CW00495433

CON

Secrets and Lies Series Book 2

B J Alpha

BJA

BJ ALPHA

CON

Secrets and Lies Series Book 2

Copyright © 2022 by B J Alpha

All rights reserved.

No part of this book may be reproduced or transmitted in either, electronic, paper hard copy, photocopying, recorded or any other form of reproduction without the written permission of the author. No part of this book either in part or whole may be reproduced into or stored in a retrieval system or distributed without the written permission of the author, except for the use of brief quotations in a book review.

This book is a work of fiction. Characters, names, places and incidents are products of the authors imagination or used fictitiously.

Any similarity to actual events, locations or persons living or dead is purely coincidental.

Published by BJ Alpha

Edited by Amy Briggs

Cover Design by Katie Evans

Created with Vellum

CON

BJ Alpha

Secrets and Lies Series
Book 2

Authors Note

WARNING: This book contains triggers. It contains sensitive and explicit storylines such as domestic abuse, mental health issues, sexual scenes with dubious consent and strong language recommended for readers aged eighteen and over.

Playlist

Remember - Becky Hill and David Guetta
Hold on (Acoustic) – Chord Overstreet
Broken – Jonah Kagen
Anyone - Justin Bieber
Save Me - Queen
Better Man (Acoustic) - Robbie Williams
Tell Me That You Love Me – James Smith
Bruises – Lewis Capaldi
Gravity – DJ Fresh
Mirrors - Justin Timberlake
Nobody Knows - The Lumineers

Dedication

Save Me For Myself
Dedicated to
TL Swan for giving me purpose
&
Bren Hawk for your support, understanding and friendship.

For Con and to all of those who suffer with their mental health.

Save Me For Myself

Broken, empty, a shell of my former self,
Desperate, despondent, void of emotion,
Useless, worthless, unwanted,
Filled with self-loathing.

Shattered into a thousand pieces, fractured,
Destroyed beyond repair.
Save me from myself,
I need you to show me you care.

Build me, help me, love my broken self,
Hold me through this misery,
Take away my pain,
Support me to stand, to feel once again.

Save me, save me from myself.
Show me that you care,
Rebuild me, fill me with love and kindness,
Show me that you're there.

Hope, warmth, love,
Strength, compassion, happiness,
Cure me for myself,
Safe in your loving arms, comfort all around me.

Save me for myself.

Written by BJ Alpha

Prologue

Two Days Before...

Con

Sitting around the table in my brother Bren's apartment, I experience the familiar tingle of happiness wash over me. I don't feel this way very often. I'm known as the jolly, happy-go-lucky brother, but truth be told, I feel anything but those emotions. I feel lost, an empty shell of my true self.

Sure, me and my brother Finn are and always have been as thick as thieves. We've always enjoyed winding our older brothers up and excelling at our notorious playboy lifestyle to the fullest. I may exude happiness on the outside, but in reality, I am void of feeling anything at all. I wish I could feel a flicker of what I let others believe I'm experiencing.

But tonight? Tonight is one of those nights I genuinely look forward to. Once every two weeks or so, me and my brothers gather at one of our apartments and release our tensions with a good old game of poker. Throw in a few beers, junk food, and the banter we all get a kick out of—even Oscar. Though he'd never admit it.

I'd never tell my brothers this, but I'd actually rather play poker with these guys than have any random fuck, or any nameless chick suck my cock. How crazy is that?

I thrive on the excitement buzzing through me when I glance at my hand. Fucking luck is on my side tonight. I refrain from grinning.

I scan my eyes over the table, analyzing my competition.

Finn has a shit hand, it's a wonder his fucking toothpick hasn't given him splinters; he's chewing it that hard. Oscar has the same impassive expression. Does he look like that when he comes too? Cal has a smile tugging at his lips. Obviously, he's my competition and useless at hiding his hand. Bren throws his cards on the table in defeat. "I'm out! Shit hand again." He declares through gritted teeth.

Cal's eyes light up in amusement. "Full house!" His smug smile full of glee.

The cocky fucker thinks he's won. Mmm, think again sunshine. "Royal Flush," I announce proudly with a wink to piss off Cal.

Groans and swearing litter the table and I smile to myself. This is turning out to be a damn good night, just what I fucking need.

Conversations go on around the table. I'm mildly amused and downright mortified about the things Cal is having to endure since his wife, Lily, had their daughter Chloe.

Poor guy has a smoking hot wife with a bulging fucking rack, and yet he isn't allowed anywhere near them because her nipples are bleeding? Who knew that was a thing? I inwardly shudder. Thank fuck my little harem of women know better than to want more from me than a good fuck.

Don't get me wrong, a couple of them keep fucking hinting at a relationship, but that's not going to happen. Ever.

Oscar tells Cal how unhappy he is about the fact he swapped Lily's pill for fertility drugs. Of course, Cal puts him in line and tells him under no circumstances is she to find out. There's fucking tension in the air. I throw another handful of peanuts in my mouth.

"So, the little charity event I attended Tuesday was interesting," Bren announces, and his eyebrows do a teasing wiggle.

"You get laid?" I ask. Because let's face it, he's so intense he needs to get fucking laid.

"I got a hot piece of ass's cell number that I might call, but I was referring to seeing Con's ex-girlfriend looking all hot on stage and giving a speech." He whistles through his teeth, trying to wind me up. Yeah, not biting pal. I roll my eyes internally.

I don't do girlfriends, therefore there's no ex. "Funny, I don't recall having an ex-girlfriend. Conquests, yes. Girlfriends, no." I give Bren a sly wink in return.

Here he goes... "That's funny. Could have sworn you once had a feisty little brunette hanging off your shoulder, a few years ago." He shrugs.

My eyebrows pull together, thinking about who he's referring to. Because there's only one girl I ever openly showed any kind of relationship behavior toward.

I glance at Cal and Finn, who both appear equally confused. Then I glance at Oscar, who is looking just as unsure.

Bren smiles widely, way too happy with himself, he sits

taller with a smug as fuck grin on his face. Yeah, he's confident, and he's got my attention. My heart is beating faster, and I sit up a little straighter, trying not to show him how much he's bothering me. "What the fuck are you talking about?" I all but snap.

"You mean *who* the fuck am I talking about?" Bren smirks trying to be fucking clever. Not the time mother fucker.

"Bren," Cal warns, "cut the fucking shit." He warns. Cal knows how I feel about her, and he's aware not to rile me up on the subject. Shit, he knows not to even broach the subject.

Bren sighs. "Okay, so I'm sitting at a boring as fuck charity event for Survivors of Domestic Abuse, when who should walk on stage and give a speech? One of their representatives, which just so happens to be Will, and fuck, is she hot!" He exhales loudly for dramatic effect.

The room is silent. However my heart is pounding in my chest so hard, I'm surprised they can't hear it. My blood is rushing around my body and at the mere mention of her name, I experience rage. I can't bear the thought of hearing her name. I close my eyes and try to pull myself together.

"Fuuuck," Finn drags out, breaking the silence.

Maybe I misheard? I open my eyes and glare at him. "Will. As in Will?"

He nods, meeting my eyes for emphasis on how sure he is. "Yeah man, it was her. Honest to God. She had us all eating out the palm of her fucking hand. She looked stunning too." Bren laughs to himself. "Seriously you'd have blown your fucking load at the table Con." Is he for real right now?

"Will?" I ask again. You know, just to clarify.

I glance toward Cal, and he fidgets anxiously, like he knows I'm a fucking time bomb waiting to go off.

Bren chuckles. "Jesus, Con, if I thought you were going to go all fucking crazy, I wouldn't have bothered telling you." I have to breathe. He doesn't understand. He doesn't know what she means to me. If he did, he'd never joke around like this. I sit looking at the end of the table, lost in my own thoughts.

"She was at a Survivors of Domestic Abuse event as a key spokesperson?" Oscar snaps in his serious tone. His voice breaks me out of my empty thoughts. And it suddenly registers. He saw Will, and she was speaking at a fucking domestic violence event? What the actual fuck?

I don't think. I erupt. My chair hits the ground as I jump up.

I point my finger at him accusingly. "You went there Tuesday night, and it's now Friday! Why the hell did you wait until now to tell me this? And what is with the fucking domestic violence? What the fuck did she have to say? Who was she with?" I'm pacing behind the table; I can't gather my thoughts quick enough, and the dip shit hasn't answered one of my goddamn questions. My eyes bore into Bren; his hands go through his hair, trying to rein his own temper in.

"Calm down Con. Come on, it might not be what you're thinking," Cal says. He's trying to be the voice of reason but it's fucking patronizing. I glare at him in annoyance, causing him to wince.

"Look man, I really don't know much and if I'm being brutally honest, I didn't hear anything she had to fucking say. I was a little taken aback by her being there on the stage. I mean, all fucking hot. The crowd liked her though." Is he for real? Did he really just call the love of my life hot? The crowd fucking liked her? My eyes must appear crazy because Finn's forehead creases in worry and his Adam's apple bobs slowly. He stares blankly at me; his mouth opens to speak but nothing comes out, causing his toothpick to fall from his mouth. He's completely at a loss for what to say, especially when I'm acting so out of character.

"Waste. Of. Fucking. Space!" Oscar snaps breaking my train of thought.

"Well, how the fuck was I supposed to know he'd go all fucking crazy over her? Last I knew, they had a fucking break up. Which was probably his fucking fault for being a dick to her as per usual and the poor girl must have come to her senses and got the fuck out of town!" I'm stunned. How the fuck can he know I screwed up? Am I that much of a fucking predictable loser? Is it that obvious I made the biggest fucking mistake of my life? He has no fucking idea. No idea what I went through, how I've fucking longed for her. How fucking dare he?

Rage bubbles to the surface, and I fly at him across the table; the snacks go everywhere, and beer bottles smash. Finn grabs my shoulders in a tight hold to restrain me. I've never wanted to hit my brother more than I do right now. Bren sits stoically still at the table in the same spot, in some sort of dazed shock.

Oscar jumps up from his chair and shouts, "Enough!" He exhales deeply. "I can access the events guest list, find the guest speakers and representatives, and you can have her information by the morning, okay? No fucking harm done." He nods toward me in confirmation, gritting his teeth.

I inwardly relax as Oscar's words sink in. I can have her details by tomorrow. Then I can find out what the hell has been going on in her life for her to be at a Survivors of

Domestic Abuse event and fuck, I could even see her again. Hope blossoms inside me.

Bren glances up from the table with a face etched with guilt. "Look man, I'm sorry, okay? I didn't realize you still harbored feelings for her. If I'd have known..."

If he'd have known? If he'd have known, he'd never have fucking mentioned her. If he'd have known, he'd have kept her as far away from me as possible. Because what I did was unforgivable.

I don't let him finish. Turning on my heel, I march the fuck out the door. I need a fucking drink.

Chapter One

Con

I groan against the window of the SUV. Fuck, my head hurts.

What's that smell? Do I smell like fucking vomit? I reach down to my T-shirt and pull it to my nose giving it a sniff. Yeah vomit, beer, and cheap perfume.

Fuck, I'm such a disaster. I curl myself up further into the passenger door. My head is pounding with each jerk of the car, and my eyes are stinging from the light.

After I don't know how fucking long, Oscar stops the car. I sit up and cast my eyes around. Where the hell has he brought me?

It's getting dark now and we're parked up on a street, nothing here apart from a fancy-ass restaurant across the road. It's one of those posh looking ones, the type with the arched canopy on the outside of the door and a small red carpet lining the entry way and a doorman in a suit that waits to greet the customers.

I clear my throat. "Where the fuck are we?" I ask, glancing around trying to figure it out.

Oscar turns to face me. Glaring down at me from above his glasses in disgust, like I'm a piece of shit, he eyes me up and down. He shakes his head silently, as if ridding himself of all the terrible things he wants to say to me. He leans into the back of the car and pulls out a brown Manila folder, dropping it into my lap with a thud.

"What's this?" I ask.

Oscar sighs with annoyance. "Will's details, as promised." He nods at the folder, prompting me to open it.

I eye him with suspicion. "You promised me them on Saturday. It's now Sunday." Okay, so now I'm being a dick.

His eyes draw in and sharpen. "You're right, but you were, what shall I call it…? Otherwise engaged, weren't you? So, I let you continue your little pity party and collected your ass this afternoon before the party starts again this evening. Now open the folder and let's deal with the next bit of unnecessary drama," he snaps with annoyance, his face in a deadpan expression.

I stare at him in utter fucking shock. The guy is as emotionally suppressed as you can get. He's some sort of fucking sociopath. Is that what's wrong with him? Is that what a sociopath is? Someone that doesn't care about anything or anyone? If that's what one is, then yeah, Oscar is a fucking sociopath. I blink, trying to come back to fucking reality, but he snaps at me again before I can. "Connor, I don't have all fucking night! Are we dealing with this or not?"

His tone startles me, making me fucking jump and my heart hammer. "Fine. Fuck. You just don't give me fucking chance to think! Jesus, you're like some fucking sergeant major, barking fucking orders at me." His lips quirk into a sly smile. Yeah, that's Oscar's version of a fucking smile, weird prick.

I take a deep breath and open the folder; a photograph falls out.

I turn it around to scrutinize the picture. My fingers shake as my eyes scan over it; there's half a dozen people in the photo, but I only see one. Will. She's smiling amongst the group in the photo. It's the charity night, and the event banner is in the background. She's clearly with other representatives. They all seem professionally dressed but Will stands out because she looks both professional and glamorous. She's the youngest in the picture and wearing a short red, fitted dress and red high heels, she's so unlike the tomboy I remember. Sure, she would occasionally wear a dress or skirt around me, and she's always looked hot, but this?

This is another level of hotness; I can see why Bren was so mesmerized. Her long brunette hair is curled and draped over one shoulder, and her hazel eyes seem like they're glaring deep into my soul, looking right at me. Her plump fucking lips are red, to match her dress. Fuck, those lips would be so fucking good wrapped around my cock again. As if on cue, my fucking cock starts to throb. I gulp and avert my gaze, feeling guilty I'm getting a hard-on sitting next to my brother while looking at a photo of a fully dressed woman. How fucking desperate. I hang my head in shame and scrub a hand through my hair.

I clear my throat. "That's her."

"It is," Oscar replies. His voice has a touch of sympathy in it as he bows his head in agreement.

My hands shake slightly as I move onto the next page. Surely, it's the hangover having this effect on me.

The next page holds some details. I read them aloud.

"Ms. Willow Chambers, age twenty-two years." I scoff at her name, Willow? She fucking hated being called Willow. Her full name she hated even more, Willowmena. Who the fuck calls their kid that? Apparently, her mom wanted Willow and her dad wanted Mena, a family name from her ancestors in Eastern Europe.

"She's divorced," he explains, breaking me away from my thoughts.

I study Oscar, then glance back at the sheet. It says Ms., "She married someone?" My heart beats rapidly against my chest and anger swells inside me. She married someone that wasn't me.

Nodding, Oscar points out the next paragraph. "Married for two and a half years, hence the Ms., and the Chambers surname. She's now divorced, recently actually. She goes by the beginning of her first name now, Willow."

I nod in agreement, but for some reason, I'm ticked fucking off. She's been married and then divorced in what? Less than five years?

I read aloud again. "Jack Chambers thirty-five, Police Officer for New Haven. A fucking pig! She married a fucking pig? What the hell was she thinking?" I erupt. My temple throbbing, the veins pulsating in my forehead. How could she do this to me?

Oscar's lips draw into a smirk. "I'd say she was thinking very well, or not so good at all. Depends on her story, I guess." He shrugs.

I spin and face him. "What the fuck are you talking about? Why do you always talk in such fucking riddles, Oscar? It takes us all forever to catch the fuck up with you!"

His lip curls up at the side of his mouth at my remark. "Well, if I was trying to get away from domestic violence, a great idea would be to marry a police officer. Would it not?"

I let his comment sink in and think about it for a minute. Of course, he's right; he's always the logical one, and he's always thought of an answer before either of us has even begun to process the question. "What if this guy, the pig, is the abuser?" I quiz.

Oscar shakes his head. "Doubt it. We're currently sitting outside a restaurant where Will is going to be attending a meal with the other representatives and her ex, Jack, to celebrate the success of the charity night."

My heart pounds, and my breathing turns erratic. He's fucking amazing. "She's going to be here tonight? How can you be sure?" I lick my lips, my throat suddenly dry with anticipation.

"Hacked her work emails." He shrugs again as though it's nothing.

I continue to flick through other parts of the file. It's mainly the usual things, birth certificate, bank statements, and so on. There's her work address and Jack-asses works address. Information on their daily routines. There are two addresses on the file. One listed as Will's, 428 Elm Tree Grove, New Haven, Connecticut, and a different one for Jack. It looks like he got the apartment in the divorce and Will got the house.

"I didn't do a detailed search on them both. To be honest, I became a little stuck in certain areas. I'm assuming Jack knows people that help to keep information hidden. They've done a decent enough job that I'd need a little longer than twenty-four hours to extract it."

I peer at Oscar, confused by what he means.

He points to the file. "There's no bank information, just a standard statement that doesn't give Jack's earnings. There are no other bank account numbers other than the statement there, no hospital records and Jack's profession is listed as a police officer. I imagine he's a little further up the chain than that, given he owns two properties and three vehicles. My guess is he's an FBI agent. Will's employment information is on there, but no details about any past employers and no salary. I mean, she could be a volunteer, but I'm guessing she earns something for her to run her own household."

I muse over Oscar's words, while keeping my eyes laser focused on the street ahead. "What time is the reservation for?" I lick my dry lips again with desperation.

He glances at his watch and sits a little straighter. "Seven p.m. Another ten minutes."

I sit forward in the seat. I can't help but chew the fucking skin on the side of my nail, my leg is bouncing with nervousness. The thought of seeing her again bringing forth a mixture a sickness and excitement. A couple of people are milling around, and I scan their faces. I see neither of them is Will as they both enter the restaurant.

Oscar moves closer to the window and points. "There, that's the ex."

I watch the guy who's just climbed out of a slick black Porsche Cayenne Turbo. He's tall, around six feet, and lean. Fairly broad shoulders, but not as thick as mine. He's got light brown hair, shortly cropped at the sides and longer on top, styled. His jaw is chiseled with a shadow of scruff.

The guy exudes confidence as he straightens his navy three-piece suit. I'll give the guy credit. He looks good. Fucking prick. He stands cross-legged, leaning against his car, with his phone out texting.

I quickly glance down at myself. Filthy white T-shirt, ripped denim jeans, and a battered pair of Converse on my feet. I look like a fucking deadbeat compared to this prick.

My eyes snap back up when I see movement come from

around the opposite corner. I freeze; my whole body stills at the sight of her. Fuck, she looks incredible. My heart pounds against my chest, the throbbing noise invading my ears. My heart fucking aches causing me to rub my hand over it.

Long dark hair flows in waves down her back. Fucking sky high fuck-me black heels make her legs a mile fucking long. A black pencil skirt sits high waisted, showing off her smoking hot body. A short cropped black top with short sleeves, giving the slightest tease of her chest with her tits pushed up. Her face is as beautiful as ever and when she sees Jack, her fucking face lights up in delight. Her smile is enormous. She used to smile like that for me. My heart sinks. I'm so fucking screwed.

Jack turns to greet her and gives a lop-sided smile; it looks teasing as he casually walks toward her. She's like an excitable child, making crazy arm gestures toward him that make her look like she's buzzing. Jack laughs at her, then grabs her hands and pulls her into a hug, kissing the top of her head. She nuzzles under his arm as they walk into the restaurant together, and just like that, my fucking mood plummets.

"They're divorced," Oscar states, picking up on my mood.

I push my messy hair from my forehead. "Yeah, they sure looked happy though." I sound like a pathetic, sulking kid whose toy has just been crushed.

"So, what now?" Oscar asks, uncertainty in his voice.

I take a few minutes before answering him. "Now I get some sleep and get showered. Tomorrow, I make a trip to 428 Elm Tree Grove, New Haven, Connecticut."

Oscar tilts his head toward me to confirm he's understood my plan.

Chapter Two

Con

The drive here took forever. After barely sleeping last night, my mind is no clearer than it was when I saw her at the restaurant yesterday.

I just need to see her up close. To make sure she's okay. At least that's what I tell myself. Get some answers to my questions about what's been happening in her life, that's all. My hand shakes nervously as I scrub it through my hair.

Bren has driven us here today. I think he's feeling guilty about dropping the bomb in the first place and this is his way of being supportive. I'm riding shotgun, while Cal sits in the backseat. Not sure what he's doing here, but he's probably the most down to earth of my brothers, so maybe that's why he came along? Moral support?

We pull onto Elm Tree Grove. It's a neat, stereotypical suburban street, with large colonial style homes. Will must love living here; this is something she's always wanted. It looks fucking perfect.

The car pulls to a stop directly opposite 428. I don't give either of my brother's a chance to lecture me before I jump out the car. I dart across the road and walk up the drive. I swallow back my anxiety and climb up the steps onto the front porch. Before I can talk myself out of it, I knock loudly on the door. Rocking backward and forward on my heels I'm briefly aware that Cal is approaching. I register him mumble a subtle "fuck" out of his mouth, but I ignore him, concentrating on the task at hand. Nervous as fuck.

I hear a noise from inside the house and what sounds like someone running down the stairs. The door pulls open and I'm stunned into silence. Our eyes meet, and what appears to be shock registers in hers. Will stands there directly in front of me. My heart thumps hard against my chest, causing me to wince. I rub at the pain.

I take her in. Her hair is up in a messy bun, a black camisole top slinks off her shoulder with blue paint on it. She wears short, cropped jean shorts and navy Converse. She's dotted in blue paint here and there, including her fingers and her forehead. I slowly rake my eyes back up to her face. Her face is a blank expression of indifference, although she appears slightly stunned. Her mouth gaping open.

"W... wh... what are you doing here?" She stumbles her words while slowly brushing her forehead in disbelief.

I glance behind me. Cal is on the lawn below us, leaning against the porch fence, and Bren has stayed in the car. I swallow thickly, a tremble to my voice. "I... I came to talk to you."

Her chest is flushed and rising faster by the second as we both stand there, in utter silence, staring at one another.

My eyes vaguely register someone striding down the

stairs behind her. Will slowly closes her eyes, deep in thought while trying to regulate her breathing.

"Willow, who's at the—" Before he finishes his sentence, the douche takes the door from Will's hand and opens it wider.

I take in the prick that is her ex-husband. He's shirtless, with low cut jeans, showing his ripped chest off. Fucking dick. He's also covered in blue paint. The dick still has the paintbrush in his hand. He stares at me and then pokes his head out the door to eye Cal. He sighs, brushes his hand through his hair, and then opens the door fully. "You best come in, and your brothers too." He nods in their direction.

Will

"Someone's at the front door," Jack says, nodding toward the open bedroom door. I sigh. Another interruption, great, we'll never get this done.

"Okay. I'll be back in a minute." I place the paintbrush down.

"Yeah. Yeah. Bring drinks back with you." Jack laughs as I head out the door to go downstairs.

My feet hit the stairs quickly, desperate to hurry back and continue. I unlock the front door without checking who's there. God, Jack would kill me for being so reckless, I shake my head at myself.

I turn the door handle, pulling it open and instantly the life is sucked out of me. There, standing in front of me, is Connor O'Connell.

The son of a bitch is standing on my doorstep. And worse, he looks fucking hot.

My initial shock is put on the back burner as I slowly take him in. Thick dark waves on top of his head, deep sparkling blue eyes, and a tanned complexion. His white button-down shirt is pulled tightly across his broad shoulders, his sleeves are rolled up to his elbow, exposing his firm muscled arms. He's wearing fitted black jeans and smart dress shoes. He also smells incredible. Bastard.

I want to say something. I want to say, "Fuck off," but nothing comes out of my traitorous mouth.

"W... wh... what are you doing here?" I stutter like an idiot. I rub at my forehead in disbelief.

He seems nervous as he shifts from foot to foot. His throat bobs, "I came to talk to you."

My mind is blank. I can't think straight. My heart is bursting through my chest, and I feel like I'm going to have a panic attack. He needs to leave; he needs to get the hell out of here and leave us the fuck alone.

I can hear Jack coming down the stairs and I close my eyes, willing him to go into the kitchen or better yet, back upstairs.

"Willow, who's at the—" His words are cut off as he opens the door wider to see for himself. I watch him tense beside me. He slowly rubs his hand down my back in a supportive gesture. My shoulders loosen, but only slightly.

But then he opens the door wider, surprising the hell out of me, and I could seriously rip his eyes out. He pokes his head out the door, gazing around the property. Then he peers down the street both ways before saying, "You best come in, and your brothers too." He gestures to the black SUV across the road and proceeds to open the door wider.

What the hell just happened? Seriously, what is he thinking?

I stand there a moment, frozen on the spot. Con moves toward me, and I snap out of my trance and move aside. Next to follow is Cal. I peek up at him and his lips tighten into an apologetic smile at me. Running across my lawn and straight into my house is Bren. Who then proceeds to bend down and kiss my forehead. "Nice to see you again, Will." I'm once again snapped out of my trance by my childhood nickname "Will." I haven't been Will in a long time. Approximately five years.

"Babe, get over here and sit down. I'll make us some drinks," Jack calls. He's in the living area, where our guests are currently seated while I'm still standing here with the door open like an idiot.

I spin on my heel. "W... w... what the hell do you think you're doing?" I screech. Completely ignoring everyone but Jack.

Jack stares at me then exhales, his face a mirror of annoyance then his expression falters and transforms into a fucking patronizingly appeasing smile. "Babe, you need to talk to him." He motions his head toward Con. Oh hell no.

My head throbs, and I press my fingers to my temples. "I don't need to do a damn thing, Jack. What I need is for them to get the hell out of my house!" I point toward the door.

I don't care that my audience can see and hear every damn word. In fact, I'm quite pleased that they can. Hopefully, it will encourage them to fuck off!

"Will, listen, I haven't come here to cause any trouble or to upset you—"

His voice grates on me. I don't want to listen to him speak. I definitely don't want to see him either. So, I cut him off before he can continue. I hold my hand up to stop his words. "Then leave. Go on. Get up and go. You're not welcome here!" I point again at the door.

I'm glued to the spot between the open-plan kitchen and the living area. Con is on the sofa, Bren and Cal are on the chairs. Jack is shooting daggers my way from behind the kitchen counter.

"Willow, you're being fucking childish. I'm making us drinks, so sit your ass down and listen." Jack's no nonsense tone pisses me off. I jump back at his words. He always does this, scorns me like a child. I slowly walk over to the kitchen island and sit on a bar stool that puts my back slightly turned away from Con. I'm sitting more or less directly in front of Cal.

I glare at Jack, then stare down at my lap. I chew the inside of my mouth to stop myself from reacting.

Silence fills the room before Cal clears his throat. "I'm

married now with two kids," he announces proudly, clearly trying to lighten the mood.

I peek up from my lap and toward Cal. His warm eyes and tight smile greet me. How can I be mad at him? "That's really nice, Cal. I'm pleased for you," I say, genuinely meaning every word.

"Thanks. My oldest Reece, he's a fucking handful, but that just makes the good days even more special." We always knew Cal was a softy but hearing him and seeing the pride shine through his eyes only re-enforces how caring he is.

Bren chuckles at Cal's choice of words. "Do you get many special days, Cal?" he jokes.

"Fuck off!" Cal responds sharply, all traces of softness gone.

We all laugh a little, but it's forced.

Jack walks around us and hands the requested drinks out. I must have zoned out because I missed what everyone had requested. Silence again. Uncomfortable fucking silence, my jaw ticks in frustration.

Con clears his throat and straightens his defined shoulders. "You weren't at your father's funeral last year?" he asks. But it's a rhetorical question.

I laugh to myself. "Why the fuck would I want to go to that?" Con's body startles at my words and his face is one of confusion.

"She hated her dad," Jack jumps in to explain.

"Since when?" Con's eyebrows furrow in confusion.

I shake my head. He's been so deluded it's not even funny. "Since always, Con. You were just too blind to see." I sigh and roll my eyes at him.

Jack clears his throat. "Listen, I'm going to have to shoot off..." He gazes at me knowingly as I nod in understanding.

"I won't be long. You need to talk, Willow. Explain." His eyes drill into mine as he says the last part with emphasis, making me scoff in objection. Jack responds with a visible sigh while his face drops, full of disappointment, well fuck him.

He leaves, shutting the front door. When it clicks, I jump back to reality.

"Seems like a nice guy," Bren comments.

"Yeah, he is. He's the best," I boast, holding my head high.

Con scoffs at my declaration. I spin around to face him. "Something to say, asshole?"

He looks directly at me. His eyes appearing frustrated, he licks his lips as if ready to do battle. "Yeah, actually I do. If he's the best, as you proudly say. Why the fuck were you at a domestic abuse survivor's event last week?" His voice rises.

I choke. I genuinely choke. How the hell dare he? I laugh condescendingly. "Do you think Jack's abusive? Is that it? You're kidding me, right? Who the hell do you think you are? What the fuck does it matter to you, anyway? You're unbelievable!" The sound of my voice is increasing along with my temper. I can't get my words out quick enough I'm so damn angry.

Bren speaks up. His tone is explanatory. "I was at the event last week, Will. I mentioned it to Con, and he wanted to check in on you. To make sure everything was okay." He tries to reason with me.

"Check in on me? Are you serious?" My eyes alight with fire, my veins pumping in anger.

"I was trying to do right," Con declares. Oh, my fucking god, he did not just say that!

"Do right?" I ask, utterly shocked my mouth open wide.

He brushes his hand through his hair and quickly looks away. Yeah, fucking guilty.

"Are you okay, Will?" Cal gently coaxes.

"I'm fucking fine, Cal. Fine!" I snap back at him.

I'm so fuming mad right now I can't speak. I take a shaky drink of my water, my hands trembling with rage.

Cal

Con has been quiet all the way here. Anxiety rolling off of him. His leg continuously bouncing, and he can't stop fidgeting. Oscar had explained what terrible shape he was in yesterday and I want to be here for him today for support. He has a habit of putting his foot further into trouble than necessary and I don't want him to say or do anything he might regret. He's been a wealth of encouragement and support for me over the years, and I need to be the same for him.

As we turn into the streets surrounding Elm Tree Grove, I start to get uncomfortable. The neighborhood is an idealistic area for families, clean and safe looking. We've recently passed a park; streets are lined with trees, and it looks like something out of a movie scene with white picket fences and perfectly manicured gardens. The houses are large without being ostentatious. It's very clearly a family orientated neighborhood. One I'm certain my wife Lily would love.

As we pull opposite Will's home, I'm getting a little concerned at the red flags that are being drawn up to me, and my brother is too wrapped up in his own agenda to realize the things staring us in the face.

Such as the home in which Will lives in is clearly very large for one person. There's also the fact that a minivan is parked in the driveway because seriously, who the fuck owns a minivan without necessity?

I walk behind Con and glance down the side of the house. Yeah, a fucking kid's scooter sits propped against the wall of the house. Jesus, this is going to be a shit show.

Looking up at my eager brother at the front porch, I can only sympathize because he is soon going to be very disappointed, and I'm fully aware it's going to completely fucking gut him. I run a frustrated hand through my hair.

When Will's husband lets us into their home, I almost don't want to accept the offer. We're clearly intruding on a very happy family set up.

I glance around the family home. Straight ahead are stairs with little sneakers at the bottom. I scrub my hand down my face. Fuck, this is going to be hard.

To our right is a large living area with open plan living leading to a large, modern kitchen. Jack kindly gestures for us to sit down while he makes us drinks. Will was obviously still very dumbfounded, and it would have been bordering on amusing if I hadn't already realized this was going to go tits up.

As we make aimless chit chat, I stand and scan my eyes around the room. I narrow my eyes in on the family photos adorning the fireplace, lifting one up, I spot the little boy instantly. Familiar eyes gleam back at me. Holy shit.

Will

The door clicks open far too soon. Jack returns, causing my stomach to sink. I close my eyes at the impending sound, knowing what's coming next.

"Mommy, I made a picture!" I wince.

"That's great buddy. Can you take it upstairs and I'll pin it up later, okay?" I smile softly in his direction.

"Sure, is my room painted yet?" My son's eager chatter makes my throat bob in anxiety.

I can see Con's back straighten at the sound of my son's voice. His jaw tenses. Luckily his back is to him, and he doesn't turn to see him. I glance at Cal; his eyes are clearly trained on Keen. Shit.

Jack subtly catches my eye and I dart my gaze toward the stairs to prompt him. He nods in understanding.

"Come on, Keen. Let's go and see how far me and Mommy got with your room, hey?!"

I can see the anger radiating off of Con, but I don't want to spare him another look.

As the door at the top of the stairs closes, his tense jaw loosens, and his venomous words spill out. "You named your fucking son Keen?!" His seething glare shooting fire in my direction.

I laugh goadingly. "Yeah Con, I named him Keenan. We call him Keen." I raise my chin defiantly.

"How the fuck could you name your son after my dead brother and think that's okay?" His leg is bouncing, waves of tension rolling off of him, and his whole body vibrating.

How dare he? "Why the fuck wouldn't I think it's okay to do that? It wasn't just you that lost him that night, Con. Stop being so goddamn self-centered!" I spit back.

His hand flies around the room aggressively. "You're

living here in your perfect fucking house, with your perfect fucking family and your fucking perfect husband, with your perfect son named Keenan." He shakes his head in disbelief, venom oozing from his words. The vein at his temple is pulsating. Yeah, he's beyond pissed.

Cal gets up slowly and starts walking toward the dresser against the wall, casually looking around. I'm hoping this means he's getting fed up with the unnecessary visit.

Jack comes back downstairs. "Keens on his console, with his headphones on." My shoulders ease back slightly, and I nod in acknowledgement and spare him a tight smile.

"Have you discussed matters?" he asks, gesturing toward Con.

I shake my head slowly, "There's nothing to discuss, Jack. I'm sure Con is getting ready to leave?"

I stare at Con, who is still sat silently fuming. His hands are clasped together; the whites of his knuckles evident.

"How old's Keen?" Cal asks.

He fucking knows. My stomach plummets.

My eyes dart toward Jacks, and he speaks up with confidence ignoring my silent pleas. "He's almost four."

Con's bright blue eyes dart to mine with shock, embroiled with anger, capturing me, causing me to take a sudden intake of breath. He gasps dramatically before snarling. "You fucking bitch! You kept the baby and took the money?" he spits out.

My body is stunned by his words. Jack's body tenses. He points his finger in Con's direction. "Do not fucking call her that, otherwise I'll put my fucking gun to your head. Do you understand me?!" he shouts back at Con.

Before Con can respond, Bren jumps in. "What baby? What money?"

I glance toward Bren and shake my head with a small laugh at Cons audacity.

"You've no fucking clue what you're talking about, Con. Unless you want all your dirty little secrets exposed. I suggest you get the hell out of my house and don't come back!" I snipe, noticing his face is paler than the flush red he was previously radiating.

"What the fuck did you do?" Cal spins on his heels. Away from the photograph he's holding to face Con.

He doesn't answer. Coward.

"I asked you a question, Connor. Fucking answer, me!" he demands louder.

Con sighs and brushes his hand through his hair. "I assumed she'd got rid of the baby." He swallows thickly his voice low. "Clearly she didn't," Con responds softly, while throwing his arm out toward the stairs. Toward Keen.

Jack is still rigid, standing beside me in his silently supportive manner.

Cal turns toward me in question, his eyebrows quirk upwards. Jack nods at me in encouragement.

I take a deep breath. "What he's trying to say, Cal, is, he gave me two thousand dollars in cash to go and have an abortion. Against my wishes, I must add." I raise my chin in determination to be truly heard.

Cal gasps. Con drops his head in his hands in shame. In the quickest move I've ever seen, Bren lunges out of his chair and flies at Con, who looks up and doesn't see the punch to his jaw coming. "Fuck!" Con screeches in the aftermath. "Motherfucker." He works his jaw from side to side. Bren paces back and forth, his face red with anger.

Jack silently pours Bren a whiskey and hands it to him, presumably to calm him down. Bren sits down in the chair, emptying the glass and glaring directly at Con who is rubbing his jaw with a wince.

Cal is still standing in front of Con with his hands on his hips, seething. "Let me get this straight. You gave your teenage girlfriend two thousand dollars to abort your baby? And you're pissed because she didn't do it?"

"I'm pissed because she kept it from me," he sneers back while glaring at me. I stare him down.

Jack breaks the tension. "How could you leave a teenage girl to deal with that shit by herself? To walk in there and have to deal with losing a baby by herself? You couldn't even be man enough to be there for her. I don't understand how the fuck you sleep at night." Jack's disgust seeps from his body in waves as he shakes his head at Con.

Con hangs his head in shame. Well, motherfucker, here comes your next bomb shell.

My spine straightens with confidence as I stand and approach him. "Well, I went as per your strict instructions, Con. I obeyed your request. Especially after the whole, 'I don't want a family with you ever and I don't even want to be with you, Will,' speech." I make finger quotes at the latter, as his words come back to me with vengeance. He winces as I repeat them.

"Unfortunately for you, I was too far along in the pregnancy, Con." My throat clogs, as the emotions grip me like it was yesterday. Gently, I shake my head, not wanting to share the worst day of my life with them, but I know I have to. I have to make them believe I tried to do what he said was best. I trusted him.

I struggle to breathe through the tears. "They said I was nearly five months pregnant, and they wouldn't terminate at that point. I'd spent all god damn morning building the courage up to go and when I got there, they couldn't do it."

A sob catches in my throat. "I tried, you bastard, I fucking tried. While you were off enjoying yourself like the selfish prick you are. I was trying to kill my baby! So don't you dare come in here and rip me and my life apart for making the best of things. And don't you dare attack Jack for manning up and being a father figure to Keen. Don't you fucking dare." I point my finger at him while shaking. My heart thrashing violently against my chest, my hands shaking in anger.

Con bends forward with his head in his hands. I have zero sympathy.

My breathing is frantic as I battle with my emotions of being both angry and upset.

"Will, are you okay?" Cal asks softly.

I shake my head. "No Cal, I'm not okay. Do you know what happened next, Con?" I stare at him as his blurry eyes meet mine. I stare through his saddened blues and continue on. Of course, he doesn't know what happened next. The bastard wouldn't know, because he didn't care.

"I went home terrified, with the two thousand dollars stuffed in my hoodie. My father sat waiting for me in his chair, with a bottle half empty in his hands."

I close my eyes as the nightmare scene comes back to me. Jack takes ahold of my hand. Cal's eyes flit to it. I gulp and continue, "He was waiting for me. One of his little minions had reported back to him where I'd been..."

"Fuck," comes from Bren. He pulls his hand down his face. It was common knowledge my father was strict and had a vicious temper. It's part of the reason me and Con would sneak around.

"He knew. Knew I'd been for an abortion. He knew I was too far gone for one. He got up and picked the metal poker up. I was so fucking scared. His eyes were glazed and black, they were soulless. He called me a slut, a whore. The usual." I watch Con and he appears genuinely surprised, so fucking oblivious. I shake my head at his naivety.

I continue on. "He hit me and hit me until I fell. He said, 'if they can't get rid of the baby he would!' He hit me with that fucking poker until I stopped screaming."

"Jesus!" Cal stares at me with sympathy and disgust in his eyes.

"A few more kicks to the stomach made me make a god-awful noise. I felt a gush between my legs and when he saw the blood between my legs on my jeans, he gave a satisfied grunt. Slammed the door and left. I was lifeless. My body wouldn't move. I went beyond pain. I couldn't feel a single thing."

The room is silent as I swipe the tears from my eyes. They're watching me, waiting for me to continue. To answer the unanswered questions. I take a drink of my water, and Jack squeezes my hand in support.

"Milo, my brother, came home. You know what he did? He picked me up. Told me, I asked for this, how it was my own fault. He drove me to the hospital and laid me down outside the doors. He bent down and whispered in my ear, 'and don't fucking come back whore.'"

Cal winces at my words. Bren's fists are clamped together, and Con's expression is empty. Void of anything.

I clear my throat and chuckle. "So yeah, Con. I guess I kept your baby and your money," I sneer.

Jack brushes up alongside me and tucks my hair behind my ears. "You did good, babe. I'm proud of you." He kisses my forehead. Con's eyes don't leave me, drilling into me.

I swallow thickly. "I was treated for broken ribs, wrist, cheek bone, amongst other things. At the hospital, I was given a cervical stitch to hold the baby in place. I was underage, so the hospital put me under the CPS, in a program for Domestic Abuse Survivors. They help you get on your feet while keeping your circumstances hidden. As far as I'm aware, my family thought I lost the baby. He came premature, his lungs weren't fully developed at the time. Eventually, we were moved into a small condo supported by the program. I used the money you gave me for his crib and furnishings. So yeah, thanks for the abortion money, Con," I say sarcastically, tears blurring my vision.

"Fuck, I didn't know, Will!" he pleads. His hands are shaking in his lap, his face white, and desperation etches his handsome features.

I roll my eyes and stifle a laugh, determined not to sympathize with him. "You're right, you didn't know. But you didn't care either, did you?"

He says nothing; he can't deny it. It's the truth, and he knows it.

Cal breaks the silence. His face a picture of fury, he's seething. "I'm so fucking ashamed of you right now, Con. So, fucking ashamed." He shakes his head in disgust.

"Don't you think I'm ashamed of myself?" he desperately tries to argue.

"It's not fucking about you, is it?" Bren snaps.

"No. You're right, it's not." His voice low. He's visibly shaking. "What happens now, Will?"

Oh, you've got to be fucking kidding me. "You leave! Do what you're good at. You turn your back, and you go!" I screech back to him, pointing at the door.

"No!" Jack and Cal say together.

My eyes dart to Jacks. Scowling at him. He tries to placate me. "Babe, you know that's not a good idea."

I shake my head, my jaw tense. Un. Fucking. Believable.

"Will, even if we left here today with no intentions of coming back. You understand it's not safe, you know we have enemies, Will," Cal explains calmy.

I gasp at the realization, a tremor rippling through my body. A new anger settling in. "So, you bastards, show up at my door and bring your fucking enemies to me? To us? That's what you're saying?"

Con winces at my words. He knows I'm right. They just opened the door up to destroy our lives.

Chapter Three

Con

Will sinks into her chair after dropping one hell of a bombshell on us. On me.

I feel sick to my stomach. How the fuck did I miss this? How the fuck did I let this happen? And now I have a fucking son?

I can't stop the tremble in my body. I want to sob like a fucking baby. Jesus, I'm such a pathetic screw up. What the fuck have I done?

Jack's hands are tender on Will, rubbing up and down her back.

I watch his hands brush delicately over my girl's body. My jaw locks in aggravation, hating him. My hands should be there. My fucking hands should be rubbing her back, soothing her.

I chance a glance at Bren; he's watching me with a razor-sharp glare. They fucking hate me. All of them do. I can sense it; I don't fucking blame them.

Jesus. I scrub a hand down my face. I hate myself.

Jack's voice is calm. "Listen, I've ordered some pizzas for dinner. Perhaps you guys can stay and when Keen goes to bed, we can discuss this a little more?"

Will scoffs. "You cannot be serious, Jack? You've just heard them; they've fucked up our entire lives showing up here. And now you want us to play happy fucking families and chat?"

Jack's body bristles at her words. "I want what's best for you and Keen. You both need to be kept safe, and at the moment these guys can do that." His eyes scan over us in approval.

Will walks around the kitchen counter and starts getting plates out. She's obviously busying herself to avoid us. The loud clatter of plates is a clear sign of how pissed she is.

"Who do we tell Keen we are?" Cal asks innocently.

"Friends!" Will snaps back over her shoulder.

Fuck that, if I'm a fucking father, I'm going to be one.

"I'm his dad, Will," I plead.

Her eyes narrow on me. "No, you are not. You didn't want to be one, remember? You're not just going to walk in here and think you can take over my family and everything I've built. Keen needs structure and stability. Not some self-centered, self-absorbed prick in his life." I wince at her harsh words.

"Will, enough. I'm sure Con is going to want to prove himself to you and Keen?" Jack asks with a raised eyebrow at me.

"Of course." I nod in agreement with him. I'm desperate for any connection she's prepared to give.

"In which case, perhaps we introduce you all as friends.

Once Will is comfortable for you to be something more, when you've proven yourself to be something more, then perhaps have another discussion about who you're going to be to Keen?" How the fuck do I argue with that? Still don't like the fucking know it all prick.

"I think that's for the best. Cons got a lot to prove. We understand your concerns, Will. But I can assure you that we're your family now. You and Keen will have us in your life, and no matter what happens with Con, we aren't going anywhere."

Well, cheers for the vote of fucking confidence, Cal. I shake my head at him. He doesn't think I'm capable or deserving, my own fucking brother.

"Thank you, Cal. That means a lot." Her voice is gentle, like the Will I remember. The Will I'm desperate for.

Before long I hear small footsteps coming down the stairs, and I take a deep breath to turn around and face him. My son.

I turn slowly. But where I instantly look, he isn't there because he's way smaller than I expected. My eyes scan over the little dude and he takes my breath away. He's barely above the height of the bannister, and when his small feet hit the floor I get a proper opportunity to see him. Keen's small and thin. My chest tightens and I gasp. His brown hair is thick like mine, wavy, and he has big blue eyes. He's my fucking double. I stare back at Cal and Bren open mouthed, my eyes asking them if they're seeing it too. They both dip their heads at me, and I'm overcome with emotion. I choke on a quiet sob and quickly try to mask it with a cough. Fuck, I need to pull myself together. I brush my hands down my jeans uncomfortably.

"Hey Keens. Come and say hello to Mommy's friends." Will holds her hand out for Keen and he goes to her. He's wearing little joggers and a T-shirt with a tiger on the front, cute as fuck.

She points. "This one here is Cal." Cal instantly bends down to Keen and shakes his little hand; Keen nervously tries to move behind Will. "This big guy is Bren." Keen laughs at Will's description of Bren. Bren moves forward and fist bumps Keen. This earns him another chuckle. He's so fucking cute.

Will's body straightens as she approaches me. I swear to Christ I can sense the tension and hate radiating off of her. "This is Con."

I get down on my knees so I'm level with him. His blue eyes meet mine and I smile softly at him. I must seem a fucking state. "Hi, Keen, it's good to meet you." He peeks at me from behind Will's leg. I'm unsure what to do or say. "I like your T-shirt dude. Do you like tigers?"

Keen steps forward a little, his voice timid. "I like all animals. My mommy's going to take me to the zoo when it's my birthday and I turn four." He holds up four fingers. I chuckle at how fucking clever my little man is.

"Wow. Dude, that sounds amazing. I bet they have tigers there; do you think I could come?" I lick my lips hopefully and stare up at Will, hoping she can see the promise in my eyes. Say fucking yes. Please say yes.

"I'll have to ask my mommy." This makes me laugh; Bren and Cal too.

The doorbell rings, breaking the small conversation and cutting the tension.

Jack answers the door and walks back through into the kitchen area with a pile of pizza boxes.

"Yes!" Keen declares, jumping up with his little fist in the air.

"Jack, did you get Coke too?" His little face is alight, and I don't miss the fact he called Jack by his first name, and relief rolls through me.

Earlier I had wondered if he called him Dad. I sink into the chair, smiling internally. I've not lost them yet. No fucking way.

"Yeah, buddy, I got Coke too." A wide grin graces Keen's face as he smiles up at Jack. Instantly my gut fucking clenches, my hopeful mood turning sour.

"Wow. You must be a big boy if your mommy lets you have Coke Keen." Cal laughs, probably thinking about his teenage son Reece, who is banned from drinking Coke.

"I am. I can have Coke on special days, can't I Mommy?"

"Yes, that's right sweetheart." Will gives Keen a solemn smile as she sets about dishing the pizza out.

Will hands me a plate with pepperoni pizza on it. It's my favorite, and she's clearly remembered. Or was it a fucking coincidence? "Thanks." She gives me a fake smile back; she's clearly playing nice.

Everyone is digging in, eating, and drinking. Brief conversations around Keen occur as both Bren and Cal ask questions about Will and Keen. I zone out and just watch the interaction. I can't take my eyes off Keen. Will has done so well with him. He's chatty, cute, and funny. The kid is fucking adorable. He even eats his pizza like me, peeling off the pepperoni and then saving the pieces until last. Will's demeanor is damn right defensive. She's pissed. I try not to stare at her, but I can't fucking help it. I'm like a magnet, drawn to her without even trying.

Inside, I tell myself to remain silent. I'm fucking scared what she's going to say if I speak. I sure as fuck don't want her throwing us out anytime soon.

We've just finished eating when Will stands. "Keen, come on buddy, it's way past your bedtime. Let's go and get you tucked in bed with a quick story tonight. Are you going to say goodbye to our friends?" Shit, I don't want them to leave the fucking room. I turn to Cal for help, but he's talking to Jack.

Keen runs to Jack for a hug, he picks him up and Keen wraps his arms around his neck. "Night, night, little man. I'll see you soon, okay?" Fuck, that's crushing. I stand and rub my hand through my hair, unable to watch the scene in front of me. I walk to the window and stare out of it, swallowing back the thickness in my throat.

"Night, night Jack, love you," I hear him say back. I rub at the pain in my chest and wince. Unable to breathe, I close my eyes and count.

Behind me, I register my brothers say their goodnights. But I don't turn around to see.

"Night, Keen," I grunt out. It fucking pains me not to turn toward him. I don't want to say goodbye, but then I don't want him to think I didn't wish him a good night's sleep either. I'm so fucking screwed.

As soon as I recognize Keen's door close, I turn around to face my brothers and Jack.

Jack's words are quick and terse. "Listen, I understand this is hard for you, Con." I scoff. What the fuck does he know? "But I really need you all to help keep them safe." My spine straightens, it feels likes there's an innuendo there.

Bren picks up on it too, his eye narrow at Jack. "What aren't you telling us, Jack?" his voice stern with a warning behind it.

Jack exhales and sits down in a chair. "Since meeting Willow, I had a friend of mine keep a close eye on her family in New Jersey. I didn't trust that they wouldn't come after Willow. I genuinely believe they think Willow lost Keen. I wasn't going to put it past them to try to make sure she keeps her mouth shut about what happened. "

"Anyway, when Willow's father passed away, her brother Milo took a more sinister role in the business." He fidgets with his hands. We're all well aware of Milo. We have been for several years. He's into dealing drugs and he's been working closely with a gang of Russians on the outskirts of the city. They're ruthless and are virtual outlaws compared to other gangs.

Jack continues. "About six months ago, my friend contacted me to say Milo had registered Willow on a missing person site. He's also been paying a private investigator in New Jersey." Jack's vein is throbbing in his temple, anger radiating from his body. "The function that we attended last week, someone took photographs of the sponsors and spokespersons. Something that isn't supposed to happen at these events, ever!" He grits the last words out in temper.

I drop into the chair. He's telling us that Milo will probably find Will because of the photo, the same photo Oscar used to find her. Shit.

"Milo is currently under investigation in both our jurisdictions and I'm hoping the case against him will be enough to put him away for life. But in the meantime, he's a fucking walking time bomb."

"She can't stay here!" I declare, almost surprising myself.

"Agreed," Bren states without hesitation.

Jack fidgets with his hands. "I completely fucking agree with you but..." He shakes his head and stares up to the ceiling, "Willow's fucking stubborn and the feelings she harbors toward you, Con, I don't mean any disrespect, but she's well within her rights to feel that way about you."

"I know." Of course, I fucking know. Shame waves through me. I rub my hand through my hair in annoyance with myself.

"They can stay with me," Bren suggests. Fuck that. My family isn't staying with him. They're fucking mine.

"Like fuck they are. They're my fucking family, not yours. Get your own," I spit back at him childishly.

"I didn't think you wanted a family, Con?" Cal challenges mockingly.

"Fuck off, and stop being a dick. They're here now, aren't they? If they're going anywhere, they're going with me!" I stab my finger into my chest for emphasis.

With Milo openly seeking Will out and with our own enemies, they sure as shit aren't safe living here unprotected.

My gut clenches at the thought of someone hurting either of them.

Chapter Four

Will

I walk down the stairs quietly and as I approach the bottom step; I listen to hushed voices. Jack and the guys are standing fairly close together. I'm surprised at this because Jack is very clearly not their biggest fans. I sense the hairs on the back of my neck prick up. Why do I get the sense they're conspiring in some way?

I walk into the room and the fuckers scurry away from one another. "What the hell's going on?" I ask defensively while crossing my arms over my chest.

Jack's demeanor screams tension, and Con appears a bag of nerves. Cal shuffles uncomfortably from foot to foot. "We think it's best if you guys come and stay with us for a little while."

My voice catches in my mouth, and I let out a surprised laugh. Is he fucking serious? "No! Absolutely not."

"God, damn it, Willow. Will you just listen to reason?!"

Jack snaps, making me jump. His fists tighten beside him. Completely unlike Jack.

I stare at him and see the stress and concern written all over his face. "What aren't you telling me, Jack?"

He has the fucking nerve to cast a scan at the others before bringing his eyes back to mine and deciding to be honest. "I have intel, Willow. Intel that concerns me. It's about yours and Keen's safety."

"What kind of intel?" I swallow deeply, a lump forming in my throat.

"Does it fucking matter?" His voice rises in irritation.

Jack doesn't lose his temper very often, and it's very rare he speaks out of line to me. But yeah, it fucking matters. Of course, it does.

"You're wanting to uproot me and Keen from our home, Jack, from our lives. Of course, it fucking matters."

"Milo." As soon as the words leave his mouth, I struggle to stand. My chest feels tight, and I can't seem to catch my breath. Jack senses the change in me and helps me to sit down. "I'm so sorry, babe, if there was something I could do, I would. I swear." His voice is sad and desperate.

"You're the fucking police, Jack." I can't help but point that out.

He ducks his head. "I know. But I can't be here twenty-four seven and I genuinely think he would run fucking shit scared if he thought you were being protected by Con and his family. Fuck, he'd probably drop the whole little vendetta he's got going on in his head altogether. As you're aware, I've been investigating his activity for a while; well, we're getting closer to finding him. Until then, you and Keen need to lie low."

"How long?"

He watches me with a confused expression. "How long what?"

"How long do I have to stay with them, Jack?" My voice is sharper. I'm fucking pissed.

I see Con shift in his chair, squirming.

"I'm not sure. He's currently MIA, fuck knows where he is. But if you stay with Con and the guys, I can concentrate on the investigation. The sooner I do that, the sooner the restraints on you loosen."

"Restraints? I'm not a fucking dog or a criminal, Jack!" Jesus, his delivery needs some serious work.

I slowly take in everything he's said. The room sits in silence, watching the exchange. We're in danger. I glance at Con, who's watching me with a painful intensity. I clench my jaw in frustration.

"We can protect you, Will. Let us help you. You've always been part of our family and nothing's changed. Keen added into the mix is a blessing, Will. We'll love and protect him. Fuck, our Ma's going to be buzzing." Bren's words resonate with me and make me begrudgingly smile.

Cyn, Con's mom, loves kids. She always showered me love and affection. Welcoming me into their home, I'd spend hours with her. I'd take any excuse not to return home to my living hell. We'd bake together, and she'd tell me how much she wished she could have had a daughter. How having sons she knew she'd lose them to their "business."

I think Cyn understood and maybe knew a little about what was going on at home because she was always so sweet, compassionate and, quite frankly, she mothered me. It was a relationship we both embraced. She never asked me about our relationship, but she wasn't blind. She knew; they all did.

"Okay. So where do we stay?" I rub my hands up my arms, suddenly feeling helpless and vulnerable. I've not felt like this in a long time, and it isn't me. There's no way I can go back to that. I shake the feeling off.

"With me," Con states while standing up, as if he's about to go to battle and he's going to come up with a verbal defense.

I splutter on my words. "With you? Seriously?"

Cons voice exudes confidence. "Absolutely. I want to get to know my son, Will. There's plenty of room in my apartment. You can have as much space as you need. I get a relationship with my son and you both get the protection you need in return."

"Makes sense," Jack agrees. My eyes dart to him with a scowl. The fucking turn coat traitor! "It's for the best, Will. Go upstairs and pack some basics. Leave all devices here. You take nothing that can be traced, okay?" He looks at me pointedly.

I stand and nod at his instructions, stunned at the turn of events.

Con

Will's in fucking shock. Like literally in shock. If I didn't want her as much as I do, I'd feel fucking guilty. But the selfish bastard in me is pleased she's coming to stay with me. Shit, she even agreed to it without an argument. That went so much easier than expected.

I can sense her enter the room without hearing her, it's something I've always been able to do with her and it's the only time I ever feel relaxed. When she's near me, with me.

I need to make her see that she doesn't need to leave when that little shit Milo is handled. I need her to see what she used to see. Apart from all the shit I put her through and the fact I was a selfish little prick, which I'd happily admit right now.

Bren stands and my eyes follow him. He takes the two bags from Will. He turns and walks out the door with Jack in tow.

"He's strapping Keen's car seat into the vehicle," Cal informs me, looking at the door.

Will is leaning against the wall at the bottom of the stairs, her head down and her arms wrapped around her middle. She looks so lost. I contemplate going over to her, I just need to touch her. Brushing my hair from my eyes, I decide to man the fuck up and check on her.

"Hey." Yeah, nice one, Con.

She lifts her head slightly and stares deep into my eyes, something she's tried to avoid all night. Her eyes are haunted, completely broken. My heart hammers against my chest as I scan her face. She's pale, her lip quivers, she has tear tracks down her face and a vulnerable, vacant expression that makes my gut twist. I've done this. I've given her this haunted, destroyed look.

Her whole demeanor a reminder of the night I told her to get rid of the baby, the night I told her I didn't want her anymore.

The acknowledgement within me makes my body jolt. I swallow thickly, the realization of the hurt I cause her just being around her almost brings me to my knees. I'm a selfish bastard and I hate myself for it. But not nearly as much as she hates me.

I'm not sure how long we stand there staring at one another. But it sure as hell feels like a lifetime. I open my mouth hesitantly to speak, but before I get the chance, Jack beats me to it.

He surges between us and holds Will's chin in his grasp. "Hey, are you okay? You're going to be okay." He scans her up and down as if checking for something out of place. She sags into him, and he tugs her tighter, his arms caressing around her waist. He places a gentle kiss on her forehead, causing her to raise her head and smile gently at him. I fucking hate it.

My fists clench beside me. He's come between us and obliterated my intensions and now she's looking at him like some sort of hero. My jaw clenches as I watch on like a fucking dumb creeper.

"Cars ready!" Bren's voice booms, breaking the moment. I spin my head toward his deep voice, and he gives me a sly grin, his lip curling up slightly, a wink at me before turning his back and walking back toward the door. Making me realize he interrupted the moment on purpose. How long was he standing there?

Did he do that for me? Why would he do that?

Will

I break away from comfort and safety of Jack's arms. He moves from my side to speak with Cal. It's only then that I realize Con is still standing there, watching me with an expression of sympathy. Guilt even? I swallow and avert my eyes, not wanting to address his demeanor, not when he's caused all of this again.

As we move out onto the porch, I overhear Jack and Cal discussing how they intend to keep in contact with one another.

The screeching sound of brakes rocks the peaceful air surrounding us. In a flash, a black SUV lowers its windows and before we know what's happening someone from inside the vehicle opens fire at us. Before my mind can summon any movement, I'm pushed back toward the door into the entrance of my home by Con, his body my shield.

I stumble backwards. I vaguely see Jack cover Con's back with his own body, as a form of protection he uses himself to cover Con.

My head hears noises, gunshots, and shouts as both Cal and Bren retaliate with their own weapons. My heart pounds when I realize the jolts of Jack's body against Con are those of bullets hitting him repeatedly.

I gasp when Cons body falls hard against my own a blanket of cover protecting me. My eyes scan over his features. I panic, did they hit him too?

"I'm okay, Will. Are you okay?"

Did I say it out loud or did Con see the question on my face? I nod my head frantically as I start to push him off of me.

He moves quickly, and we both turn in tandem toward Jack. Con grasps my hands and pushes them against a bloodied chest wound. He quickly tears his shirt over his head to use as a compress.

He stands and walks toward the door with his back against the wall, his hand raised as if telling me to stay put.

I shake myself off from the initial shock and quickly survey Jack. He's breathing heavily. Blood seeping from his chest, another wound in his shoulder.

My lip trembles. "Why did you do that?" Why did he shield Con?

My trembling hands press harder on his chest, causing him to suck in his breath. Slowly Jack brings his hand to my face, "Because, you need him, Willow. You just don't realize how much yet." I glance away from him, scared to acknowledge his words. Scared to admit Jack cares enough about me to not want Con hurt. "You need him." He smiles softly at me, his handsome face grimacing in pain.

Tears pour down my face.

Chapter Five

Con

Cal approaches the door first. "Jack took two bullets. He's stable." He dips his head in acknowledgment.

"Bren's going to wait by the car. We need to get out of here," he pants, looking over his shoulder at Will and Jack on the floor.

I glance back at Will, she's in pieces beside Jack. I brush my hand through my hair. There's no way she's going to leave him like that.

As if hearing my thoughts, she says, "I'm not leaving him!" Her voice trembles.

Me and Cal walk toward Jack, he's trying to shuffle something from underneath him. "My phone," he pants.

I delve into his ass pocket and hand him his phone. He quickly sends a text. "My partner Stan..." his breath stutters as he goes on to explain, "... will be here in five minutes with medics. Get Keen and *go!*" His voice is stern, leaving no room for argument.

Cal takes off up the stairs. Willow stares at him blankly causing Jack's lips to straighten in annoyance. "Willow. Do as I fucking ask before someone else gets hurt. I'll contact you tomorrow. Now get the fuck out." His chest struggles as he kicks the words out, but they have the desired effect on Will she needed to hear. She gingerly backs away from him and I move around her to help her up.

Before I reach her arms, she descends on him again and presses a hard chaste kiss to his lips. "I love you." Jack's face softens at her words, and he ducks his head timidly at her.

I guide her stunned body to the car with my hand digging into her waist to stabilize her.

I tuck her in beside me in the back of the SUV, strapping her in like a helpless child. Tears drip from her shocked face.

Keen is already strapped inside, sound asleep. Fuck, the kid can sleep through a hurricane by the look of him. I'm not sure whether to be in awe or envious. The thought makes me chuckle to myself as we pull away from the side of the road.

Cal and Bren share muffled words in the front. Cal brings the phone to his ear, no doubt calling Oscar.

I tune out my brothers in the front seats and turn my body toward Will. Her trembling hands are covered in blood, she pulls a blanket higher on Keen's sleeping body but quickly drops her hands into her lap, as if only just realizing they're covered in blood.

Before she has time to contemplate those thoughts, I unlock her seatbelt and pull her toward me. I palm her head and push her to rest on my bare chest. I use my hand in her hair to keep her head in place, I'm not sure if I'm trying to comfort her or me.

Her tense body loosens as she crumbles into me with heart-wrenching sobs, her hands grip my waist as she clings to me, causing my chest to tighten in response. I never want to let her go.

Cal turns his head and peers back at us. He gives me an approving tilt of his head before facing forward giving us some privacy.

I nuzzle my nose into her hair, capturing her familiar scent. Vanilla and lemon. My eyes squeeze closed at the memories, emotion racing through me. I band my arms tighter around her, ensuring she can't move away, can't leave me. I swallow away the thought.

Will's tears hit my chest and the sounds emitting from her rip my heart open, causing a lone tear to trail down my own cheek. I never thought I'd see her again, let alone hold her. My heart pounds against her. I'm never letting her go.

Never again.

Will

At some point during the drive, Con's hold on me loosened. I could move away from him, I could continue my fight against him, my hatred. But right now, I need him. I need his strength and support. I need him to be everything he wasn't, maybe everything he isn't. My arms drop at my thoughts.

"Don't." His voice is stern with a little desperation to it.

I tilt my head to peek up at him, his beautiful blue eyes shining with emotion. "Whatever you were thinking, don't. Please."

His soft voice is a plea. His eyes hold such vulnerability, he looks utterly broken. How can the man I fell in love with, the hard talking joker who showed little genuine emotion, seem so broken? I swallow thickly. "Please, Will." His hands squeeze me again as I realize he needs me. I nod my head in agreement and bury my face back in his chest.

Con kisses my head slowly, whispering gently, "Thank you." I clutch him in response, so he knows I heard him. His hand brushes lazily up and down my back.

We pull into an underground carpark and the lights come on automatically as the car descends further inside. "Won't they have tracked our car?" I ask, bolting upright in panic my eyes darting around us.

Cal's commanding voice fills the car. "Maybe. But the car is clear of bugs and trackers. It's likely they're aware this is our car by now. So, if they were coming for you, Will, they know you're here."

My body tenses at Cal's words, causing me to involuntarily whimper. "Shhh, it's okay, Will. We've got you. We've also got the best security available; I swear it." Con brushes his hand up and down my back gently, coaxing the tension from me.

"Come on, let me get you both settled." He opens the door and I follow him out, taking the hand he offers me, his slick muscular body greeting me. Fuck, he needs to put a shirt on.

Cal unstraps Keen with ease; I smile at the fact he is a well-practiced daddy. We follow behind Bren as we enter the elevator. "We're the third apartment from the top. Finn is above us, and Bren has the top floor." Con informs me as he pulls me protectively by my waist into him. Keen is resting his head on Cal's shoulder, completely zonked out. A trail of drool building on Cal's shoulder.

We enter Con's apartment and when he switches the lights on my eyes dart around the room. It's an open plan modern concept, which would be appealing, but the place is a shit hole.

My body stills beside him as I take in the trash strewn across the room, it looks like a party was taking place at some point and he never got round to cleaning it. Empty takeaway cartons, upturned furniture, and broken glasses.

Then, right there on the kitchen counter, an open foil with white powder. I gasp.

What the actual fuck?

I spin my head toward him, accusing eyes drilling into his.

Con

As soon as the light illuminates the room, I tense. I'd completely forgotten how I left the apartment. Obviously, I didn't intend to bring Will back here quite so soon, and I sure as shit didn't expect to bring my son here too.

Will freezes beside me, taking in the room the same time as we do. I quickly dart my eyes to the kitchen counter and internally groan with disappointment at the open cocaine on display. There's no chance Bren will miss that, that man can sniff out anything.

"They're not staying here!" Cal spits the words out, not caring if he disturbs Keen. His body solid with anger, the vein on his neck pumping.

"Damn fucking right they're not. They can stay at my apartment." Bren's shoulders broaden further, like he's ready for a fight. The disgust on their faces is evident. The sickening sensation of failure in my stomach is all too familiar making my body shake with panic at losing them already. I lick my lips as my throat goes desperately dry.

I don't want them to go anywhere. They're my fucking family. Mine.

If they leave now, will they stay with Bren indefinite? How would I prove myself? Would Will make me a part time dad who sees his kid when she decides, and I have no say? Would I even be allowed to see him?

If they think drugs are involved, they have every reason not to. My family would side with Will. I know they would. But I need them, the thought of losing her all over again is too much to bear. My legs feel like they're going to buckle. My heart pounds rapidly. Panic floods my veins.

"No," I spit the words out harshly. "I'll clean it up. It won't happen again. I swear. Will, please, by the time you wake up, it'll all be gone. I swear. Please, just give me a chance. I want you here, both of you. Please." Will's hazel eyes meet mine; she looks torn. Probably wondering what the right thing to do is.

She looks at Keen and then back at me. I bite my lip and brush my hand through my hair, anxiety reeling off me, "Please, Will." I'm hoping she can see the sincerity in my eyes, the desperation in my voice.

Her eyes flick back and forth over my face, likely seeing how pathetic and desperate I am.

She gently nods her head, "Don't make me regret this. It needs to be right by morning."

I nod frantically, eagerly, before letting out a deep sigh of relief.

"Where should we... erm, where should we sleep?" Will stands with her arms around her middle, hugging herself vulnerably, the blood still coating her hands. I want to hold her, pull her into me. I stop myself knowing I'd be rejected.

I swallow thickly and avert my eyes. "Cal, can you show Will where the spare room is? There are fresh towels in the closet." I point in the direction of the room. Cal gestures for Will to follow him as he steers her and Keen to a spare room.

"You sure it's suitable in there?" Bren's deep, uncertain voice breaks my thoughts.

I brush my hand through my hair. "Yeah, it's suitable." I don't dare to look at him. But instead survey the room, staring at all the work that needs doing. Shit, it's going to be a long ass night.

"You got a problem?" Bren tips his head toward the cocaine on the counter, cutting into my thoughts.

I dart my eyes to his, "No man, I don't. I just use it occasionally when I party." I shrug as if it's no big deal. But let's face it, I know it's a big fucking deal.

"Party?" His eyes bore into mine. As if he's trying to dive into my soul. Searching for a lie.

I make sure my voice is confident and hold his eyes. "Clearly, I won't be doing any of that again. So, no need to worry about it." Bren dips his head, as if satisfied with my response.

Footsteps on the marble floor draw my eyes toward Cal. "What the fuck, Con! This place is a fucking shit hole. You can't have drugs around kids, for Christ's sake." Yeah, he thinks I'm that dumb. He stands there with his hands on his hips, seething.

His eyes narrow on me, while exhaling a deep breath. "What the hell happened to Maureen?"

I scoff, he means our cleaner. "Her name was Brenda, and she was a whiney bitch, so I fired her."

"Well, perhaps you need to rethink that decision?" His eyes rove over the room again.

I blow out a deep breath. "Ya think?"

Cal nods, clearly missing my sarcasm. "Will and Keen are settling in. Come on, I'll help you clean and get rid of that shit." He tilts his head toward the drugs.

"Oh, and tomorrow we're going to have to tell Da."

"Fuck." My stomach plummets, yet another disappointment for them.

Fuck. My. Life.

Chapter Six

Con

I crashed on the couch a couple of hours ago. Grateful yet again for my brother's help.

The sun seeps through the window blinds and the soft creak of Will's bedroom door alerts me it's definitely morning.

I shoot up and scan the room, we did an amazing job in a few hours. Cal told me he would organize a team of cleaners to come this afternoon to give it a thorough clean and a team to childproof the apartment. He's like a kid-whisperer now days so I'm grateful for his help.

I listen intuitively for her footsteps but don't hear them. I rise from the couch and make my way past the kitchen counter toward the hallway leading to Will's room.

Just as I approach the hall, I almost stumble over Keen, he's so small and with the dim lighting, I almost wipe the poor kid out.

He gasps, probably scared shitless.

"Oh, shit." I clamp my mouth closed as quick as I opened it. You're not meant to swear around kids. Fuck.

Keen giggles, pointing his finger at me. "You said a naughty."

I crouch down beside him. "Yeah, I did. Sorry about that, little man." I clear my throat. "You remember me?" My voice shakes with vulnerability but hopefully my kid doesn't notice. Although I bet he's smart, just like Will.

He scrunches his nose up. He looks cute as hell. His wavy hair is a mess. His hands fidget in front of him. "You're Mommy's friend."

I grin at him; my little dude is fucking clever. "Yeah, my name's Con. You remember?" I nod encouragingly.

He bows his little head. "I did a pee-pee."

I stare at him, a little shocked. Where the fuck did that come from?

My eyes scan his body before landing on his little tiger pajamas, they're soaked.

Shit, what the fuck do I do? I tug on my hair in a bit of a panic. I take a deep breath and steel myself; I need to man the fuck up and show everyone I can do this.

I soften my tone. So he knows he's not in trouble. "Okay, little man. Do you need a diaper change?"

He wrinkles his nose and then straightens his little shoulders with confidence. "Nope. I don't wear diapers because I'm a big boy. Big boys don't wear diapers, they pee in the potty."

O-Kay then. I scan his face, unsure if he's joking. His face is impassive as he stands proudly. Nope, he's definitely fucking serious. I mean, clearly, he's not a big boy because he pissed his pants but... What. The. Fuck. Ever. I'm sure as shit not going to have my kid upset with me.

"Okay, so we need to change you, right?" Completely unsure if that's what we need to be doing right now.

"Yep." he rocks back and forth on his feet, grinning.

"Okay, little man. Should I bathe you or something?"

"Yep. With bubbles."

"Bubbles, right, got ya." Do I even have fucking bubbles? I scan around the room as if bubbles are going to jump out at me. Then, as if the fucking bubble gods have shone light on me, my phone vibrates on the counter. Right next to the liquid dish washing bottle, bingo! Bring on the bubbles. I grin back at Keen.

I turn on the taps as Keen curiously investigates around the bathroom, he's opening the cabinets and occasionally sitting in them before closing the doors and moving onto the next one. I sit on the toilet lid, watching him with amusement. His whole-body language and gestures are so comical, so like me.

"Keen, the bath is about ready. Wow, can you see all these bubbles, man? I think I might lose you in there." I point to the tub with a grin.

Keen spins around on his feet, his eyes bugging out at the overflowing bath, his face lights up and his belly laughs. His little fist shoots into the air. "Yeah. Werhoo!" I grin at his excitement. I did that, and it feels fucking good.

He cocks his head to the side, a thoughtful expression on his little face. "Did you check the water?"

I study him his face in question. "What?"

"The water. Jack said you always have to check the water. So, you don't get burned." His face all serious and his finger shakes at the bath as if telling it off.

Oh shit! I nearly burned my fucking kid. I shove my hand in the water, then relax when I realize the temperature is fine. My shoulders sag with relief.

Before I understand what's happening, he scrambles to undress and then stands there in front of me with his arms up. Like I know what the fuck he wants.

He sighs at my lack of movement. "I can't climb into the bath. It's too high."

Oh shit, poor little dude. I lift him into the bath, his grin even bigger as he sinks into the mountain of bubbles.

When I finally get Keen out of the bath, he's all crinkly and chatting a mile a minute about some television show with a pig on it. Sounds insane if you ask me, this pig wears fucking boots.

As I help him dry off, I scratch my head, realizing we don't have any clothes for Keen. I mean, I think there's a change in Will's room, but I don't want to disturb her. I need to prove to her I can handle hard shit like this on my own.

"I'm wondering what you can wear while your mommy is in bed. I don't want to wake her; she had a tough night," I explain to Keen.

Keen's forehead wrinkles as if he's thinking hard. His little eyes draw together. "I can wear one of your T-shirts?"

I nod at him, but then I point to his legs. "I mean, what can you wear instead of your boxers, you know, as pants?" Do they even call little man panties boxers? I put my hands on my hips. "Come on, I'll call Cal, see what he thinks."

Keen follows behind me, tripping on his towel as I dial Cal.

His voice sounds a million miles away. "Yeah?"

"Cal, what should Keen wear? He doesn't have any boxers and the ones he came in are wet."

"You called me at six-thirty a.m. to ask me what to dress your kid in?" I pull the phone away from me slightly, staring at it. His tone fucking stinks.

I put the phone back to my ear. What the fuck is his problem? "Yeah."

"Chloe has been up teething all night. Lily is pissed I came home only a few hours ago. Now you wake me with some dumbass question? Handle your own shit, Con."

He cuts the call. I stare at the phone, confused. What the hell is his problem? What just happened?

I glance down at Keen and shrug. He stares back up at me with an expression of inquisitiveness about him.

"I'll try, Bren." I smile down at him, and he grins back at me and overly nods.

"Bren, dude, minor dilemma. What do I dress Keen in. Will's asleep and I want to leave her there. Any suggestions?"

"Not got a fucking clue." He cuts the call; I stare at the phone. Seriously, what the fuck is wrong with some people?

I peer at Keen, his eyebrows knitted together. "Don't worry, little man, I've got more brothers." He nods and gives me a mega-watt, encouraging smile.

I pull up Finn's number, taking a deep breath knowing he isn't aware of my current situation.

"What?" he snaps.

"Finn, purely hypothetical. If you didn't have access to any boxer shorts and needed them, what would you use instead?"

I can hear Finn's steady breathing. Has he fallen back to sleep? "Finn?" I all but bark.

"Go commando."

I shake my head at his suggestion, "No dude, it's for a kid."

His voice comes out confused, "Kid can't do commando?"

"No, no pants. Nothing."

"Jesus." I listen to him rummaging around, and then a sigh, as though he's thinking about it. "How about a pillow-case? Cut the legs out or something?" See, this is why Finns my favorite. He's a fucking genius.

"Thanks man." I cut the call with a smile on my face.

Chapter Seven

Con

I sit Keen on the couch; a long T-shirt covers him. Underneath that is his makeshift boxers. We worked as a team and cut some legs out, then I used tape to secure the waistline. He's now sitting watching the pig program while I sit watching him. I'm feeling quite impressed with myself, even if I had to ask for Finn's advice, I still achieved it all.

Me and Keen work well together, that's for sure. A great team.

"I'm hungry." Keen whimpers while looking at me.

I jump from the couch and walk over to the kitchen area, walking around and opening the cabinets for inspiration. "Okay, little man, you like cereal?" I pull down the Captain Crunch and Beaver Balls.

He nods his head frantically. Then points his finger at me. "No nuts. I'm allergic."

My heart misses a beat. Fuck, I could have killed my kid.

"Are you allergic to anything else?" my heart pounds waiting for his reply.

His eyebrows furrow together, then he ticks things off his little fingers. "Peas, lettuce, and those little tree things."

"Little tree things?" I ask, completely confused.

He nods his head. "Jack has them at dinner, but I don't. I'm allergic."

I think about what he's saying. "Do you mean broccoli?"

"Yeah, that." Keen points his finger at me.

Shit, what else is he allergic to? What if I give him the wrong thing and something happens? Fuck, this is some serious shit. I glance at Will's door, biting my lip, unsure of what to do. Then I gaze back at Keen. What the fuck do I do?

He's now sitting on the kitchen stool watching me, waiting for me to feed him.

"How about a drink? You want a drink?" I try to divert his attention from being hungry.

"Yeah, but no apple juice. I'm allergic." He points at me again, with all seriousness.

I open the fridge and see the milk and orange juice. Do I let him have those? Fuck no. I'm not making that mistake.

"How about water? Can you have that?" He smiles with a tight grin.

Will

Surprisingly, I slept really well. I think I was that exhausted that after I showered, I literally dropped on the bed and slept through until this morning. eight-thirty to be precise. I turn over and realize Keen isn't there.

Listening carefully, I can hear chuckling from the living area. I smile to myself.

I stretch my arms wide, before forcing myself out of the bed, I freshen up in the en-suite bathroom before entering the living area. Con is in the kitchen looking a little stressed. His hair is tussled, his white T-shirt clings to his delectable muscles, and his gray sweatpants hang off his hips. Of course they do.

A throat clears and my eyes dart up to meet his, a smug smirk on his face. "Morning, beautiful," he practically sings with a handsome grin.

I tug awkwardly on my T-shirt, attempting to cover my thighs. Con's eyes follow my hands, his blue eyes drinking me in. Slowly his eyes draw up to meet mine once again, but this time there's fire behind his eyes, and not in a playful, flirty way. No, now he's angry, his jaw clenching.

"Everything okay?" I ask cautiously moving toward Keen.

"Yep, I had a bath with lots of bubbles!" Keen beams as I kiss him on his forehead.

Thankfully, the tension has been broken by Keen's declaration. "And I'm wearing a pillowcase as pants."

Con winces as I turn to him in explanation with raised eyebrows.

Con swallows, his eyes darting down, almost looking embarrassed with himself. He tugs on his hair. "I, erm... didn't want to disturb you, and Keen had an accident. I wanted to fix it myself." He doesn't meet my eyes as he speaks, looking completely vulnerable. My heart aches a little for him.

"Oh, thank you. For sorting him, I mean. And for not disturbing me. I appreciate it." I try to sound as genuine as possible. Inside, I'm bursting to laugh and hug him all in one.

"Does he pee like that every night? I wasn't sure if he was meant to be in diapers?" Con asks with all seriousness.

Oh jeez, he really has no idea, does he? "No, it's just because he woke up somewhere strange and probably didn't know where the toilet was. Right, buddy?" I peer over at Keen.

Keen points at me. "Yep. And I didn't pee in the bed. I peed when I got out." I stifle a laugh and pull my teeth between my bottom lip as I gingerly stare at Con. He's got his own grin. Our eyes lock and something passes between us.

Keen drops his feet to the floor and wanders over to the couch, watching Peppa Pig.

"So, Keen wanted breakfast, but to be honest, he scared the hell out of me with the whole allergy thing." Con is back to brushing at his hair in both frustration and anxiety.

"Oh shit, his nut allergy. Jesus, with everything that happened yesterday, I completely forgot! Oh, my god. You must think I'm such a terrible mom." I start pacing with frustration, rubbing my temple, my heart pounding. Shit, I screwed up.

Con rounds the kitchen counter to stop me. He pulls me toward him, ducking his head until our eyes meet. "Hey Will. What the fuck? It's okay, you wouldn't know he'd wake and want food, right? I understand now and I'll make sure everyone else knows too, okay? No more of this pacing bullshit, it's sorted out. No harm done." He talks with such confidence and power; I believe it myself. I breathe out a sigh of relief. No harm done.

Con walks back round to the counter and fills the coffee machine.

"I'm sorry. I just had such a rough time with him, and everyone seemed to criticize everything I did. They looked down on me for being a young mother, you know?"

He stops what he's doing in an instant. His eyes dart to meet mine, his tone deepening. "They looked down on you?" his eyebrows furrow in concerned anger.

I meet his eyes, feeling completely open and vulnerable with the admittance. I laugh nervously. "Are you kidding? I was a young single mom, who didn't have a clue about changing diapers, bottles, colic..."

"Colic?" Con's eyebrows pull together.

I swing my hand in the air. "Oh, you don't want to know, trust me. Luckily for you, you skipped that stage!"

There's silence between us as the weight of my words hang there, "Luckily for you." I hadn't meant it like that, but I'm not taking it back. He deserves some shit for the mess he all but left me in.

Con breaks the tension, slowly working his jaw back and forth. "So, he told me about the nuts, peas, lettuce, broccoli..."

I hold up my hand. "Wait, he's just allergic to nuts. The others... he doesn't like them. He's probably trying to get out of eating it or he hasn't quite worked out the difference between like and allergy."

We both glance over at Keen. He flicks his gaze between us, his eyes wide. "They make me sick." He shrugs innocently. And there's the answer. Con stifles a grin with his lip trapped between his teeth.

We eat our breakfast at the dining table in virtual silence. Luckily, Peppa Pig and Keen's giggles fill the tense atmosphere.

I drop my spoon into my empty bowl and take it over to the sink. My eyes avoiding Con's.

He stands and follows me with his bowl in his hand.

Leaning against the countertop his voice low and uncertain. "When are we going to talk?"

I avoid the meaning of his question, not wanting to talk about anything at all. I'm so damn angry with him. I really don't want to talk. "Talk about what?"

He sighs. Knowing I'm not making it easy on him, but why the hell should I? "About everything, Will."

"Everything is a pretty broad subject, Con." I'm being a petty bitch, I realize. But again... Do. Not. Care.

He stands fidgeting on the spot while I tidy the kitchen. How the hell can he make such a mess of serving cereal to three people? "Okay, so do you want to talk about it? What happened between us?"

My spine straightens, my voice low but laced in venom. "You mean the fact you didn't want us? Didn't care to even try to search for me? Search for us?" I scan his eyes for guilt.

His head drops forward. "I didn't try to find you because I was ashamed of how I'd treated you, Will. Honestly, I thought you'd be better off without me." He gulps thickly at his admission.

"Yeah, well, you should be ashamed. And you're right, we are better off without you, but you came anyway. You came and ruined everything. Every God damn thing." I practically shout the last few words, causing Keen to jump up and peek over at us, craning his head high like a little meerkat.

"Fuck." Con breathes out slowly, dragging his hand through his hair. He licks his lips, contemplating his thoughts and words, his voice low. "I'm fucking sorry, Will, for everything."

I nod. "You should be because of what you did to us was unforgivable, so don't even think about asking for it." I dry the bowls a little too harshly with the kitchen towel. I'm bubbling inside.

Con nods again, his head still hung low. "I get that I fucked up Will. I'm not sure how I'm going to show you, both of you, that I can be a better person, but I promise you I'm going to try my best. I swear to you." His words sound stronger filled with determination.

Chapter Eight

Con

This morning with Will and Keen went surprisingly well. Apart from Will's dose of reality in the kitchen, it was really enjoyable. I can see myself waking up like that regularly. Having Keen around has already given me a sense of purpose, the feeling of someone needing and depending on me and not seeing me for someone who is known as the screw up.

As soon as I can get through to Will how much they can both depend on me and maybe even need me, then I can work on getting her to marry me and maybe even have a couple more kids like Keen. God, that would be amazing.

"What the hell are you sat there grinning about?" Bren's sharp voice breaks my cheerful mood, his nostrils flaring with annoyance. "You realize we're on our way to see Da, right? That you'll probably be walking out of the house with two black eyes and a few broken ribs. If you walk out of there at all?"

I fidget uncomfortably in the passenger seat of his Mercedes G-Wagon.

Fuck, he's right. My parents are going to hate me when I drop this clusterfuck on them.

I shuffle in my seat and spin my cap so it's backwards. "You said Cal is going to be there, right?" I'm aware I'm sounding completely childish.

Bren scoffs. "Do you think that sappy fucker can save you?" He raises his eyebrow to me in question.

I ignore him and zone out, peering out of the window.

The car slows down as we approach the security gates before passing through when the guards are reassured it's us.

Bren parks the car behind Cal's, and I breathe a desperate sound of relief, knowing he's there as moral support because fuck am I going to need it.

"You good?" Bren asks, as he watches me closely while switching off the engine, I shrug in response, because of course I'm not fucking good. There's a good chance I'll leave here minus a few limbs. My face must pale at my thoughts because Bren's eyebrows knit together before softening slightly. "We got ya. You know that." I dip my head in thanks before taking a deep exhale and vacate the car.

Cal gets out of his car and approaches us with a face of determination. "You okay?" I just nod in response to his words.

Cal glances at Bren, and they huddle together a bit closer with their backs toward me and the house, very fucking inconspicuous. "So, how are we doing this?" I hear Cal ask Bren.

I watch them both, they're having their own conversation about my fucking life and they're deciding how to figure it out for me. Well, fuck that shit. I need to step up and take control. I might be the youngest, dumbest brother, but I've got responsibilities now. And I need to show them I'm capable.

I stride between them, both breaking up their little pow-wow. "I'm doing it. My fuck up. I own it. So I'll deal with it." I throw behind them as I stride with purpose toward the house.

I don't take my time to take in our family home, I head for the kitchen door and walk straight in.

The smell of homemade bread fills my nostrils. Ma welcomes me in her usual tight bear hug, her dark hair pulled up in her tight bun, silver glistening in it. She kisses both my cheeks before moving on to my brothers.

I sit at my usual spot at the family table, the last one at the end next to Ma, who sits opposite Da. The king of the table.

Finn normally sits next to me and if he's not there, his place would be empty, so I'm a bit fucking shocked when Bren drops in his spot instead of his usual one beside Da. Then I'm even more shocked when Cal doesn't take his usual place but sits opposite me next to Ma. I turn toward Bren in confusion. His shoulders widen in a protective stance, his eyes trained on Da coming through the door.

Fuck, they're sat ready for Da to explode, so he'd have to go through one of them in order to get to me. They're acting as my fucking bodyguards; I don't know whether to be thankful or fucking panicked. My Adam's apple bobs in nervousness.

Da drops in his seat, his wide body filling it. His posture rigid as normal, on the defense. His famous fighting hands tighten into fists before him. I swallow, not feeling as confident about this showdown anymore.

Ma sits down, wiping her hands on a towel she then throws it onto her shoulders.

"Why ya sat down there?" Da's voice bellows and fills the room. Ma's eyes dart to mine in worry, she's clearly noted my brother's protective barrier.

The room falls silent as words evade me.

"Asked ya a feckin' question. Why ya sat down there?" His stocky finger points at Bren.

Clearing my throat and sitting up straighter. "I... I've something to tell you both." I gulp but continue. "And you're gonna be pissed." I can't help but hang my head low in shame and fiddle with my hands on the table.

"Stop fucking stuttering and spit it the fuck out, haven't got all feckin day!" his intimidating voice barks.

"Okay so..." I clear my throat again and gaze up to catch Cal's eyes. He nods at me in support, and I raise my head to my father. "I've recently discovered I've got a son."

And just like that... *boom*... he erupts... the chair goes back; his palms slap down on the table making us all jump. "What? Another fucking kid we know nothin about? Have you learnt nothin from dipshit here?" He waves his hand toward Cal, who rolls his eyes at his nickname.

Not too long ago, poor Cal had to endure this very same treatment when he told our parents he was the father of a teenage son, Reece. Luckily for him, he didn't screw up anywhere near as bad as me and therefore managed to keep his O'Connell good looks. He did, however, have to jump through hoops to get out of an arranged marriage in order for him to marry Reece's mom, Lily.

"How many times do I have to tell ya, to wrap ya cocks up!" His hands shake against the table before he lets out a deep breath and rights the chair before begrudgingly sitting back down.

"Well, who the fuck is she? She better not be a whore. I ain't having no whore bastard in this house."

I wince at his suggestion. "She isn't a whore, Da." I pull off my cap and brush my hand through my hair, anxiously avoiding the truth. *Rip off the band aid, rip off the band aid, you can do this, Con.* I chant in over and over in my head.

"Con." Bren gently prompts.

I can sense their eyes boring into me like lasers. Shit.

I man up, sitting straighter. "It's Will."

"Will?" ma questions, her knowing eyes meeting mine, a small smile graces her lips. She and Will always had such a special bond. My ma loved Will and Finn's ex-Angel like they were her own daughters. I tilt my head to her in confirmation.

"She kept the boy from you?" Da's eyes widen full of shock. He knew Will and also knows that wasn't her type of behavior.

I shake my head in disgust with myself. I lick my dry lips. "No. She didn't."

"But you just said you recently found out you had a son. So, which one is it?" Da's voice is laced with annoyance.

I sit bolt upright and straighten my shoulders. "She told me about the baby," I admit weakly.

"Ya, talking in fucking riddles. Fucking explain!" Da's finger stubs the table. No doubt seeing through my shit show of an explanation.

My breath stutters and I glance out of the corner of my eye at ma, knowing what I'm about to say will destroy her belief in me. "I'm sorry." I tell her. Tears glisten in my own eyes as she gasps.

"What have you done, Connor?" she asks, her voice trembling.

"I... I... shit." Brushing my hand through my hair and staring up to the ceiling. "I asked her to get an abortion." My words come out choked with emotion. But even as I say the words, I realize what I'm saying is wrong. So very wrong because I didn't ask. I told. "Correction. I told her to get an abortion."

Ma visibly shakes. Her body rigid yet shaking.

Her shuddering hand goes to her mouth as she sobs.

My ma is Catholic through and through, this poor woman has lost babies herself.

Hell, Bren and Cal can remember her being heavily pregnant, but the baby never appearing. We never discussed it with her, but in our hearts, we believe ma must have lost her precious baby. And here I am, demanding for my teenage girlfriend to kill ours. Absolute shame consumes me. My gut roiling with sickness.

Ma doesn't look at me as she stares at the table in shock.

"I'm ashamed of what I said and did to Will. If I could take it back..." I leave my words open and try to peek at ma. She shakes her head, not wanting to acknowledge the words. Not wanting to look at me, her gut-wrenching sobs deepen.

Da's quiet, too fucking quiet. "You told her. To get. A feckin abortion?" Each word poised with venom.

"I did." I admit, while inclining my head down at the table, guilt-ridden.

Da's chair goes flying as he comes storming around the table at lightning speed.

Bren jumps to his feet and Cal moves swiftly around the table behind my chair. "Sit the fuck down Da, come on," Bren practically pleads.

Da's face is red, his eyes bulging. His veins popping, his fists clench shut as he launches at me through Bren. "Fucker," Bren grunts when Da's body lands on his.

Da swings his arm in my direction, but I stay stoically still in my chair, prepared to face whatever punishment he sees fit.

His arms flare in all directions as Bren holds him back. "I'll fuckin kill ya. Ya little shite. See how ya like that, eh? She was too good for you, that girl. Too fucking good!"

Don't I know it. I nod agreeing with his words.

Da tries his best to overpower Bren, but it's near on impossible to shift the big fucker.

"Da, you need to calm down. We've more to discuss, and it's serious." Cal tries to talk over the scrummage.

Ma's sobs break through me, and my hands shaking. I'd rather my da beat the shit out of me than hear her cry. She sobs gently into a small blue teddy bear she keeps in her apron pocket and chants the words "Teddy, Teddy." Over and over. She always does this when she's hurting or emotional. She always chants the same words. When we were kids, I asked Cal about it and he said not to mention it to her. He surmised she'd lost a baby and the pale blue Teddy she clung to was meant for the baby. The thought of her losing a baby and me openly pushing Will to kill ours makes me want to vomit.

I don't deserve a family, that's for sure. I don't deserve anyone.

I'm not sure how long it takes Da to settle down back into his chair. All I know is my face and body are intact, but my chest fucking hurts. My heart ripped open. How the fuck did Will feel when I asked those things of her?

"You said there was more. More than him wanting to

kill his kid?" Da spits the words out like poison, making me wince with the truth behind them.

Cal clears his throat as he sits straighter. "That's right, there's more. Con gave Will the money for the abortion and ended their relationship. When she went to the clinic, they were unable to perform it because she was too far along." Da nods his head for Cal to continue. I chance a glance at ma, but her body is tense, and she's staring emptily into space.

"When Will returned home, her father beat her. He was aware of the baby and tried to... tried to kill the baby." Cal swallows thickly. Ma's chair drops back in shock as she stumbles to get up from the table. We watch as she walks away, closing the door behind her. Her sobs can be heard echoing from the room.

Da stares at me with utter hate in his eyes. His fists clench and unclench. "Ya having it, boy, I'm telling ya. Ya ain't leaving here walking." I nod my head in agreement.

Cal continues talking, ignoring Da's tirade. "Will was dumped at the hospital by her brother. The baby Keen barely survived." Da's eyes meet mine when Cal mentions Keen's name. He dips his head sharply with pride and, if I'm not mistaken, his eyes glisten too.

"He's a fighter then? Just like my boy." Da confirms.

"Yeah, he is, Da. A little on the small side with the problems Will suffered, but he's perfectly fine," Bren admits.

Da waves his hand in air. "Plenty of time for him to grow big and strong. In the kid's genes. He's an O'Connell." Da's shoulders become broader with pride. "Now, when ya bringing them to see me?"

"There's more..." Cal grimaces.

"Like feckin what?" he seethes, again his tone changing in an instant.

"Like Will had to hide from her family to protect herself and Keen. Like she married an FBI agent."

"They're divorced," I cut in quickly to lessen the blow.

"A feckin cop? She married a feckin cop?" Da's temple throbs, his nostrils flare like a bull.

Cal ignores his outburst and plows on, swallowing thickly. "She did, and as Con explained, they're now divorced. However, when we met with Will and Jack, her ex, he explained Milo, Will's brother, has put a hit out on her. We're unsure if he's aware of Keen."

Da erupts, yet again. I clench my teeth in annoyance. How the fuck can you give the guy full details when he constantly blows up like this?! And I'm the childish one.

His face is red, his veins bulging in his forehead.

"This is all your feckin fault." He points. I nod in agreement, because he's right.

"Da, enough!" Bren snaps and bangs his fist on the table, causing the silverware to rattle. Like father, like son. I almost roll my eyes at the blatant replica. "Carry on Cal," he coaxes Cal with a wave of his hand as Da takes his seat again.

"As I was saying. Jack explained the situation to us and agreed it was best for Will and Keen to move in with us while he investigates further."

"Damn feckin right, they move in with us. We're family," he chimes in.

"As we were leaving the house, a black SUV open fired on our asses and shot Jack in the chest..."

"Good hope the fucker is dead!"

My eyes snap to Da's. He did not just say that. My glare venomous.

He shrugs, unbashful. "He's a cop."

Cal seethes, "That's beside the fucking point. The man

stood up and took responsibility for Will and Keen. Protected them and loved them when Con clearly wasn't willing to!"

Wow, Cal's words fucking hurt. I wince at the pain in my chest and fidget awkwardly in my seat. I scrub my hand through my hair before daring a glance at Cal. His eyes fixed on mine in a fighting stare-off I'm not prepared for. I turn my head away in defeat.

His words are right, of course.

"Wouldn't have got shot if he was doing his job properly," Da nonchalantly throws in.

"What the fuck ever. Point being, Milo is a threat, and we need to step carefully with the FBI being involved." Bren gets to the point.

"I want him dead. No fucker touches our family. Will's ours, she always has been, always will be." He glares at me. I peer down at my sweaty hands shamefully, placing them flat on the table to stop myself from fidgeting.

"You better be stepping the fuck up, ya little shit. You hurt that girl again and I'll kill ya. Ya hear me?"

I work my head up and down like a fucking puppet. "Yeah, I hear ya Da. I won't hurt her." Confidently I sit straighter and stare at him in the eyes, hoping he can see the truth in them. "I'm going to marry her, give her and Keen what they deserve."

Bren snorts. "She know that?"

My eyes narrow and spin to meet his. "She will, soon."

While giving Bren my attention, I hadn't noticed Da getting up from his chair. He moves over toward Cal so he's now opposite me.

His demeanor has changed. He's calmer, almost lighter as he watches mine and Bren's exchange. Cal's eyes narrow suspiciously on Da's, unsure of this change in him.

"So, you're gonna marry her, yes?"

I dip my head again in confirmation. "I am."

"Well, ya best crack feckin on because you ain't gonna be able to jerk yourself off for a while." My eyebrows knit together in confusion.

Before I even see it coming, I experience it. The bastard has stabbed me in the fucking hand with a dinner knife.

"Holy fuck, that hurts! Jesus, Da. Did you have to?" My eyes meet his accusingly.

"Shit!" Cal throws out while moving toward my hand... that's fucking stuck to the table!

"Ya lucky it wasn't ya cock ya little shite. If I didn't think that would hurt Will, it would have been." He smiles smugly and I know without a doubt he'd do it, too.

Thank fuck for Will.

Da moves back to his chair and pulls a cigar out of his shirt pocket, lighting it in the process. "Now, about this Milo fucker. Kill him." His pupils dilate and his grin turns sinister.

Chapter Nine

Will

This morning Cal called to say Jack was stable in hospital and being guarded by a couple of trusted colleagues, to say I was relieved is an understatement. Jack has been an incredible part of mine and Keen's life. I don't honestly know what we would do without him.

I spend the afternoon with Keen in Cons apartment while he's gone to explain our situation to his parents. I experience a small nervous flutter in my stomach when I imagine what Con will be up against at his parents' house. I quickly shut that emotion down. He deserves it; I tell myself.

I make myself at home. Luckily, Cal's wife Lily had the forward thought to send us a grocery order so I could stock the cupboards and fridge. I've never been so grateful for some fresh produce. How Con survives I'll never understand but judging by the state of the apartment when we arrived, I probably don't want to know either.

I also may have done a little snooping around to keep myself busy, but when I opened Con's bedroom door and his familiar masculine scent hit me, I automatically closed it. I couldn't face going in there, being drawn in again. No, I need to keep my defenses up and keep him at a safe distance. There's Keen to consider this time around and there's no way in hell is he going to hurt my son.

The elevator pings and Con strides in the room, his aura automatically surrounding me, causing my breath to still. How can he still have this effect on me?

His eyes dart to mine instantly, before dipping to my chest, my tight camisole top leaving nothing to the imagination. I'm without a bra, due to the fact the only one in my possession is in the washer. My nipples pebble under his scrutiny. He licks his lips and I'm sure he's not even aware he's doing it, my breath hitches in response.

His heady voice laced with need. "Will."

"Mmm?" I snap my eyes up to meet his, trying to ignore that tongue, those lips. God, those lips.

"Miss me?" his cocky grin asks.

I shrug. "Not really," I lie.

How can I not miss him when he's everywhere in this apartment, yet nowhere at all?

He walks toward me with purpose. "I missed you," he scans my face, "and Keen. Where is my little dude, anyway?" His eyes dart around the apartment.

I nod toward the corridor leading to the bedrooms. "He's putting some toys away. Lily sent some over for him."

Con scrubs a hand through his hair then winces, causing me to notice the poorly wrapped bandage on his hand, blood seeping through it. "Yeah, he's going to need his own room, isn't he?"

"What happened to your hand?" I ask, while pulling his wrist toward me.

He exhales deeply. "Da, fucking stabbed me. Prick." He spits the latter out with hate.

My eyebrows shoot up. "Your Da did it?"

"Yeah, said I was lucky it wasn't my cock." He chuckles. Actually, freaking chuckles.

I shake my head. "You're insane, the both of you." I walk him into the kitchen and start unwrapping his hand. "Why would he do that?" I ask as I reach for the first aid kit above the cooker.

My top lifts as I stand on my tiptoes to reach for it. Before my feet touch the ground, I feel a soft hand snake around my waist. Con pulls me to him, so my back is against his front. His breath causes goosebumps over my body, he moves his mouth to my ear, "You want to know why he stabbed me?"

My words clog in my throat, so I nod, those pesky words evading me.

I'm consumed with Con's hand sprayed across my stomach, under my top. His head in my neck, breathing me in. His hardness pushing against my back.

"I told him I was going to marry you."

Like a douse of cold water over me, I bristle at his words, my spine rigid. All thoughts consuming me gone in an instant. "Don't pull away from me, Will. You're mine. This is happening." His lips tease my neck. I shake my head. He tightens his hand on me and pulls me to him. Closer. Tighter. "I'm never letting you leave, Will." His gentle but confident voice pissing me off.

I shake my head again. "You don't own me, Con."

He chuckles in my ear. "No, maybe not yet. But you own me." He rubs his cock against my ass for emphasis.

I gasp at the sensation. "You always have, Will. I was just too dumb to realize it. It's always been you." I close my eyes at his admission. Determined not to cry. I can't.

When I don't react, he pushes my boundaries further, goading me for a reaction. The right reaction. "I love you. Do you hear me?" My heart skips and I break at his words. My knees give way, I can't stop the wail that leaves my mouth.

"Shhh baby. I've got you." He coaxes gently while holding me up. His fingers dig into my hips. "I've got you." Kissing my hair. "I'm all in." He kisses my head as I bend over, quietly sobbing at his words. His promises. He holds me close, letting me cry.

How many times I've wanted to hear those words, feel this support. So many times. I stifle my emotions by biting my lip.

"Mommy, I did a poop!" Keen proudly shouts from the bathroom, breaking our moment. I've never been more grateful for hearing those poop words declared in my entire life.

Con chuckles to himself. "I got this." He gently releases me and kisses the back of my head.

I clear my throat and avoid his eyes. "Don't forget to wipe his tush."

Con stops on the spot and spins round, a blank expression on his face. "Huh?"

"His butt. He needs it wiping." I gesture with my hand swiping up.

"He doesn't do that?" I stare up at Con, his handsome face looking all sorts of unsure.

"No Con, believe me, he tries. Be grateful he's shouting he's pooped from inside the bathroom and not from another room."

Con's face grimaces at the thought, but he nods and moves on toward the bathroom. I listen, hoping to hear what their hushed conversation is about but can't make it out. I stifle a small giggle at the thought of Connor trying to wipe a very independent but not competent Keen.

Con ended up bathing Keen while I made a start on dinner, something about it being easier to wash the shit away than wipe it.

I made spaghetti with a side salad. Con grins from ear to ear when he scrapes the last of his meal into his mouth. "Fuck you can cook."

My eyes go wide at the cuss word, then they instantly dart to Keen, whose eyes are bugging out. "Oh shit. I'm sorry. Keen don't say that word, okay?" I glare in his direction. I mean is he serious? Like shit is okay to say?

"I don't. I'm not a naughty boy." He sits proudly in his chair, a smug little smile on his face makes him appear even more like Con, his bright blue eyes mirroring his fathers.

Con's face of shock soon turns into something more playful as he gazes at me. "Am I a naughty boy, Will?"

My eyebrows raise. Is he serious? Yep, that sly smile tells me he is. I sharpen my tone. "Yep, he's very naughty, Keen. Don't repeat the naughty words." I decide not to play Con's game. I eyeball him.

"Are you naughty, Will?" Con grins, undeterred.

I peek at Keen, his eyes darting between mine, and Con's trying to figure out if either of us is naughty.

"Nope, can't say that I am." I give him a sarcastic, tight smile back.

"Pretty sure you are." His smile encompassing his face with childlike glee in his eyes.

I roll my eyes at him. "Nope. Definitely a good girl."

Con watches me and brushes his hand over his jaw. "Mmm, I'm not so sure."

The elevator pings, causing all our eyes to dart toward the door.

In walks a tall platinum blonde, in a freaking trench coat and high heels. The whole stripper thing down to a tee.

Red lips, right red nails, red heels. "Hey, handsome." She purrs with a sultry wave. My mouth drops open.

I watch on mortified, as Con jumps up from his chair so fast it hits the floor. He runs toward her, pulling her coat shut as she opens it to reveal a red bra and panties. "Oh fuck! Cher, don't open the fucking coat." Yeah, pretty sure she's just opened the coat, Con.

I watch in complete shock as Cher proceeds to open the coat wider before trailing her nails down Con's chest. "I want to play." She pouts with her thick fake lips. She seems completely oblivious to the family at the table.

My stomach churns.

"Can I play too?" Keen calls as he stands on his chair for a better view.

Oh god no! "What the hell, Con?" I screech over my shoulder as I stand and block Keen's view.

"Fuck. Outside. Get the fuck outside." I hear him snapping at her while I'm coaxing Keen to bed with a cookie and promise of a visit to the park tomorrow.

I glance at the door and realize they've both gone through it. My shoulders sag in defeat. I pick Keen up and march him to our room.

My heart is full of annoyance and yeah, as much as I hate to admit it, disappointment too.

Con

Shit. I fucked up, again.

Cher comes by twice a week for our little rendezvous. I'd completely forgot about her. I mean, why the fuck would I even think about her when I've got Will consuming every second of my mind?

By the time I manage to get her out the fucking door and explain I'm not interested anymore, I felt fucking sick at the thought of letting Will down again. What the fuck must she think of me? Cher might have been an okay fuck, but that's all she ever was, and she was fine with it.

I message Oscar and ask him to change the security details, so we have no more unexpected guests. I sure as hell don't need any of the guys who I party with showing up here.

I walk back into the apartment ready to apologize, but when I see Will in a long baggy T-shirt, my anger morphs. It's not just any baggy shirt, it's a man's T-shirt. And it's not fucking mine. My jaw clenches so tight my fucking teeth hurt.

Will's soft voice cuts through my tension. "I put Keen to bed. He was exhausted."

I nod in understanding, but I'm pissed she put him to bed without me.

I storm to my bedroom and rummage angrily through my drawers. If she wants something to wear, I'll fucking give it to her.

I rage through the apartment to where Will is wiping the kitchen surfaces. My face must scream pissed. My temples throb, my hands clench, and my nostrils flare.

"What the hell are you wearing?" I spit.

Will turns to face me, her face a picture of shock. She

looks down at herself, then back up at me, completely confused.

"You're wearing another man's shirt in my apartment," I explain to save her apparent confusion.

Her eyebrows rise, then her expression changes as she chokes slightly before giving me lip. "You have got to be fucking kidding me Con! I've just had a front-row seat of some pumped up strip show and you're lecturing me on what I'm wearing?" her chest rises angrily pointing at the door.

I shrug off her comment. "You have nothing to worry about where Cher's concerned. She doesn't matter. She means nothing to me."

If I thought that would pacify her, I was fucking wrong. Apparently, very wrong.

Her nostrils flare with rage. "Nothing to worry about? What the hell are you talking about? I don't give a shit who you screw. Just don't flaunt her in front of me and Keen. We deserve respect, Con." Her voice softening at the end, just enraging me more. She doesn't care? My heart races wildly. Doesn't care?

I scoff. "Take the fucking shirt off, Will!" I spit.

Her chin rises in defiance. "No."

My chest heaves with anticipation as I stare into her defiant eyes. They're gleaming with a dare.

I step toward her and hold her shirt by the scruff of the neck. I twist my face to match my fists as I roar and rip the shirt from her body. It hangs loosely on both sides of her body. Her hands hang beside her in shock, her lips parted beautifully. Fuck, she's gorgeous.

I seethe with barely restrained rage as I take in her gorgeous body. She trembles under my gaze. Her tits hanging free, her perfect pink nipples on display, begging to be sucked. I lick my lips.

Her small black lace panties barely cover her pussy. Fuck. I gulp thickly.

I work my eyes back up to her face. My eyes meet hers and she can't mask the want in them, the need. But she also can't mask the hurt still shining through.

I can't fucking stand it.

"Turn the fuck around!" I spit. She doesn't turn, she just looks at me in a trancelike state. "Turn, Will. Fucking turn." I demand, spinning my finger in a motion I expect her to understand.

She slowly begins to turn, but my impatience takes over, I spin her around and push her hands onto the worktop.

"Co... Con?" her soft voice wavering.

"Shut up. Shut the fuck up. I need this." I bite into my lip.

She goes still as I roughly tug her panties down. "Did you love him, Will? Did you love your fucking husband?" I snipe the words out with bitterness.

"Ye... yes, of course."

I nod even though she can't see me. My heart pounds violently against my chest with her admittance. "I never felt a goddamn thing for any of them. Not one. Do you hear me? You. Fucking. Own. Me!" I punctuate each word. I'm so beyond pissed at her. For the shirt, her loving someone else, for hating me. I just want her to want me, to need me. Like I need her.

Before I give her a chance to think about what's going to happen, I make it a reality. I don't even test the waters, so to speak. I fucking plough in.

I roughly tug my buttons down my jeans. If I could rip them off me, I would. My dripping cock springs free, hitting my stomach. The soreness from not wearing boxers and my cock rubbing against my jeans just adds to my heightened, aggressive state. She'll fucking pay for causing that. I grind my teeth with annoyance when Will tries to turn her body around.

I roughly push the middle of her back down slightly and kick her legs further apart. Gripping my cock with fury, I ram it into her, not caring if she's ready. Not caring if she wants me as much as I want her. I know she wants me. She'd have voiced it if not.

Air rushes from her chest at the sudden intrusion as she sucks in air. I smirk and grip her hips as she wiggles her ass from side to side to accommodate me.

"Fucking take it!" I grit out.

Her breathy moans urge me on. "Ah. Oh god, Con." Her hands clench tighter on the countertop.

I spit my words out. "Fucking standing here, dressed like this." I pound into her, taking her to her tiptoes. "In another man's shirt? You're fucking mine. Do you understand me?" I grip her roughly, no doubt leaving bruises as my cock thrusts into her relentlessly. "Say you fucking understand." Her pussy clenches around my cock at my words.

"Fucking. Say. It!"

Her breath ragged. "Yours. I'm yours."

My body eases at her words, my words coming out softer this time. "Yeah, you are. You're mine." I nip at her neck, then kiss away the bite.

Her pussy clutches me like a vise. I move my uninjured hand to her tit and grip the cushioned breast forcefully, tweaking her nipple. Fuck, it feels good. My mouth waters for them, my balls tighten at the thought. I've never felt the need to fuck someone so much, so hard, so desperately.

"Will, I'm close baby. I'm fucking close." I clench myself to try and tame my cock.

I gaze down at our combined bodies. My body pounding against her sweet ass. Ramming in and out of her pussy.

"Fuck, you're still tight. So tight." My mouth falling lax with pleasure.

"Oh, fuck, Con. Like that." My naughty girl loves her tits being squeezed. "Yes. Oh, I'm going to..." Her words end as she drops her head forward. Her pussy grips me with intensity.

I throw my head back with the force of my orgasm, my cum flooding her pussy with vigor.

"Fuck yes, take it, Will. Take it all."

Her hands turning to fists on the worktop as our orgasms consume us. I push one final time, ensuring my cum is as far in as possible. Her body collapses against the worktop with such force, she winces. My heavy body stumbles onto hers.

We pant in unison, our bodies laced with sweat.

I straighten slowly as I hold her hips and gently stand her back upright. My cock slips from her, my cum coating her thighs. I watch in awe as it covers her, marking her. I use my bad hand to push the cum back up and into her swollen pussy. The thought of owning her inside and out possesses me.

"You... you didn't use a condom." I still at her words. She turns her head over her shoulder to stare at me with desperation evident in her eyes.

My shoulders tense once again. "I'm clean Will. I've never..." I leave the words hanging there as I wave my hand in her direction, her pussy's direction.

She nods her head with uncertainty. A vulnerable look

appearing in her eyes as she turns and tries to cover herself with the remains of the shirt. "I'm on birth control." She ducks her head down. Is she meaning to reassure me? What the fuck? Does she not get it? Does she not understand? My eyebrows pull together in confusion; how can she not understand my intentions?

I shrug. "Stop taking it."

She sucks in a dramatic breath before she throws her head back and mock laughs. Is she for real right now?

"Jesus Con, you've had us here for two days!" She all but shouts, her tone laced with condescension.

I shake my head sharply, licking my lips. "Doesn't matter. You're not leaving."

She lets out an exaggerated exhale, before holding her hand up and shaking her head. "I can't deal with this shit right now. I'm going to bed." And with that, she turns and walks away. Leaving me standing there with a throbbing hand, a semi, and my T-shirt.

Chapter Ten

Will

I've just showered and I'm still in a post sex daze from the night before. I stand in front of the mirror. Tilting my head from side to side, I survey the bruises on my hips, left by the aggressive sex with Con yesterday.

I clench my thighs at the reminder. My pussy still swollen and, surprisingly, still needy.

When I woke again this morning, Keen was already awake. I could hear him with Con chatting away together and giggling. It's become a bit of a morning routine, a routine that melts my heart. Keen wakes early, Con sits watching Peppa Pig with him until I get up. Then we all have breakfast together, like a family.

I tug on a camisole top and pull on a pair of leggings. I'm running dangerously short of clothes with very few selections available. That's definitely something I need to resolve. I sigh in defeat, pull my hair up into a messy bun, and head out to the living room.

I stop short as I approach the living area. Con is laid on the couch bare chested with Keen sitting on his stomach, happily munching on a cookie, his cute face coated in crumbs.

Con's abs are on full display, his wavy hair wet, probably from a shower. He lays in grey sweatpants with an arm tucked behind his head looking every bit the sexy man he is. I lick my lips, imagining running my tongue down his toned body. Keen's giggle breaks my stare.

"Morning," I say as I approach Keen. I bend down and kiss his messy curls. As I do, Con's hand brushes up the back of my thigh, pulling me closer to them both. I reluctantly meet his eyes and he smiles softly, his blue eyes unsure of himself and my reaction. His gentle touch and brushing motion giving me goosebumps, I push away the memories of his hands roaming desperately over my body.

I brush the crumbs from Keen's cheeks and smile to myself. My little monster is covered.

"Morning Mommy, I'm hungry," he says, struggling to watch me and not Peppa Pig.

I roll my eyes. "You're always hungry, little man."

I go to move away, but Con's hand tightens slightly. I study him, but his face is transfixed on my braless breasts. Typical. I internally roll my eyes.

"I need to get some new clothes. I'm a little limited." Grimacing, I try to explain, a little embarrassed at the display.

Con clears his throat. "I don't know. I think I like you limited." He chuckles with a smirk, and I playfully swat his hand away from my thigh and move toward the kitchen.

After filling the coffee machine, I start working on breakfast.

Con has left Keen on the couch and followed me into

the kitchen. He bends over the countertop, watching me move around the kitchen. His broad shoulders on full display, his elbows on the counter. I try not to pay attention to the way my body is craving his.

"You can order some clothes online if you want?" he suggests.

"I have clothes at home." I remark, without turning to face him.

He sighs. "Don't be difficult, Will. Just order some new shit, okay?"

He's right. It wouldn't be wise to go home just for clothes. I sigh and duck my head in defeat. "Sure."

I decide to change the subject to something a little lighter. "I promised Keen I'd take him to a park today."

Con's body tightens. "That's not a good idea. Not until I speak to Bren, anyway. Besides, I made plans for us today."

I turn sharply, irritated. "Plans?"

He looks unsure of his words and brushes a hand through his wavy locks. "Yeah. Lily and Cal invited us over. I thought it would be nice for you to meet Lily, so you'd have a friend here. Then Keen could have a playdate meet Reece and Chloe? They have a garden full of stuff, like a pirate ship and shit." His words come out fast and persuasive.

I soften at his thoughtfulness. I quite like the idea. It'll be nice to meet Con's niece and nephew, he's told me so much about them and Cal speaks with such pride it'll be nice to finally put faces to their names.

"Great," I smile back at him genuinely. "Keen, come on little man, breakfast!" I call over Con's shoulder, his grin broadening at my enthusiasm.

Chapter Eleven

Will

We pull into the gated community where Cal and Lily live. Con had explained they previously lived in one of their apartments, but when Lily found out she was pregnant, Cal surprised her with a family home. And wow, did he do good.

The mansion is nestled behind manned gates but being surrounded by trees, they're not visible, giving the illusion of privacy.

The car rolls along the cobbled driveway. I stare out of the window in awe, imagining Keen climbing the trees.

"You like it?" Con asks, watching me closely as the SUV slows approaching the mansion.

I turn to meet his eyes. "What's not to like? It's beautiful."

He grins at my remark. "Good. I was hoping you'd say that." He smiles to himself.

What the hell is that meant to mean?

I watch Con a little closer, searching for answers, but all I see is an excited man-child—correction a hot, excited-man child. His hair is in a baseball cap sitting back to-front, with curls poking through, a white tight T-shirt stretching his muscular shoulders, and his denim clad thighs stretch the fabric. He eyes me again before giving me a knowing wink, causing my eyes to roll at his cockiness.

We exit the car and Con expertly unstraps Keen. "Come on dude, time to go meet some new friends." His voice laced with enthusiasm.

"No!" Keen stomps. My poor little man is nervous, he tugs his hair a little and then sucks his thumb, completely unsettled and unsure how to act. He then comes running around to me and clings to my legs for reassurance.

Con watches him with a look of pain on his face. His Adam's apple bobs, no doubt hurt by Keen's actions. Yeah, he needs to get used to little strops and tantrums.

I swallow my pride and decide to take pity on Con, I bend down to Keen. "Keen, Con has all sorts of fun things planned today. He said that little Chloe has a jungle gym and a pirate ship. Would you like to see it?"

Keen nods silently.

Out of the corner of my eye, I see Con visibly relax. I glance up at him and he mouths an appreciative "thank you" to me. I offer him a small, tentative smile.

We turn to walk up the steps toward the front door and Con automatically goes to reach for my hand, but I pull away. "Fuck, I'm sorry Will. I can't stop myself." He doesn't meet my eyes as he quickly tries to explain, while glancing away.

The funny thing is, I get it. I understand how natural it is to hold him. That's why I'm trying to stay closed off with him. I can't step over the line and give myself to him again, not yet. Maybe not ever.

"You said a naughty!" Keen is quick to chastise, suddenly forgetting he's nervous.

Me and Con eye one another, probably thinking the same thing. I stifle a laugh, clamping my teeth over my bottom lip.

Con's hand brushes against the small of my back as he leads us through the front door, his breath whispering in my ear as he tells me. "I'm rock hard imagining me stuffing that pretty mouth of yours with my cock, Will." I choke. Literally choke on my spit. What the hell?! My eyes bug out as I spin my head up to his grinning face, his gleaming teeth on full display. Proud of his confession, he then proceeds to lick his lips seductively. I dart my eyes back down to Keen; he's completely unaware, his eyes taking in the room.

A throat clears in the hallway. "Finished with the games, Connor?" Cal's stern voice cuts through the sexual tension. He stands in navy shorts and a white t-shirt, looking completely unlike his usual businessman self.

Con chuckles. "Actually no, I haven't even started." I elbow him in his stomach, earning an "Ouch."

Before I can move further forward to greet Cal, I hear running of feet and a very flustered looking brunette. She's petite, with her hair tied into a messy ponytail, she wears an off the shoulder shirt and ripped jeans. Lily pushes past Cal, and she virtually flings herself at me. "Hi, I'm Lily. It's sooo good to meet you. Oh my god, wow! You are a mini-Con aren't you?" she declares, staring down at Keen. Then, realizing her mistake, she clamps her hand over her mouth. "Oh, my god. I'm so sorry. Oh god!" Her face is a picture of mortification when she realizes her mistake.

I take her panicking hand. "It's fine. He's a little out of

sorts and I'm not sure he'd put it together anyway," I try to reassure her.

Lily nods. "Okay. Okay. So come on, follow me." She takes my hand and literally pulls me down the corridor, guiding me outside.

I chance a glance at Con over my shoulder. He's still standing in the doorway with an anxious-looking Keen.

Lily waves her hand around. "Oh, don't worry about them. I've given Cal strict instructions to leave us the hell alone and amuse the kids with Con." I laugh at her declaration. "Honestly, it's so good to have another female in the family." She babbles while leading us outside.

Lily shows us to a patio area overlooking a generous, enclosed pool that looks like a lagoon. Beyond that is a children's play area, complete with a jungle gym and wooden pirate ship. I take it all in while Lily pulls out her seat, gesturing to the surrounding chairs. I move to sit opposite her.

"Erm, how old is Reece?" I ask, confused. Thinking I thought I already knew the answer.

Lily bursts into laughter. "I know, right? He's fifteen now. Oh, don't for one minute think any of this is for him!" She waves her hand at the play area. "Nope, that's all for Chloe! You know our nine-month-old daughter!" She rolls her eyes at my wide-eyed expression. "Oh, I completely agree. Cal is absolutely insane; I mean, by the time she can play on it. She'll need a new one." She sighs dramatically while dropping into her seat.

"Wow, I thought Con was the O'Connell man-child."

Lily beams at me. "I think they all are. Secretly anyway." She winks.

Lily offers me a drink from the various selections of slush cocktails she has on the table. She's really gone to town; she's even made a fruit platter. I smile as she pours me some sort of orange cocktail, complete with fancy decoration. "This, this is all Cal," she explains, motioning toward the fruit and cocktails. "I have to stick with juice," she sighs a little, pouring herself a fruit juice. "I'm still breastfeeding. Well, weaning anyway," she explains.

"Well, he's done great." I smile back.

"He has, hasn't he?!" She smiles dreamily.

"So, where's Reece?" I ask, my eyes searching around the grounds.

"Oh, I'm so sorry. He's at Oscar's. I swear those two are thick as thieves. They're constantly trying to outsmart one another." She shakes her head while smiling. Her entire personality is infectious. "You'll meet him at the family meal on Sunday, of course," she declares.

My drink stops before it reaches my mouth. "Meal?"

"Yeah, we have to attend every week." She grimaces.

I forgot about the family meal. I used to look forward to them, but after Brennan stabbed Con with a knife, I'm a little apprehensive about taking Keen. He's not used to Brennan's whole brash demeanor. Keen's timid. Sometimes a little too timid.

"Don't worry, we'll all be there to support you. And apparently, Brennan can't wait to see you and meet Keen. Cyn is bursting at the seams, of course." Lily pats my hand in support.

"Thanks. It's just a lot to take in." I swallow harshly.

Lily nods in understanding. "So, how's it going with Con?" she asks tentatively.

I blow out a breath. "Fine. I mean, we get on. We always have. It's just I wasn't prepared to see him again, let alone have him back in my life with such bold determination." I admit on a fake chuckle.

Lily watches me closely, seeing through my facade. "Yeah, Cal explained what happened. I'm so sorry you had to go through that, Will. I understand it's none of my business and it's the only thing I'm going to say, but Cal has always said Con has never been the same since you left. He's always said his heart was broken."

I scoff angrily at her words. *His* heart was broken?

"I hope with the way he treated you, you're making him pay, though?" She raises her eyebrow in jest. And just like that, my anger dissipates.

A loud giggling interrupts our easy conversation. Cal strides over with a beautiful baby girl in his arms, her pretty frilly pink dress on display and her chubby hands pushed into Cal's mouth as she babbles away. She's utterly adorable, with untamed brown curls and a little pink bow in the front.

"She wanted to see mommy before going to play," Cal explains while lowering Chloe onto Lily's lap.

"She was having nap time," Keen informs me, his smile wide.

"She was?"

Keen nods. His head now covered in Con's baseball cap, and I wonder to myself if he had to give it to him to coax him from the front door.

"Oh, you're such a beautiful girl, Chloe," I tell her, as Lily bounces her on her knee. Chloe reaches her arms out for me, and Lily nods in approval for me to take her.

I lift her into my lap, instantly loving the reminder of having the weight of a baby on me. A smile gracing my face as I snuggle into her scent. Chloe pushes her fist into her mouth, babbling away.

"She's trying to eat her hand, Mommy!" Keen giggles to himself as he kneels before her. Causing us all to laugh at their cute interaction. "She's a silly girl, aren't you Chloe?" he coos.

I smile to myself, then lift my head up and instantly find Cons' eyes on me. Drilling into me, they're like laser beams.

When he realizes I'm watching him, he swallows thickly and quickly glances away.

"Come on, little princess, let's get you on that swing," Cal declares while lifting Chloe from my arms.

Keen fist pumps the air and follows suit, with Con trailing behind them.

Once they're out of earshot, Lily turns to me. "Sooo, Con looked like he was about ready to knock you up just then."

I splutter on my drink and act innocent. "He did?"

"Mmhmm. He looked like he was ready to take you right out here. His eyes never left you and Chloe. I hope you're on birth control, Will. In fact, scrap that, make sure you're on birth control and use condoms," she tells me while pointing a finger at me tauntingly. "Cal knocked me up while I was on the pill." She exhales for effect.

My eyes bug out. "No way?!"

"I know, right?! What are the chances?"

"Well, there will be no pitter patter of tiny feet from me," I say, while raising my chin in the air in defiance.

"Yeah, that's what I said." She laughs to herself.

We chat for a while about kids, Cal's obsession with creating the perfect family environment, and how great a dad he is to his children and how they came to be together. Lily appears completely and utterly in love with Cal as he is with her, and I can't help but experience a small pang of jealousy at their beautiful family life.

"So, Will, you were married previously? And Cal says you're good friends with your ex? That's pretty impressive." A genuine smile graces Lily's lips.

"Yes. Jack and I met when I was at a hostel for single mothers needing help. He was volunteering with legal advice, that sort of thing. Anyway, he helped a lot when I explained about my circumstances." I shuffle from side to side, slightly uncomfortable sharing my story, but I continue with determination. "So, we basically got close. He was great and patient with Keen, amazingly supportive, actually. We grew close quickly. Before I knew it, we set up a family home and were married."

Lily listens inventively, her eyebrows furrow. "So, what went wrong?"

I think about her question. "Nothing per se. I just think we both wanted a perfect family, but in fact, we were better off as just friends."

Lily stares at me a little shocked, so I decide to elaborate a little deeper. "Jack has a hero persona. He had a high school romance that ended through the girl suffering from abuse within her family. Anyway, it was for those reasons he joined the FBI and volunteers at hostels. When we got together, I think we needed each other as a crutch? Does that make sense?"

Lily nods softly. "I understand. You supported one another when you needed it. Your relationship was based on the support for one another."

"Exactly. Don't get me wrong, I love him. I'll always love him. But it's not the same kind of love." Not the same kind of love I have for Con is what I don't say, as my eyes catch onto him tickling a giggling Keen on the grass. My heart instantly beats fast. I swallow away the emotion their interaction brings.

As if reading between the lines, Lily grins. She subtly changes the subject when I school my expression. "Keen never called Jack Dad?" she asks, but it's more of a statement.

"No. Neither Jack nor I encouraged him. It's almost like we both knew that Jack wasn't in it for the long term. We actually both openly corrected him." I wince at the memory.

"You did right, Will. You're doing right." I meet Lily's eyes and they're filled with love and admiration; she's going to be such a great friend; I can sense the sincerity in her eyes. I'm so lucky to have met her and be welcomed as part of the family once again.

Con

Being with Will and Keen at Cal's today has been absolutely incredible. How the fuck anyone can live their lives without their own family is beyond me.

No sooner do I think that thought I have the usual jolt of reality that, that is exactly what I was doing. I was living my life without my family; the thought instantly sickens me. The pain returns to my chest, clogging in my throat.

I watch Will throw her head back, laughing at something Lily is saying, and the expression on her gorgeous face gives me an instant boner.

Not great when my three-year-old kid insists on running into me every three damn seconds. Knocking the fuck out of my dick and balls.

I wince as Keen rebounds off of me to climb the pirate ladder for the hundredth time. His energy is unreal. He reminds me of my brother, Keenan. My mouth automatically goes dry, and I push the sadness aside.

Glancing back at Will, I swallow thickly. Her beautiful brown locks hang down her back, her light blue summer dress exposes her slender shoulders. The neckline of the dress dips down to her tits, which are fortunately covered by a new bra. Otherwise, I'm pretty sure those edible nipples would be on full display, too. Fuck yeah. I scrub a hand down my face with a painful groan. I'm not sure this is the distraction I need right now.

I scrutinize her a little more. She's so fucking beautiful it hurts. I'm going to be a better man for her, for Keen, and my brother.

My eyes follow her chest as she laughs and her tits bounce. Fuck, I need to touch them, mark them.

I was pretty fucking glad when a bundle of clothes was delivered to us this morning. Now Will can leave the house with underwear on, and no fuckers can see her sexy body on full display. Even if we are only going to my brother's, I still don't want him looking at her like that. No, I'd knock the pricks out for even daring to peek.

"What are you looking so pissed about?" Cal asks while standing by the picnic blanket, he laid down for Chloe.

I glance down at my hard dick and lift my T-shirt to show him.

His face morphs into utter revulsion, his eyes bug out. "Jesus Con! Seriously? Around the kids?" he scowls.

"I can't fucking help it. It won't go down!" I spit back in equal, measured disgust.

Cal's eyes search around, and he waves his hands around his property, his voice turning lighter. "Think fucking trees, bushes or something like that." He breathes out sharply.

I choke. "Bushes? Now you've got me thinking of Will's lack of bush. And that isn't fucking helping." I shake my head. "No. You gotta help me out, man," I ask desperately.

Cal's head spins toward me, his wide eyes drawing in. He lowers his tone dangerously. "Help you out how? What the fuck are you talking about?" he swallows harsh. His words bitter.

I chuckle at his panic riddled voice. "I need some alone time with Will." Nodding in her direction with hopeful eyes, I watch Cal's reaction.

Cal's shoulders visibly relax before instantly tightening again. "Absolutely not," he all but spits.

"Fuck man, come on. Do you really want me to sit at the dinner table eating lunch with Lily around and my rock-hard dick?"

His lips tighten into a firm line with the thought, his fists flaring at the side of him.

"Fucking fine," he spits. "You can have the garage. Twenty minutes. Tops." He presses something on his phone, and I can only assume he's switching the cameras off in the garage.

"The garage? Can you not do better than that? Like a bed? Fuck Cal, you've got like eight rooms here." I gesture to the monstrosity he calls a home. Selfish prick can't even spare a bed?

"No, Con, you're not coming over here for a fuck-fest. You either use the garage or sit in tight jeans." He triumphantly grins.

"Fine," I snap out, annoyed at the moody fucker. If I sit in front of Will with her delectable body on display, I'm liable to cream my jeans.

Garage it is.

Will

"Will, follow me I want to show you something!" Con shouts as he walks across the manicured gardens heading toward the garage, looking like a man on a mission.

I lift my eyes over my drink and stare at Lily for guidance, she just shrugs. Glancing over at Cal with the kids in the play area, he has an unamused expression on his face. His hands are on his hips, watching Con with a disgruntled look in his eyes.

"Will!" Con barks out at me.

I roll my eyes at his impatience. "Excuse me, Lily, I'm sure I'll be back in a few minutes." I push my chair away and make my way over to the garage on the far side of the property. I follow with uncertainty through the door that Con walked through a few moments ago.

Apprehensively, I walk into the dimly lit garage, my eyes attempt to adjust to the poor lighting. Before I have a chance to call out for Con, I experience his presence behind me. The hairs on the back of my neck stand up in excitement.

His breath trickles down my neck as his hands gently sweep my hips. He pushes himself into me. "Fuck, I need you Will. So fucking bad." He kisses down my neck as his hands massage my hips before moving down and creeping up inside my dress. "I need you so bad, I'm going to fucking explode." His voice is already ragged with need.

"Con," I pant out.

"Fuck yeah, say my name again." His lips tug on the sensitive skin beside my neck. Soft exploring lips trail kisses, tugs and gentle sucks along my neckline and shoulders.

"You smell so fucking good, Will." He breathes in my scent.

His hands rotate around my thighs, caressing, and massaging, causing wetness to pool between my legs.

He pants out his words, heavily. "Say you want me. Say you want me as much as I want you."

I say nothing, scared to admit the truth. I let him nuzzle into my throat and neck. A sharp bite to my upper shoulder, "Say it." His voice is firm and demanding. I shake my head in defiance.

"You fuck up my head, Will. I can't think straight with you around me. I just need to be inside you all the time." He grits the words out as though they pain him. "Making you mine all the time. Owning you all the time. Because I do own you, Will. Every bit of you."

"Your mind." He spins me around and kisses my forehead.

"Your tits." He bends down and kisses my tits, one by one. My nipples pebble in response.

"Your pussy." I suck in a breath as he lowers to his knees. Moving my dress aside, he kisses me over the top of my panties. Before he spins me again so I'm facing the wall.

"Your ass." He dips back under my dress and kisses both ass cheeks before caressing them in his hands. His damaged hand long forgotten.

"Take off your dress, Will," he commands.

I hesitate for a moment too long; he growls in response and sharply slaps my ass. "Do it!"

I jump at his gruffness and tug my sundress over my head, allowing it to pool to the garage floor. "Now put your hands on the wall."

I do as I'm told, my palms hitting the wall.

Con tugs down my panties to my knees. I can hear him

shifting behind me. His jean buttons popping open. I expect his cock to push into me at any second, but when I feel his breath in the crook of my ass, I gaze over my shoulder. And holy hell, the sight has me almost coming undone on the spot.

Con is on his knees with his engorged cock in hand, stroking himself while licking his lips in anticipation. Our eyes meet and he smiles a cocky grin. He lunges himself forward and, using the other hand, he parts one ass cheek and pushes his face into me. His warm breath and wet tongue giving me sensation overload as he licks around my ass. Con's tongue pushing in for deeper access. His groans rumble and my pussy clenches in response. I shift my hips to push back into him and give him better access.

I can feel the rhythmic thrusts of his hand, jerking his cock. My moans escape me with ease.

"Oh, Jesus Con, that's hot. Don't stop." I bite my lip.

He pulls away quickly. "Play with your pussy, Will. I'll lick your ass, baby, now you finger fuck your pussy." Oh, sweet Jesus, this filthy man. I throw my head back in ecstasy as my fingers thrust in and out of my wetness in rhythm with Cons tongue, probing my puckered hole. It's so dirty, so erotic, I'm struggling to remain on my feet. I use one hand on the wall and push my cheek against the wall to help stabilize me.

His whole body is matching the pace of his facial thrusts. He's fucking himself and my ass in sync. I'm enthralled by how absolutely erotic the moment is. My orgasm is fast approaching, but I need more. I want more. He's right, I want him!

"Con, I need you. I need you to fill me." I pant in unison with his groans.

"Oh, sweet fucking Jesus, Will." He quickly pulls away, as desperate for more than I am. "Fuck yeah, you do! You need me, Will."

He stumbles to get up with haste before he slams his cock into me. "Fuck that's good. So, fucking wet Will." His cock slams inside me again, as he repeatedly draws all the way back and pushes in further. My hips buck in time to meet his.

"Oh god. Right there, Con." My pussy clenches his cock, desperate to hold him inside.

"Too fucking right. You like me tongue fucking your ass, Will?" The juices drip down my thighs at his filthy words.

His dirty, crazy mouth sends a thrill shooting through my body, making me unbelievably wetter. "Yes. Oh fuck. So good." My hand clenches into a fist against the rough texture of the wall.

He brings his mouth around to my head, his hand grabbing my hair and pulling my neck to the side so he can thrust his tongue into my open mouth. A crazed, possessive kiss descends on me like a starved man.

While his thick cock fills me. His fingers dig into my hip, tightening to the point of pain. His balls hitting my ass. The many sensations throw me over the edge.

"Oh, fuck!" he screeches. "Fuck, yes come! Come, Will. Come on my cock. Fucking own it." My wetness floods his cock.

I throw my head back as Con pistons inside of me, ropes and ropes of warm cum coating my inner walls. My throbbing pussy milking his orgasm with my own. "*Con!*" I yell before my orgasm descends, leaving me a trembling mess from the most powerful orgasm of my life.

Con stumbles against me, struggling to hold his own

weight with the force of his own orgasm, consuming him with ferocity.

"Oh, fuck Will. How the fuck?" He pants and gently kisses my neck. "Fucking incredible."

His soft cock falls from me as he spins me around. He cups my face in both hands, "I love you, baby." He gently kisses my lips with tenderness before pulling away to watch me. His blue vulnerable eyes meet mine, but whatever he sees in mine causes his shoulders to drop and his Adam's apple to bob before he redirects his gaze to the floor.

He steps back and swoops his arm to the floor to tug my panties up and collect my dress. "Come on, Cal only gave us twenty minutes." He smirks.

"What?" I gasp.

Con's playful demeanor is back. "I know, right? No time for round two. Looks like I'll have to wait until I get back to the apartment," he says while pulling my dress over my head.

"Con, I don't think..." He presses his finger to my lips to shush me, before removing it and dropping a quick peck to my lips. Effectively stopping all conversation. He pulls me back outside as if nothing ever happened.

Chapter Twelve

Con

Dinner with Cal and Lily went well, perfect even. The girls get on like a house on fire. They're going to give me and Cal a run for our money, that's for sure. Keen absolutely adores Chloe and, watching him interact with her did something to me. It made me want that even more. A baby. With Will and Keen.

Then we can be a proper family, like we should have been.

The determination in me is something I've never felt before. It's fierce. Nothing is going to stop me. Even Will. She'll come around; I know she will. I just need to show her I'm becoming a better man. The man they both deserve.

"Hey, are you okay?" Will asks, breaking me from my thoughts.

I glance at her, her hazel eyes sparkling and the cute pink blush still on her cheeks from our garage fuck. Jesus, she's hot.

"Yeah. I'm fine." I smile back at her softly.

"You're kinda gripping the steering wheel a little tight." She nods toward my hand. Sure enough, my fingers are white with the grip.

I sigh and brush my hand through my hair with my confession. "I've got to meet the guys at the warehouse."

Will's body slumps. "Shit. I'm sorry, Con."

I swallow thickly and try to shrug it off, lifting my shoulder for emphasis. "It's okay. I should be used to it by now."

Will sits forward, her tone gentle and caring. "It's okay, you know. For things not to be okay. You don't have to pretend." She takes my hand off the steering wheel and gently kisses it. All the tension in my body eases instantly. How can she have this effect on me? How can she know me so well? She sees me. The real me. And it just cements it in my mind all the more. She's mine. And I'm hers.

After settling Will and Keen in the apartment, I make my way over to the warehouse.

I pull the car through the armed gates and automatically I can feel the tension radiating into my neck. My body coiled tight as I shift the car into park.

I glance down at my trembling hands and squeeze my eyes closed, willing the memories away. Anxiety coursing through my body. My mouth is dry as I desperately try to gain air into my lungs. My lips tingle. My heart pounding ferociously.

Shame consumes me, shame for being so weak and vulnerable. I'm losing control. I squeeze my eyes tight and bury my head in my hands, clenching my hair to the point of pain. "Fuck!"

I suck in a deep breath, and I steel myself. I exit the car and walk toward the warehouse. Each step is like walking to my end, an impending doom, dread.

I feel like I'm outside of my body. Empty and exposed.

A shell of nothingness.

I nod politely at our security guard, his broad body filling the door as I enter.

The thrum of my heart against my chest, so loud I feel like it's echoing through my ears into the empty space. Thrum. Thrum.

I can vaguely hear the guys in Bren's office. The laughter in their voices.

I glance at the window. My eyes squeeze shut as my chest vibrates with the rhythm of my heart. Why? My mouth dries and I struggle to swallow.

Why do I do that?

Why do I always have to look?

And then it hits me, it always hits me, I suck in a breath...

Six years ago.

Music blares out in the car as we head toward the warehouse. Knowing we can make it in and out before anyone knows we've even been makes the excitement bubble within me. I glance back at Will from the rear-view mirror. Fuck, my girl is hot.

She catches my eye and licks her lips seductively, no doubt remembering why I left my wallet in the warehouse in the first place. I smirk in memory.

"How the fuck did you leave your wallet there in the first

place?" Keenan asks, completely unaware of the sexual tension radiating off of me and Will.

I grin. "I was busy, entertaining." I glance at Will. She's stifling a laugh, her teeth tugging on her bottom lip. She's so fucking beautiful.

Keenan huffs beside me. "Seriously? You guys were in there this afternoon? Da would blow his motherfucking stack if he knew!" He exhales sharply, causing me to laugh at his seriousness.

I turn my head away from the road and stare pointedly at Keenan. "He isn't going to know though, is he?" My younger brother and I are tight. We cover for one another, and tonight's just another example of that.

He shakes his head in laughter. "Guess not. So where to once we get your wallet? I need food!"

"You always need food!" Will leans forward and hits Keenan on the back of the head.

He waves her hand away playfully. "Well, you do too. Since you had that bug last week you've barely eaten; don't think I haven't noticed," he chastises while looking back at her.

Why didn't I notice? Fuck, she's my girlfriend. I should be aware of these things. I drag my hand through my hair in annoyance with myself. I've been that busy with this shit Da has us doing, I didn't even realize my girl was sick. I shake my head in frustration with myself.

I divert my attention. "Keenan's right. Wallet then food." His grin widens. My little brother is like a mini-me, only he has dimples, and the ladies call him cute.

Will ducks her head up and down in agreement.

I turn the music down as we drive through the gates of

the warehouse without issue. Security is always low when Da is out of town and no shipments are due in. It's how I snuck in with Will to fuck her on Da's desk. It was a big fuck you to all the extra hours he's had me working lately, dragging me into the family business when I don't want to be.

I park the SUV and roll my head toward Keenan. "Go fetch my wallet, dude."

His face morphs into shock. "Ya kidding me? What am I, your fucking slave?"

"Come on dude, don't be a cock block." I glance back at Will; she hides her head in her hands in embarrassment.

"Fucking Jesus. Give me the goddamn keys. You owe me!" Keenan throws his head back, laughing.

I grin at him. And clasp my hand on his shoulder. "Thanks bro." I wink.

We climb out of the car simultaneously, but while he takes off for the warehouse, I open Will's door. "What are you doing?" she asks shyly while licking those fucking plump lips of hers.

"Feeding you!" I smirk, "now get out the car and on your knees baby."

I take her smooth hand in mine and help her out of the SUV. As her feet touch the floor, she drops to her knees. Such a fucking good girl for me, she's always submissive and ready. The thought hardens my cock.

Her dark hair is tied into a ponytail, perfect to wrap my hand around. Her hazel eyes shine seductively under the dimly lit car park. I pop the buttons of my jeans and shuffle my converse forward, my dick straining painfully against my boxers.

My eyes scan around the empty space surrounding us.

"I'm gonna be quick baby, swallow me down like a good girl, yeah?" I stroke her hair gently.

Will nods and opens her mouth. I take my cock in my hands and paint her lips in my pre-cum. "Mine!" I growl. The action alone causes my balls to tingle. I tug her head toward me by her ponytail. She uses her hands on my thighs to steady her. I smirk cockily.

Slowly I push in through her lips, her tongue flattening to offer me access. I rub my cock along her tongue, using my hand, in and out, in and out. Fuck, that feels incredible. I close my eyes to the sensation.

"Ah fuck baby, that's incredible. That's it, suck it in."

I thrust forward so my pelvis hits her as she begins to suck me down. My hand tightens in her hair, and I use my other hand to steady myself on the car. I fuck her mouth. "So fucking good." I pant around Will's encouraging moans.

A piercing noise interrupts me, making me stumble slightly. My Converse grate on the pebbles around Will's knees. Now my senses are on high alert. My eyes dart around the parking lot in panic.

I glance down at Will, and she's stopped moving. She's staring back at me with a face of sheer terror, my cock still stuffed in her mouth.

The fear in her eyes penetrates into my soul, and a feeling of sickness washes over me as I quickly pull out of her and begin buttoning up my jeans.

Will jumps to her feet. "Wh-what was that, Con? Was that a gunshot? Was it?" She panics as I straighten myself out. I need to calm her down; her chest is heaving up and down, her hands flaring at her sides. "Fuck, Con, you said no one would be here. Shit! She tugs on her head."

My heart races in panic, but I can't show her. I take her face between my hands to reassure her. "Hey, it's fine. Probably some of Da's guys shooting their shit outback." I nod at her, and she dips her head in agreement.

Her face pales and her glazed, panicked eyes meet mine. "Keenan."

One word sends me spiraling into utter turmoil. My fists clench as I gaze back at the warehouse. Shit! I'm so fucking dead for this.

I rush to the driver's side of the car and pull my gun from the glove box.

"Get in the car and lock the doors, Will. Keep your head down."

"What? No way! I'm not leaving you." She stands still, her chin held high. Fuck, my girl is stubborn.

I brush my hand through my hair again. I don't have time for this shit.

I glance back at Will and sigh. "Fuck! Fine, just stay behind me, okay." I grit my teeth, not liking this plan.

She nods following behind me.

We stalk against the perimeter of the warehouse, following the shadows of the building. I stop when I hear a commotion at the back of the building.

I pull my phone from my trembling hands, knowing I'm going to be in deep shit for this. I hand it to Will. "Message Cal, tell him to come to the warehouse quickly." She ducks her head eagerly as I walk away from her and make my way through the warehouse door.

It's empty, eerily fucking empty.

I take in the dark room, cold cement floors and dripping leaky pipes. Nothing out of place.

Yet a sickening feeling is stuck inside my stomach, tugging at me to get out. The hairs on my arm rise and I sense something is wrong. I scrutinize the surrounding space again with my gun in hand.

A muffled groan leads my eyes to the window. A crate lying overturned as if someone was trying to escape.

Then I see them, his sneakers hidden behind the crate. Oh shit! My heart plummets.

I rush to him, dropping to my knees. His body is shaking. Is it shock?

"Keenan, what happened?"

He keeps trying to open his mouth, but nothing is coming out. Panic consumes me. I scan my eyes over his body. Only now do I see the puddle of blood he's bathing in. Oh, sweet Jesus, no!

My hands shake as I hold his face in the palms of my hand. A scuffle of feet moving toward me makes me snap my head up to meet with Will's panic-stricken face. Her face is pale and her eyes are wide with fear.

Before I realize what's happening, she's pulled her hoodie off and has it pressed against Keenan's chest. My phone is out, and I can hear her scrambling to get her words out. I don't hear what she's saying. I can only see and hear the trembles of Keenan's body.

Cradling his head between my hands, I stare down at him. He's pale, too pale. His soft blue eyes are missing their shine. I lean down to his face, noticing something wet on his cheeks. I gently brush it with my thumb, wondering where it came from. Then I realize it came from me, my eyes are leaking. I can't remember the last time they did that.

"The paramedics are on their way. He's going to be okay, Con. Do you hear me?" Her stern, controlled voice has a

tremble to it, and I know she's lying, I know she's trying to tell me what I want to hear.

I stare up into Will's eyes and shake my head at her, knowing the truth. My little brother is not going to be okay.

I peer back down at his lips, still trying to move. I kneel down further so my ear is next to his lips. "He... did... it," he gently pants out.

I pull back to study him, and when I do, a wail erupts from Will. The noise startles me. Her expression is pure devastation. Her eyes trained elsewhere; they're staring below me. My body feels like it's floating, like something else is happening that I'm not aware of.

I peer down to see what caused her wail and stare straight into the eyes of my brother. His empty blue eyes. I can't breathe. Air can't get in. It can't get out. I can't breathe. He can't be dead. He can't. I can't breathe.

My hands tremble and my heart sinks. Please God, no. Please help him. Someone help him. "Please." I can't breathe.

"Con. Con. Connor!"

My body physically jolts, breaking my train of thoughts.

My tight chest hurting. I can't breathe.

"Are you okay?" Oscar watches me with something very close to sympathy in his sharp eyes.

After Keenan was killed, Oscar made it his mission to take over the family security. Da retired and Bren stepped into his shoes, taking over the office. Cal does the wining and dining with clients and Finn takes a more hands on approach. He enjoys the violence, actively participating in our illegal fight clubs as a hobby. And me? I do whatever they want me to do. Errands, paperwork, overseeing the clubs or casinos. I don't want to belong here in this world. But I don't want to let them down either. I can't let another brother down.

"Yeah. Yeah, I'm fine." I nod my head vigorously, almost trying to convince myself. Oscar's eyes are trained on me as he opens the door to the office. He glances back at me, his eyes unconvinced, but I turn away to mask my pain.

I step into the office and fall backwards into Oscar when a sharp pain erupts across my jaw.

I wince as my fingers find the sore spot. "What the fuck?"

"That was for Will, you little fucker!" Finn spits at me. His body is bouncing on the spot with anger.

Shit. I take it they filled him in on everything then.

I drag my feet further into the room. Pain radiating from my jaw, I shift it side to side, grateful it's not broken.

The room resembles a boardroom with enough chairs around the table for each of us. Bren sits at the head of the table with his large frame filling the space. Cal, his second in command, to his right, looking the part in his business attire. Oscar moves to sit to his left; his white shirt and suit pants make him look the part with his glasses perched on his nose. He looks every bit the geek he is.

Finn throws himself in the seat beside Cal, his whole body screams bad boy with ripped jeans and a leather jacket to finish off his bad-boy appearance. His hair has grown out, looking shaggy on the top but still shaved at the sides. Not a curl in sight now.

I sit beside Oscar, slowly dropping into the chair with trepidation. I move my jaw from side to side again, testing it out. Fucking prick.

I peer up straight into Finn's fucking evil eyes. He gloats

at me with a smirk. I shake my head and turn my attention to Bren. He nods firmly and begins the meeting.

"Tell us what you have, Oscar," he prompts.

Oscar pushes his glasses up his nose and glances down at his tablet. He reads from his notes. "So, it appears Milo has been working with a small Russian gang unconnected to the Dimitriev brothers. Jack and his colleagues are working on a case against them for drug distribution across borders."

I jump in, cutting him off with my angry words. "I want him dead. He hurt Will, hurt Keen and put a fucking hit on her. Fuck, he tried to shoot us."

Oscar's spine straightens. His voice sharpens, sounding deadly. "If you'll let me finish."

He exhales deeply and then softens his tone. "Now Da requested he dies. I've worked with Bren and Jack; Jack has agreed that because of the hit outside of Will's house, it wouldn't be safe for Will and Keen if Milo lives. Therefore, he's going to help cover up whatever we do. He's going to pin it on someone else in the investigation."

"Can we trust him?" I can't help but shoot out.

Oscar scoffs. "Can you trust the man that took a bullet for you? Am I correct in that, Cal?" his eyes dart to Cal's for reassurance. "Jack took a bullet for Con, didn't he?" Cal's head ducks knowingly. My heart plummets. He's right, of course he did.

"Yeah, he did. He jumped straight in front of you, Con."

I stare down at the table, my hands fidgeting in front of me. My tone softens. "Why would he do that? Why did he do that, I mean?" I meet Cal's eyes with vulnerability.

"Because he loves Will and Keen. And he knows how much you mean to her," Oscar explains with no emotion, almost in a robotic tone.

How does he know that? The man's a fucking emotional

robot. The expression on my face must say what I am thinking, because he rolls his eyes and explains further. "I might be emotionally void, but I'm not stupid. She loves you for some reason, and he knows it will only ever be you. He did it for Will and Keen." I dip my head in understanding.

"So, where the fuck is Milo?" Finn demands.

My eyes shoot up to meet Bren's. He shakes his head. "He's gone deep. Not got a fucking clue where he is. Even his crew are deep. They're avoiding the FBI." He shuffles slightly in his chair. The man is a machine and never shows vulnerability, but now he looks uncomfortable. What the hell is going on? My eyes narrow at him. He drags his eyes up to meet mine. "We're going to need to draw him out."

I erupt. Portraying my best impersonation of Da, my chair hits the floor with a loud clatter. "Absolutely. Fucking. Not!"

"Calm your shit!" Bren exhales, dragging his hand over the top of his short, cropped hair. "She's not in danger, Con. If you'll just sit down, I'll explain everything."

My heart thunders beneath my t-shirt. My eyes dart around the table, all their eyes fixed on me. I must appear like a wild animal because that's sure as hell how I feel.

Angered and caged, ready to tear something apart.

Cal holds my gaze and gestures at me to take the seat.

I sigh in defeat, knowing I can't do this alone.

"You're not putting them in danger. I won't have it." I point at them all, needing the last say. They're my family, after all.

"Of course, not Con. Fuck, what do you think we are? We protect our family. Now come on, screw your head back on. We need you in this." Cal's eyes drill into me, his voice calm and reassuring. I take my seat and sit ramrod straight, glaring daggers at Bren for even daring the words.

"So, may I continue? Is the tantrum over?" Oscar deadpans.

I spin to face him. My nostrils flaring in fury. He swallows harshly and then clears his throat. "As we were saying before, we were rudely interrupted..." Is he for fucking real?

"There's a charity event on Monday night. It's a Voices Against Abuse event, basically something Will would normally participate in. We are leaving the fact she is going out. But the circle of people who will attend is the same as the last event. The one where she was photographed. So, we know Milo will have people there searching to see if she attends."

"What do you plan on achieving from her going?" I ask as calm as possible, my palms clenching.

"We're basically showing him she's in *our* circle. He knows where to come for her. If he dares come for her. Which he will," Oscar replies with certainty.

"Why are you so sure? I mean, what's it matter to him? Why is he so adamant about hurting Will to begin with?" All valid questions from Finn.

"Will explained that Milo helped dump her at the hospital the night her father attacked her. Maybe he regrets helping her. Or maybe he fears the backlash from us?" Cal muses.

We sit thinking for a moment when Oscar breaks the tension. "Actually, that may well be a reason, but I highly doubt it. That man has a god complex and would quite happily rain a war on us. No, there's actually multiple reasons the man has a vendetta against Will."

I sit taller. What the fuck is he talking about. I scan around the room and we're all listening to him attentively.

"First, I believe that Will witnessed her mother's death at the hands of domestic abuse of her father. Milo probably helped cover it up." I gasp because fuck, how the hell did this happen? Will said her mother left when she was a young girl. A wave of sickness washes over me. How much was she hiding? How much did she need me, and I wasn't there?

Oscar continues on. "Secondly Will's grandfather is originally from Russia. Meaning the family have ties with Russia, hence Will's birth name, Willowmena..." Oscar shakes his head at the injustice, his lip curled up in disgust, "Anyway, it appears Will was due to marry someone within their Russian ties. An arranged marriage, of sorts. Once her father found out about his daughter's..." Oscar shuffles slightly, uncomfortable, "promiscuity, he couldn't very well pass her off to be married as a virgin Russian bride now, could he?" He looks at me accusingly. "He eventually told the Russian family that Will had been involved in an accident and died." His voice is void of emotion.

I splutter his words out. "Died? He told them she'd died?"

Oscar tilts his head toward me. "Exactly. They paid good money for Will. They took pity on him for losing his beloved daughter and settled on a business deal. The one Milo currently helps with. Now if they were to find out all this business was built on a lie, then..." Oscar leaves his sentence open to our interpretation.

"And finally, he probably blames Will for the death of his father. According to his headstone, he was broken without his daughter but now reunited." Outrage floods my veins. How the fuck dare they treat her like this? My girl. Mine. My palms turn into fists.

I let out an audible scoff.

Wow, what an absolute clusterfuck. How the hell do I get my head around this? I run my hand through my hair.

"So, what? We showcase Will and hope his rats run back to him with the information?" Finn sneers.

Oscar taps on his tablet, not raising his eyes. "Exactly that. In the meantime..." Oscar's hand waves, gesturing at the door.

The door swings open and in walks Uncle Don. "Evening boys!" His deep voice cutting through the air. He slaps me on the back, hard enough to make me wince. He's like a fucking bull. "Con ya little shite, got ya self into a state, I hear?" he says with a deep chuckle.

I nod in annoyance and grimace. "Could say that."

"Don't ya worry, mi lad. I've got ears to the ground."

My head pops up in hope. "You have?"

He takes a puff of his cigarette, blowing it along the table. "Aye, reached out to a few of my Russian friends. I've given them enough shipments over the years for them to return a favor. They're well aware of how well their loyalties will be paid for information on Milo and his little shites." He flicks his cigarette on the floor, causing Oscar to throw him a venomous glare. Don seems oblivious to the anger and disgust radiating off of Oscar.

"So, what else do ya need from me?" he asks while throwing himself into the seat opposite Bren. Now, we have two kings at the table. I roll my eyes at the thought, looking up into Finn's eyes, he smirks back at me as if knowing what I'm thinking.

He pulls a toothpick from his jacket and begins chewing on it to stifle his grin.

"We're wanting to create a perimeter around Will and Keen until Milo is dealt with. So, if you could take over the security of the warehouse for the time being, then we can use our current men to be undercover and cover the family.

Security will be upped for Lily and the kids too. Just until things settle down."

Cal eases in his chair. Shit, I hadn't thought about how Milo may actually try to get to Will. He could use one of us to get to her. Shit.

"So, you've got yourself a kid, then?" Don laughs.

I meet his eyes. "Yeah."

He nods sharply. "Quite the little empire you lads have got going here. Nice to leave your kids something to run. A legacy." He nods his head as if he's talking to himself.

"Aye, nice to have a family. Strong lads to hold the fort together." He taps his finger on the table, deep in thought. "Right, I best get going, boys."

We all say our goodbyes to Don as he stands and leaves as abruptly as he entered.

When I hear the final door close, I scan the guys. "He seemed a little deep today?!"

They nod in agreement. "I think he regrets not having a family of his own, that's all," Cal states.

"He's got us!" Bren winks. "Lucky fucker, has us!" His grin widens, and his eyebrows dance, making us laugh.

Chapter Thirteen

Will

Con left us alone while he went to the warehouse for a meeting. He told me they had updates from Jack to discuss.

Knowing that Jack is okay and working with the guys brings a sense of ease to me. There isn't the initial competition I first encountered. I like the fact they're working together, for me and for Keen.

Con had told Keen he had a surprise for him in his gym room, so as soon as we entered the apartment, Keen took off and an excited squeal came from the room.

I smiled to myself as I made my way to the room next to mine. When I walked in, I gasped at the transformation. Con had clearly hired someone to come in and redecorate the room. It's now a beautifully decorated LEGO themed bedroom, complete with a Peppa Pig toy box. Keen goes wild inspecting the room as I watch him opening and closing the drawers, closet, and toy boxes. His happiness is infectious.

I bathe Keen and settle him in his new bed, complete with story and a cheesy smile from my little dude. My heart warming as his little smile and his heavy eyes struggle to stay open. I brush his curls from his forehead and kiss him goodnight.

Once I'm showered, I await anxiously on the couch for Con to return.

The state he was in earlier made me want to hold him tight and never let him go. The vulnerability shining in his eyes taking me back to the night that changed him. Changed us.

I can't believe after five years he's still fighting his demons with such intensity. He needs to see someone before they swallow him whole.

The blame and guilt he holds over himself for the death of his brother is agonizing and crushing his soul and heart.

He's pushed me away before, and I know he's capable of that again. It's not something I'm prepared to go through, not with Keen in tow.

Unease spreads through me the longer the night goes on.

Is he coming home? Has he gone somewhere else? Is he getting high? I nibble my nail in annoyance.

The click of the door has me bolting to my feet, and I rush over to him. His head is downcast, his body tense. I swoop in and pull him toward me, and without thinking I hug him tight. His body drains against my touch.

Con's hands band around me, his fingers digging into my spine with the pressure of his hold. His body trembles with relief and his breath tickles my neck as his head nuzzles into me. "Thank you." His words soften my encased heart.

I pull back to scan him. But his eyes dart everywhere

but at my face. I gently grasp his cheeks in my palms, forcing him to stare into my eyes. "Are you like that every time you go to the warehouse?"

He swallows thickly and tries to move his eyes away from me. A small nod. "Yeah."

I shake my head and hold him tighter, his blue eyes locking with mine. Unsure how he's going to react to my words, I swallow harshly. "You need to speak to someone, Con. You can't keep going through this. It's consuming you. You're going to snap and it's going to be at the wrong person."

I hold his gaze and his guilt filled eyes dart over my face. He bites his bottom lip vulnerably, as if holding himself together. He nods gently, his throat slowly rolls. "I know."

Then he pulls away and buries his head in the crook of my neck.

"Just hold me, okay?" His voice sounds exhausted, and his body seems drained.

I tighten my hold on him. Then turn my head delicately to place a gentle kiss on his neck. Goosebumps break out on his skin as he shudders into me. The force of him pushing me slightly.

I pull away and take his hand. He follows me over to the couches. I spin on my heel, losing all seriousness in my face as I stare up at him and gift him with a playful smile. I know just what he needs tonight.

He smirks back at me and licks his lips. I turn to him and then push him to the couch.

His fall exaggerated; he sits with his jean-clad legs wide. His palms twitching beside him. His eyes meet mine, laced with uncertainty. Licking my lips, I drop to my knees between his thighs. I want to give him this, give him the power back, the control he loves, the part of him that lets him be strong. I need to give him this, to help him forget.

I stare into his heavy eyes and his tongue darts out over his top lip with a cocky smirk.

"Give it to me, like you wanted to..." I don't say anymore, but he knows. By the sharp look he gives me and the subtle nod. He knows to give it to me like he wanted to that night. Keenan was taken from us.

His voice comes out stern, deep, but ragged. "Take me out."

I shuffle forward slightly. Popping his buttons open on his jeans, he hisses as my hand grazes his hard cock.

He shuffles his jeans down slightly. I move my hand to the waistband of his boxers. Peeling them down painfully slow. "Will." He warns in a deep rumble.

He lifts himself again for me to take them down enough to free his throbbing length. His hard smooth cock hits his stomach and leaves a trail of sticky pre-cum on his chiseled abs. My pussy clenches in response. I move my hands to his thighs before dipping my head to lick his cock. I trail my tongue from his balls, painstakingly slow to the tip. He uses his damaged hand to hold it upright toward me, offering me his cock. "Lick the slit. Lick it good."

I watch him as I lick his slit. He hisses in response, and I do it again. His eyes burn with desire. He thrusts up slightly, his other hand goes to the back of my head. His fingers tangling into my hair.

"Again." His voice trembles with grit and need.

I lick it again, but this time I use my entire mouth to suck the end and swirl my tongue around the head. "Fuck, yes!" His teeth clench as he speaks.

"You're driving me insane, baby. Now suck down my cock like a good girl and show me what you've got." He smirks. I raise my eyebrows to him and smile around his throbbing end as I keep my eyes focused on his aroused face, his pupils dilated with need.

I cup his balls with one hand and stroke him with the other as I lick him from top to bottom. Tugging gently on his balls, I swallow more and more of him.

"Fuck, Will."

His hand on my hair tightens as he thrusts up into my mouth. "Gonna fuck your mouth, baby." I nod and hum in response, knowing the vibrations will send him wild. His cock hits the back of my throat, but I take it. "Fuck. Swallow it. Fucking swallow my cock."

"Fuck. Yeah!" He pants and clenches himself, trying to wane off the impending orgasm, his body rising off the couch with his vigorous thrusts. "Fuck, fuck, I'm gonna..." His hot cum shoots into my throat. I swallow it all, watching his face ease back into a post sex relaxed state.

"Come here," he holds his hand out for me. I take it and rise into his lap, as he tucks himself back in one handed.

I sit on his knee and pull his head against my chest, hugging him. "Thank you," he whispers. I melt against him.

I wake to a clatter in the kitchen. Taking in my surroundings. I slowly come to realize I slept on the couch.

Then I remember falling asleep with Con holding me close against his chest all night, my back to his front. He told me he loved me in my ear when he thought I was sleeping. I touch my ear, remembering the tickle of his breath.

"Morning, beautiful. You hungry?" My eyes dart up and catch an amused Con bare-chested with a kitchen towel thrown over his shoulders. God, he looks hot. My gaze tracks his chiseled body. The wolf tattoo showcased on his left upper arm on full display.

"Are you cooking?" I ask in confusion. Since when does Con cook?

He rubs his hand through his hair, appearing a little embarrassed. "Actually, I kinda bought these." He holds up a pre-packed pack of pancakes, waving them in the air. I stifle a giggle at his discomfort. "I got Keen nut free chocolate, and I saw this site online that shows you how to make meals appear like characters. So, I figured I'd make him muddy puddle pancakes." He shrugs, looking everywhere but at me.

My heart soars at his words. This beautiful man in front of me is making Peppa Pig pancakes. I tug on my lip with my teeth to cover my smile.

"Sounds great." I smile back at him, his own grin spreading proudly across his face.

Chapter Fourteen

Will

We drive the familiar roads to Con's family estate. I'm both nervous and excited at the thoughts of seeing Cyn, Con's mom.

It's been almost five years since I last saw her, and she was the closest person I had to being a mom. The thought of her hurting at me leaving so abruptly or resenting me for not telling them about Keen makes me nauseous. My stomach flutters with butterflies.

As if sensing my inner thoughts, Con takes my hand and gently kisses it. He's slowly working his way back into my heart and that in itself fills me with uncertainty and anxiety. I can sense him watching me, so I turn my head toward him. "Everything will be fine, Will." Con's blue eyes sparkle with conviction. I dip my head and offer him a small smile in return before setting my gaze back to the road ahead.

We pull up to Connor's family home. Nothing has

changed. The vines are still overgrown onto the roof; and the lawn is perfectly manicured. It feels like home. A warm sensation travels through my body. This is where I belong.

I get out of the car and Con unstraps Keen. He strides around to me with Keen's hand in his he offers his other hand to me. I watch him. He chews on his bottom lip with a clear sign of uncertainty and nervousness. I place my hand in his, his grip tightens ever so slightly before loosening a little.

We head up to the house. Smiling to myself, I remember it's always a hive of activity. As we approach, I can hear the rumbustious noise of Con's family on the other side of the door. Keen hides behind Con's leg, stopping us from walking.

Con bends down and talks softly to him. "It's okay dude, nothing to be nervous about. Bren's in there and Cal. Little Chloe too. You can show them what a big boy you are today. Can you do that?" I watch the interaction with warmth. Con stands back upright and places his arm around my waist, gifting me with a soft kiss on my neck. "You ready?" he asks with a raised eyebrow.

I roll my eyes to feign confidence causing him to throw his head back with a laugh and totally changing the nervous energy between us.

The door swings open before Con's hand even touches the handle. And Cyn comes barreling out of the door, pushing past Con and straight into my arms. I'm squeezed and kissed and looked upon, "My baby. My poor girl!" She kisses my forehead, looking into my eyes. Her own eyes are glistening with tears as she holds my arms out to scan me from head to toe.

She shakes her head. "Beautiful, just beautiful!" Then she goes back to squeezing me once again.

"Ma, gonna let up?" Con's voice chuckles behind me.

Cyn's eye narrow and she spins on her heel as if she's about to give hell. But when Keen pokes his small head from around Con's leg, she lets out a mighty sigh. "Oh, my goodness! Look at him." Her eyes snap back at Con with a death glare. Before glancing away in disgust, going back to Keen, she bends down to his level. "Hello there, sweetie, I'm your Nana. Would you like to come inside and have some fresh lemonade? Little Chloe is desperate to see you." Keen nods shyly.

We follow Cyn into the kitchen diner, the table already full of familiar voices.

A chair scrapes and pushing past Con is his older brother Finn. He tackles me into a hug, kissing the side of my face. "Good to have you back, darlin."

I swallow away my emotions. "Good to see you, Finn." He pulls back to scan me. "Your hair's grown." I laugh, covering my emotions.

Finn strokes a hand through his hair, "I know, right? Only took me five years for it to grow this long," he jokes. I take him in, his legendary leather jacket still smelling of weed. His handsome face has a few extra scrapes, but he hasn't changed a great deal.

"Come and join the party?" He gestures toward the table.

All the greetings from the guys are lovely and welcoming. Brennan greeted me with a hug. Lily explained Reece didn't like to be touched, so I politely introduced myself and Keen, to which he nodded his acknowledgment.

I nodded a small, "Hi," toward Oscar because I know like Reece, he doesn't like physical greetings. He smiled at me with his usual smirk and a polite duck of his head, "Will."

We all sit around the table chatting.

Cal chuckles loudly. "Keen, do you need a cushion or two? You don't quite reach the table." I move forward to peek over at Keen, who is sitting beside Con. Sure enough, his little head barely reaches the table.

Con jumps up in a clear panic. "Oh, shit, sorry, little dude. Let me help you." He rushes off to get some cushions before returning to the table and plumping Keen up on them. Keen is enjoying the attention and laughing to himself.

"You're like a king sitting there, dude." Con grins at him.

Keen grins proudly. "Yep. I'm a king!"

We all chat away around the table while Cyn happily delivers the food. She, point blank, refused any help from me. Lily explained she's like it every week. She just loves looking after her family. Chloe sits in her highchair, babbling away, Cal coaxing her to eat with a spoon and then wiping her messy mouth with a small towel. He's adorably devoted to her. Lily doesn't seem to get a look in.

"I like your fluffy cat, Reece," Keen declares with a mouth full of potatoes.

Reece looks up from opposite Keen, his bright blue eyes mirror images of Cal's. He's stroking the Tortoiseshell fluffy cat that's sitting with its own bowl of food beside his plate, much to Brennan's disgust. He keeps sending filthy looks at the cat.

"Name's Pussy," Reece spits out.

Keen tilts his head to the side, his innocent voice

breaking the tension. "Can I stroke your pussy? I love your pussy. It's very hairy."

Brennan drops his fork. Cal and Lily go as still as statues. Finn chokes on his dinner. I glance at Con, who has tilted his head up to the ceiling, pinching the bridge of his nose. "Sweet fucking Jesus," he mumbles. I bite my lip to stifle the laugh bubbling in me at the change in atmosphere.

I peek at Oscar, whose lip has curled up at the side in amusement.

Clearing my throat, I speak up. "Can Keen pet your cat, Reece?" I ask softly.

He glances up from his meal, completely oblivious to the change in mood of the room. "Pussy."

I lift my eyebrow in question, unsure what he's getting at.

"You want to stroke my Pussy?"

My words won't come out right, "I... I..."

I gaze toward Con for help, but he's still looking at the ceiling as if that's going to give him answers on how to deal with this. I pass a glance at Finn beside me, his cocky megawatt smile in full force. He's loving this, the little shit.

I sigh in defeat, unsure of what to say next. Luckily, Bren puts me out of my misery. "Reece, let the kid pet the cat." He points the fork from Keen to the cat.

"Reece, don't be so goddamn difficult. You know what you're doing!" Cal chastises in an annoyed tone while wiping Chloe's messy hands.

Reece huffs out and begins to mumble a string of curses, something about us being dicks, it's his cat, go suck cock. Amongst other lovely liturgies of sentences.

Keen peers at me from beside Con, and I nod in approval.

However, I wasn't expecting him to literally climb the

damn table to get to the cat.

"Oh Shit!" Con exclaims as Keen knocks the jug of lemonade over, the mashed potatoes dish and the peas go flying.

All to stroke the Pussy.

Keen sits on the table as proud as punch with Pussy on his lap eating the mash from his pants. Con and Cyn rush around, trying to tidy up. Brennan curses up a storm. Bren ignores us all and sits, eating his meal completely unphased. Oscar taps away on his tablet.

Cal and Lily have surrounded Reece, trying to explain how they perceived him as being difficult, leaving little Chloe happily playing in her highchair with mashed potato between her fingers.

I sit back and take it all in, a small smile dawning on my lips.

Finn leans forward in his chair, "Miss us?" he whispers with a chuckle.

Smiling, I turn toward his grinning face. "I hadn't realized how much," I admit, biting my lip. His cocky smile softens.

Chloe continues babbling, but the noise seems to be clearer. I go around to her and wipe her hands with one of the napkins. "What's that, little princess? What are you telling me?"

Her lips pull together, and she blows bubbles, trying to talk. "Pppss."

"Are you trying to say please? Such a good girl," I coo proudly at her sweet attempts.

Lily and Cal stop and watch our interaction. I smile at them. "She's certainly telling me a story. I'm sure she's trying to say please."

"Pushy! Pushy!" she suddenly shouts, pointing at the

cat, her hands clamping open and closed.

I swear to God a pin could drop and you'd have heard it. The room goes deathly silent. "Pushy, Pussssy," she repeats clearer. Louder.

You hear Cal breathe in a lung full of air, his face turning to rage, his chest visibly vibrating through his shirt.

Shit, the guy looks like he's about to have a coronary.

Then he erupts.

He throws the towel off his shoulder at the table. "Her first fucking word! Her first fucking word is Pussy?" He spins and glares at Lily, as if it's her fault. His chest heaving, he's struggling to reign in his temper, that's for sure.

Lily's mouth opens and closes before she shrugs innocently. "It could be worse!"

He glares back at her. "How the fuck could it be any worse?" His chest rising, his fists clenched as he waits for a response from poor Lily. Her mouth open and closes again, like a fish.

"I was going to call her Cock." Reece sits back and smiles with a smug grin. Lily spreads her arm out toward Reece as if to say, see.

"Pussy!" Chloe screeches while trying to shuffle her cute butt closer in her chair.

"That's it! I'm out! I'm fucking done!" Cal, all but kicks his chair in and storms from the house. My eyes go to Lily, who rolls hers at his dramatic exit.

"I like Cock!" Keen muses, tilting his head side to side, looking at Pussy. "It suits her. You're a hairy Cock aren't you?"

Both me and Con jump in at the same time, "No!"

I shake my head at Keen. "No, sweetie, maybe call her Puss. She likes that best." I nod in encouragement. He pats Puss on the head with a cute smile.

Chapter Fifteen

Will

After dinner, I follow Lily out to the gardens. Reece has taken it upon himself to show Keen how to play basketball on the O'Connell's court.

Cal is on a bench, sitting with his legs and arms crossed on the other side of the garden away from all of us. An expression of pissed off and sulky on his face. I spare him a glance over my shoulder. Yep, definitely looks like he's been chewing a wasp.

"Don't mind him." Lily throws her arm out in Cal's direction while tackling the picnic blanket on the floor. I help her out as she places Chloe on the top of it with a selection of toys, which instantly go into her mouth.

I meet Lily's eyes, and she stifles a laugh. "He's being dramatic. Let him have his time out and he'll be fine in five."

I peek back at Cal. Yep, definitely looks like he's in time out.

Me and Lily chat away about the kids. She vaguely

fills me in on how she and Cal got back together. I cannot believe Reece orchestrated it all. The child is a genius but by the same token he's struggled so much in day-to-day life. Lily tells me about getting Reece on the right medication and the right doctor. It sounds awful and I cannot imagine what it must be like on a daily basis for them. Thankfully, they seem in a more stable place at the minute, although Lily pointed out it can all change without warning.

A shadow covers the blanket, and I glance up to Finn peering down at us. A cocky grin is plastered on his handsome face.

"What's got you so smug?" I ask him with a raised eyebrow.

Finn's smile stretches across his mouth playfully. "Con just took another fist to the jaw," he says while trying to stifle a laugh.

I gasp in shock. "Another? Seriously? He won't have a jaw left if you lot keep insisting on hitting him there!"

"Would you prefer we hit him in the balls?" He looks at me pointedly, but with the smile on his face, it's clear he's digging for information on our relationship status. I pause thinking of my come back but don't get a chance.

"Yeah, didn't think so. Jaw it is." He chuckles.

Finn joins us on the blanket.

He's laid back with his arms under his head, aviator sunglasses covering his eyes, his dog tags hang proudly on his chest. His signature black tee has risen, showing off a smattering of hair around his beltline, impressive golden abs on display.

Wow, I forgot how much these O'Connell guys are hot.

Lily makes a noise in the back of her throat, causing my head to shoot in her direction, her eyebrows raised with a tight smile on her face, letting me know she saw me checking out Finn.

"So Will, you ever hear from Angel?" he asks nonchalantly, but with the change in his posture, it's easy to tell it's been a calculated move sitting with us.

I smile softly at him. "No, sorry, Finn. I'm still as shocked as you," I sigh in defeat. "Honestly, I expected her back a long while ago." I pick at the strands of grass as I chat to him.

"Did you ever try to find her?" Lily asks Finn directly.

He shrugs off the disappointment but it's clear in his tone. "Na. If she wanted me, she'd be here. I'm not chasing her. Besides, last I heard she was happily married." He sits up and stares out at the garden, deep in thought, almost talking to himself.

"Well, I was as surprised as everyone when she went away, Finn. I don't care what bullshit her mom told you. She was crazy about you, and she'd never leave you hanging."

My body breaks out in goosebumps, the entire conversation making me uneasy. Something definitely wasn't right about Angel's disappearance. It was completely out of character for her, she absolutely adored Finn and would never, ever hurt him. No, there's more to it, I'm certain of that.

"Could you speak to her mom again?" Lily suggests.

Finn shakes his head and scoffs. "She died not too long after Angel left."

Bren's loud voice breaks our conversation. "Cal, Finn, get your asses inside. There's shit to discuss." Finn sighs and rises from the blanket, brushing himself off.

Cal stomps across the garden like a petulant teenager. I can see where Reece gets some mannerisms from that's for sure.

Cyn comes outside a few minutes later, leaving the men inside to talk business as she brings with her some fresh lemonade. I rise from the blanket and join her at the patio table.

She clasps my hand in hers as I take a seat opposite her. Her eyes glisten with protectiveness and love and I give her a genuine smile and nod of my head in acknowledgement of her feelings.

Cyn swallows down her emotion. "You know I'm not proud of how my son treated you, and his boy..." she glances over at a giggling Keen, being chased by Reece, "and I won't try to apologize for the words he spoke to you, Will." I nod at her so she knows I'm listening. "But when you love someone, you can hurt them with words much more than actions." I incline my head at her and listen to her soft voice. "Those words cut deeper than any knife, hurt harder than any fist, become harder to forgive than any physical reaction. When that person you hurt loves you, you don't forget the hurtful words, but you love them too much to lose them. So instead, you choose to forgive them and move forward. Forgiving them does not mean you forget about the words they said, but you understand that they lashed out with words because they couldn't lash out with actions, and you make the choice to accept it. Those words they spoke probably ate at them as much as they ate away at the person, they said them to."

I sit and digest her words. I want to move forward, and I can never forget the words Con said to me, nor his actions. But can I forgive him? I watch my son playing with Reece, his family.

I look at the gardens and Lily with Chloe. I know deep in my heart that Con said those words out of grief, anger and sadness, but I needed him, and he wasn't there.

As if hearing my thoughts, she says, "He's here now, Will. He's here and can you tell me you really think he's going anywhere else?" Cyn asks as she strokes my hand gently.

I shake my head at her. No. There's no way in hell Con will ever not be in our lives now.

I peer up at Cyn's expectant eyes and see a fleeting emotion of honesty and experience, as if she has felt the same feelings as me. The same hurt.

"Brennan hurt you?" I ask, my heart clenching for her.

Her eyebrows rise slightly in surprise before her body relaxes. She swallows deeply. "A long time ago, yes," she admits solemnly.

"Do you want to tell me about it?"

Cyn smiles gracefully before shaking her head. "No, sweetheart. Like I said, we don't forget, but we can move on. We can choose to forgive the person and that's what I did, and I promise you, if you love someone enough to do that it strengthens your love more than any other action."

Breaking us out of our deep conversation, the kitchen door flies open and Brennan storms toward his wife. He stands like a mountain above her, before bending down and softly kissing the top of her head.

Cyn peeks at me and smiles gently. Before Brennan breaks our connection once again. "That little shite will get his balls cut off the next time he steps out of line, sort him the fuck out Will!" He wags his finger at me in all seriousness, but I have to stifle a giggle between my lips at Brennans clear nonchalance of breaking a special moment apart. Cyn rolls her eyes in jest, making me grin.

I glance up and see Con standing in the doorway, his signature cap on back to front, his muscled body showcased in his tight white t-shirt, ripped jeans, and Converse. He's the epitome of hotness.

His eyes find mine instantly, his teasing smile aware of me checking him out. I scoff at his smug grin.

Can I forgive him?

I think I already have.

Chapter Sixteen

Con

I've been on edge all fucking day. Scrap that, ever since that fucking meeting at Da's yesterday. It was all going fucking well until we had a meeting while the girls and kids were outside.

I knew we were going to discuss the charity event that me and Will are attending tonight, but the feeling of not being in control made me act like a bigger ass than usual.

Bren fucking clocked my jaw because I pointed out he's a heartless cunt with no idea what it feels like to lose someone he loves. I mean, Jesus, that guy doesn't want a permanent woman or kid, so how the fuck can he understand how protective I am over mine. Because that's what they are, they're mine! Not the O'Connell family's. Mine!

And other people telling me what's going to happen, and I have no say? Yeah, fuck that.

In the end, I fucking relented. Because what fucking

choice do I have? But I wasn't relenting without voicing my opinion, even if it meant my jaw feels like it's fucking broke.

How the hell am I meant to be a great husband and dad with a broken fucking jaw? I mean, it fucking kills just to make those damn dog noises Keen goes mad about when I put him to bed. And what happens when I want Will to sit on my face? Because fuck do I want her to sit on my damn face.

Yeah, now I have a fucking hard-on and I have to go to this goddamn, mother fucking charity event just to showcase Will. Fucking flaunting my girl in-front of everyone. I swear to fuck, I'll kill anyone that looks at her. I seriously need a line of coke. Just one to settle me, to make shit easier. My eyes lock onto my drawer, the one that I used to keep my party drugs in. I had to empty those when Will and Keen moved in. I couldn't risk anything hurting them. The realization hits me hard.

I can't do coke.

I don't want to hurt them.

I fume as I stomp around my room, adding my watch as a finishing touch. I draw my eyes up into the full mirror in my room. And what do I see? Scum. A loser. Hopelessness. I swallow thickly.

A knock against my door breaks my stare. "Con, are you about ready?"

My voice comes out too harsh as I panic out the words. "Yeah, don't come in the fucking room, Will." Shit. I tug on my hair. Shit, I sounded like an ass.

I hear her huff and her heels click away. Fuck. Get it together, Con.

I take a deep breath and exhale, straighten my shoulders, and turn the knob on the door.

I walk into the living area, and my steps falter as I see Will standing by the countertop.

Our eyes meet instantaneously. Fuck, she's stunning.

Her legs are longer in her heels, a slit goes all the way up to her waist, exposing her golden legs. The shimmery silver dress hugs her hips and showcases her tits where it dips at the front. Her long waves are up in a ponytail, and she has this smokey makeup going off that makes her hazel eyes look deep and fucking epic. Her lips are painted in a plum color, making them look a little bruised, and I want to bruise them with my cock. Fuck, how hot would she be with my cum on those bruised lips, dripping down her chin?

My cock presses against my waistband. Shit, that hurts.

"Wow, you look hot!" Will announces while waving her hand over my tuxedo. My lips curl up into a grin when I realize she was checking me out as much as I was checking her out. We're so fucking good together.

The doorbell rings and I know it's showtime, security is here to escort us. I tense and stand taller. "Come." I hold out my hand for Will. As soon as her soft hand falls into mine, I immediately embrace a sense of calm. My eyes drift to her face one last time before we walk through the door. Her beautiful eyes meet mine, and I lean over and kiss her forehead. "Love you, baby." Then I pull her through the door before her refusal hits me.

I stare out of the window in silence as our driver weaves through the traffic. Will's soft voice breaks through the atmosphere. "Are you okay?"

I clear my throat and meet her eyes. "Yeah, I'm okay. You, okay?"

Will laughs and shakes her head. "You've been in a mood since dinner at your parents' yesterday. What's wrong?" She cocks a brow.

"Nothing." I gaze back out of the window.

She swallows harshly, her voice vulnerable. "Is Milo going to be there?"

I spin my head around to face her. I unclip my seatbelt and move toward her, grasping her chin between my fingers. "Fuck no. Jesus, is that what you think? You think I'd let that piece of shit anywhere near you? No fucking way would he be in the same room as you, Will. Trust me, baby." My eyes drill into her, imploring her to trust me.

Her eyes duck down before rising to meet mine. "Okay, I trust you. I know something is going on and you won't tell me, I just didn't know what to think." Her voice is riddled with helplessness.

I release her chin and think about her words. She trusts me. Me.

I study her before giving in. She needs to hear this. "We're going tonight to show you off. So word gets back to Milo that you're in town. We have security everywhere, Will, and I won't let you out of my sight."

Her eyebrows rise as she gasps out. "You're using me as bait?"

I tip my head back and pinch the bridge of my nose. "Yeah, I wasn't too happy about it either."

Her soft hand grazes my jaw. "Is that how you got this?" She brushes delicately over the bruising, tingles spreading over me at her gentle touch.

I nod, swallowing thickly at her mere touch. "Yeah."

"You know, I wish they'd stop hitting your face. I kinda

like it how it is." She smiles with her top teeth biting into those lips.

"I kinda like those lips of yours around my cock instead of in-between your teeth," I tug her lip from out of her teeth and brush my fingers over her bottom lip. She teases me by licking over my fingers, before tugging my forefinger into her mouth with said teeth. Then she sucks on my finger, her tongue swirling around my finger. Fuck, that's hot.

My cock twitches in response.

My eyes grow heavy, and I shuffle in my pants, trying to rub some of the ache of my cock against something, anything.

The car comes to a stop and draws us out of the moment. We both pull away from one another.

"We're safe?" Will asks again her eyes shining with vulnerability.

I bring her hand to mine and kiss her fingers. "Perfectly." She nods her head.

Security opens the car door and I step out first before going around the SUV to help Will.

Chapter Seventeen

Will

The ballroom is adorned with white drapes and crystal chandeliers. It really looks beautiful. The event tonight is a fundraiser for Voices Against Abuse, a cause close to my heart. I scan the room, looking for anything out of the ordinary.

Con leads us to a round table where Bren and a dark-haired woman sit. Bren rises to kiss me on both cheeks, his stubble catching my skin, making me jump back with a small laugh. He chuckles before introducing me to the dark-haired woman sitting beside him in a tight red dress and bright red lips. Bren's deep voice makes me jump into action when the woman, Marianne, holds out her hand for me to shake.

To say I'm a little on edge and not with it is an understatement. I scan the room again. Con's hand grasps my elbow. "Will, chill the fuck out."

"I feel like someone's watching me," I whisper back at him.

His eyes soften on me. "They are. We've got security everywhere. I'm by your side all night, remember?"

I nod and ease myself down into the chair opposite Marianne, her tight smile watching my every movement as she raises the champagne glass to her red lips. Bren sits stoically still beside her.

The event has numerous speakers and auctions. The O'Connell family have donated a break away to their luxurious holiday retreat in Barbados. It sold for $250,000. And the proud winner? Marianne. She sits there looking like the cat that got the cream, giving Bren a smug smile and flirtatious lick of her lips before throwing her hair over her shoulder. I watch them both and she makes no attempt to hide her lust for Bren, who does not hide his unphased attitude. I'm not sure if it's some game they're playing, where he acts like he's not bothered, and she does all the chasing? Nope, totally confused.

Con's hand brushes against my shoulder. He's spent the entire evening so far with his arm banded around my chair, either playing with my hair or stroking my shoulder. A clear sign of possessiveness. Making it obvious that we're together when, really? Are we?

"What are you thinking?" Con's voice snaps me out of my daze.

I glance at Bren and then Marianne, who is laughing away and touching Bren's arm while whispering in his ear. The guy is like a stone mountain. He gives absolutely nothing away.

"Are they together?" I ask, a little confused.

Con throws his head back and laughs, drawing attention to us both.

When his head comes forward, he shakes his head, clear amusement on his face. "I doubt Bren will ever be with anyone. I mean, have you met the guy? He's an emotionless prick. I doubt he even cracks a smile when he comes." He waves his hand in Bren's direction, laughing at his own joke while Marianne narrows her eyes at us. I shift a little uncomfortably. It's clear we're discussing them both. I glare daggers at Con, causing him to splutter into his wineglass in entertainment.

Marianne sits straighter in her chair, shifting her shoulders back as if preparing for battle. She swirls her red fingernail around her wineglass. "Sooo, Will, what is it you do for a living?" She raises her eyebrow at me in question. Wow, she's a pompous bitch. She's obviously expecting me not to work for a living.

I smile sweetly at her. "I'm a Family Liaison Officer and Advocate for Domestic Abuse helping families find themselves again. I support them in becoming a stronger unit." Con shuffles forward in his chair before kissing me on my forehead and drawing me into him for a hug. I melt against his chest. "You're fucking incredible, baby," he mumbles against my hair. Something inside me melts against his encouraging words.

I slowly pull away from him. "So, what about you, Marianne? What do you do for a living?"

She sits taller and smiles a mega-watt smile before flicking her hair provocatively over her shoulder. "I'm a lawyer." Of fucking course she is. I almost want to roll my eyes.

I fake a smile. "In what area?" I ask, already knowing the answer.

"Corporate law." She grins smugly. I glance at Bren; he's completely zoned out. Yeah, there's a reason why this woman is sitting beside him and I'm pretty sure it's nothing to do with her flirting, red lips, and fake tits.

Marianne looks from me to Con and then points her glass in our direction. "So you two are?" She leaves the question in the air but does so with a knowing smile. As if to say, you aren't a couple either.

"Engaged," Con spits out. I almost choke on my saliva. Marianne glances at my finger, my empty ring finger, before smiling smugly once again.

Yeah, I officially want to bitch slap her!

Con has also watched the movement of her eyes; his hand tightens on my shoulder in contempt. He sits forward in his chair, a menacing coldness in his eyes. "She's the only woman I will ever love. Only woman I will ever need. And she will be my wife," he shrugs, "she just needs to come to terms with it."

I don't know whether to be enraged or turned on by his possessive, demanding, determined words. My chest rises and falls with both annoyance and passion.

I flick my eyes over to Bren, who has now taken notice of the conversation. His lip curls up in a smirk at Con's words.

Marianne sees me looking at Bren and quickly puts her hand on his arm, his eyes land straight on it taking in the possessive action. Wow, this woman is something else. Con has literally sat and poured out his feelings toward me. We've acted as a couple all night, yet she still feels the need to show me Bren is hers? I roll my eyes at her pathetic, desperate move.

Good luck Bren, you're going to need it.

Bren's chair pulls back, his deep voice gruff with a tone of annoyance. "I'm going to the bar."

I eagerly jump up to follow him, ready for a break from this table and the conversations surrounding it.

"Me too."

Bren smirks at me and then glares at Con, who moves as if to join me. Bren gives him a subtle head shake that makes him sag into his chair, like he's defeated. Conscious of the bitch over the table, I lean down to Con, and move my lips to his. His mouth plunges against mine before I can reach him, his touch desperate, desperate for my lips, for my kiss, for anything I'm giving him. The thought makes me clench my thighs together in arousal.

Bren clears his throat, snapping me out of the kiss. I jump back and watch Con's lust filled eyes follow me as I sashay my way over to the bar with Bren.

Chapter Eighteen

Con

Watching my girl walk away with my brother takes everything in me not to follow, I grip the arms of the chair to keep myself pinned down. Anxiety rippling through me. I scan the crowd and then dart my eyes back to Will and Bren with haste.

"You're coming across a little obsessed, you know? You could tone it down a little." Marianne clucks her tongue in disapproval at my behavior. I scoff. Tone it down? This *is* fucking toned down.

I don't even turn my head to speak to the bitch, I just reply. "That's rich coming from you. If you shake those tits any harder in Bren's direction, you're going to give him a concussion. You're coming across as obsessed yourself. Perhaps tone down the desperation too, not a good look," I challenge back at her. She huffs and I can hear her trap open, but then I zone out because all I can see is some motherfucker approach my girl. Fucking smiling at her. And Will? She fucking hugs him.

Hugs him.

I fly out of my chair before Marianne finishes her sentence. The pounding in my ears intensifies with each step. She's laughing while he speaks to her. Flirts with her.

My temper rockets. I stalk across the dance floor, pushing past people trying to talk to me. She's putting something on her phone. His fucking number? She's going to fucking leave me for this prick?

My fists clench and my jaw throbs. My teeth hurt. I see my security team close in slowly as I descend toward the bar. His hand is on her mother fucking arm.

I snap the prick out of his gaze when I push against his chest so hard he stumbles back against the stool, sending drinks flying. "Hands off motherfucker!"

Will gasps beside me. "Con," she's trying to move in front of me, but I don't let her pass. I'm staring the prick down as he glares back at me, waiting to see what move I'm about to make.

Bren jumps in front of me, he growls into my ear. "Con, calm the fuck down. This guy knows Will. He's an associate of Jack's. I've been listening in to the conversation, man, nothing to worry about." His eyes drill into mine as if trying to make a point. I relax a little at my brother's words. But my head is still pounding with such intensity it hurts.

The douche sees this as a sign to move away. He straightens his jacket. "Willow, hopefully speak to you soon. Have a good night." He tilts his head at Will and turns to stroll away.

"Don't fucking count on it, buddy." I spit loudly in his direction.

As I turn to face Will, I'm greeted with a face of fucking

thunder. Oh shit, I scrub my hand through my hair and swallow. "What. The. Actual. Fuck. Was. That?" she grits out while staring at me with venom in her eyes.

I study her, unsure how to handle the situation. I move from foot-to-foot because honestly all I fucking want to do right now is fuck her in front of everyone, so they know she belongs to me. But I know she's not down with that.

No, she's expecting some apology or dumb shit and that's not happening either. I glare back at her and cross my arms over in a standoff.

She huffs and stomps her fucking foot before turning on her heel and making her way to the restrooms. I move to follow her, but Bren takes me by the elbow. "You need to calm the fuck down before you cause damage you can't fix," he warns.

Yeah, I don't take advice from someone who's never had a relationship in his life. I shrug out of his hold and go after Will. Bren's heavy sigh leaves me in my wake.

Turning into the ladies' restrooms, I nod at our security detail. Knowing he's cleared the restroom for Will to enter makes what I'm about to do a lot easier. I smirk knowingly as I enter the ladies room.

Will stands at the sink with her chest heaving, she's taking deep breaths, no doubt trying to calm down. I grin to myself, how riled up she is. So beautiful when pissed.

When she notices me in the mirror, she darts toward one of the cubicles, and I almost want to laugh at how ridiculous that is. Does she really think she can get away from me? Again? My chest bubbles with adrenaline.

I dart into the cubicle with her and slam the door shut

behind us, both our chests rising and falling with anger, almost in unison. Fucking beautiful.

I cross my arms over my chest in anticipation of her next move. My eyes dart to her purse, her knuckles whitening as she clutches it.

I grab the purse from her and begin rifling through it. "What the hell, Con? What are you doing?"

I grab what I was searching for and throw her bag to the floor carelessly.

Holding up the offending item, I jerk it from side to side, holding it higher, taunting her. "You put his number in your fucking phone?" I snip out.

Her bottom lip wobbles as she stares at the phone as if it's a fucking lifeline. She sighs. "He's a colleague of Jack's. He asked me to view some case files for him." I scoff at her dumb reply. That guy wants in her fucking panties and she's too naïve to see it.

I lean over and drop the phone in the toilet, then flush it.

"What the hell have you done?" she panics.

"Pretty fucking sure that was obvious. Flushing the fucking competition!" I point at the toilet.

"They have photos, videos of Keen on there, Con. How could you?" Her voice wavers. But I don't give a shit at this moment in time. I'm too far gone, too hyped up.

I roll my eyes at her dramatics. "Oscar can get them for you," I reply nonchalantly, because honestly, I couldn't give a fuck. My brother is a fucking genius. He'll get everything important and anything not? Well, it can fuck right off.

Will's chest moves up and down rapidly, drawing my attention to her glorious tits, her chest a tinge of red in anger. "You're fucking insane. You've lost it. Absolutely fucking lost it," she fumes, her voice rising.

"Turn around." My voice is calm and a little unnerving even to my own ears.

"What?"

"Turn around." I nod to the toilet door.

Will's eyes bug out when she realizes what I'm insinuating. "Absolutely fucking not!" she seethes.

"Yeah, not the answer I wanted." I lunge forward and grab her hips, forcing her around. I drag her flaying arms above her head. She spins her head around, trying to see what I'm doing, whilst trying to unhook her arms. I grasp my belt buckle with my free hand and unhook my belt, ripping it from my pants.

"Con. Don't you dare!"

My nostrils flare. She doesn't get to tell me no. Not after the torture she's put me through all night. No fucking way.

"Con, I'm not fucking you." Her eyes are ablaze with determination. This just fuels my need for her.

I thread the belt around her wrists and hook her onto the door hook. "Are you wet, Will?"

"No!" she spits out. She's fucking lying. I know my girl and I know she likes it rough. She likes the games we play.

I shove her dress over her ass. Her mother fucking ass. I could come just staring at it. My eyes scrutinize it, the toned globes smooth. I palm my hands over one cheek, stroking gently. Before bringing my hand down on it hard. The smack penetrates the room with an echo.

"Shit," she grunts pushing forward with the force. But eases back against my hand, my cock jerks in response to her.

I stare down at her red ass cheek, its then I realize. "No fucking panties?" The anger inside me bubbles. She's been fucking flirting with some douche, and she wasn't even wearing panties to cover my pussy? Smack!

"Ah." A sweet moan from her lips makes my cock jump in anticipation. I can feel myself wet against my boxers. I ease down my zipper and boxers, freeing my weeping dick. I adjust her footing, kicking her legs out and pulling her hips up a little.

"Are you wet?"

"No!" she snipes back. Liar.

"Too fucking bad." I spit on my hand and rub it over her pussy, just in case. But she's fucking drenched. I laugh tauntingly; I fucking knew it.

Not giving Will further chance to grumble and bitch, I plow my cock in, causing Will to shove violently against the door. "Jesus," she rasps.

"Fuck that's tight," I clench my jaw. Her pussy grips me, molding to my cock. I hold myself still inside her, where I'm meant to be.

I nuzzle into her neck, taking in her scent. Fuck, I wish I could stare into those eyes right now. I wish they would mirror my own. I draw back and push again, hard, causing Will to groan.

I grab the skin on the side of her neck with my teeth and pull. She gasps at the pain. "Con. Fuck!" I sink my teeth in further to mark her. If I could mark her forever, I would.

I continue the process of slowly pulling back, then pound her into the door. "Who do you belong to? Tell me," I demand.

"You. I belong to you."

"Damn fucking right you do." She squeezes my cock with her pussy, making my eyes roll as I fight off the orgasm. Her juices flowing between us, the sound makes me grip my girl tighter.

"Say you fucking need me," I spit out through clenched teeth. "Say it. Say you'll never leave."

She shakes her head. I draw my cock out of her, with my right hand I move to her clit and smack her hard. "Oh, shit, Con."

"Fucking say it and I'll let you come." Sweat beads on my forehead. My shoulders tense, desperate for her words. Please fucking say it.

She shakes her head in refusal. I take my left hand and draw it up to her throat, adding pressure to it tightly. I nip at her shoulder. "Say it." Her pussy tries drawing me back in. But I don't allow my cock to move. I want to hammer her through the fucking door, but I don't move. I lick up her neck, gently, almost in a caress. As one hand stays on her throat and the other hovers over her clit. I kiss her just below her ear as she melts against me, her head turning into mine. "Please," I slip out, almost on a beg.

She pants out the words I'm desperate to hear, sounding almost broken. "I'll never leave you."

And that's all it takes for me to snap. I push my fingers against her clit and thrust back into her pussy. I'm hammering her against my hand as the other holds her throat in place. My balls tingle, and I can feel my orgasm coming. I growl as I thrust in and out of her, her sweet moans filling the air.

"Cum for me," I demand. Her wetness coats my thighs as my balls hammer against her ass. I stare down at her tight pussy, swallowing my cock. I pinch her clit causing her pussy to squeeze me as she screams out my name. "Con!"

My balls tighten at her release, and my cum floods her pussy as I roar her name.

My arms tremble as I work to unhook her from the door. She shuffles her dress down and stumbles forward, but I catch her by her hips. She spins around in my arms and throws her arms over my neck, drawing me down for a kiss.

Her sweet lips meeting mine, I close my eyes and drink her in. This. This is what it's all about. I open my eyes to meet hers, my stomach flipping at the expectation of the usual disappointment in her eyes, but it's not there. My body sags in relief and before she can change her mind and hate me again, I take her chin in-between my forefingers. "Marry me!" I rasp.

Her eyes flare in anger. She pushes back from me, the unexpected shove making me lose my footing slightly. Her body shakes in anger. "No. Get the fuck out, Con." Her chest heaves as she points at the door, her eyes filled with unshed tears... What the fuck?

No? After I gave her an epic fucking orgasm? Seriously?

I need a fucking drink. I'll gladly fucking leave.

I swing the toilet door open; it ricochets off the wall. I storm out the door and nod at the security details to let them know to stay with Will as I make my way to the bar.

Will

I eventually make my way back to the table while my legs tremble with a mixture of disgust and anger.

I cannot believe that Con had the nerve to be so jealous over a fucking phone number. To go as far as flushing the phone down the toilet, fucking me against the door, then being pissed at me because I refused his marriage proposal in a goddamn bathroom, for Christ's sakes.

I mean, how the fuck dare I expect better?

What's with the making me face away from him bullshit too? He can't even face me when we have sex now? Am I not good enough?

I feel like shit. Used. Rejected. Utter shit.

I sigh and shake my head at my thoughts as I plonk myself begrudgingly in my chair.

Con's chair still vacant. My eyebrows furrow in confusion as I search around the ballroom for Con. Did he leave? My blood slowly boils.

Marianne's smarmy voice cuts through my thoughts. "If you're looking for your future husband, he's over by the bar with his mistress." Her smile fills her gloating face as she trails her finger over her champagne glass smugly.

Both mine and Bren's heads snap in the direction of the bar on cue.

My eyes zone in on some pumped up tramp brushing her hand up and down Con's arm. Her tits pushed into him. He smiles sweetly at her but makes no move to stop her blatant flirting. What the fuck? I swallow thickly at their interaction. Hurt grips my throat as I consider my marriage proposal and now this? Yeah, I'm hurt.

"Let's go," Bren snaps before pushing his chair back and gesturing for me to stand. He completely ignores his date and comes around to guide me out of my chair. My trembling hands grab my purse as Bren pulls me protectively into his side.

"I'll kill the son of a bitch," he mumbles to himself as we weave through the crowds. My heart hammers in my chest as I take one more glance back at Con. His head is thrown back in a laugh. Her hands now on his thigh. Disappointment curdles inside me, sickness rolling my stomach.

No thought as to where I am or what I'm doing.

No thought to the fact his cum is currently trailing down my leg, making me feel like a whore for fucking him in a bathroom.

No thought at all.

Chapter Nineteen

Con

I fucked up.

Again.

I brush my hand down my face as the light seeps in through the blinds, making me squeeze my eyes shut.

Shit, my head hurts.

The banging from somewhere in the room vibrates around inside my head. Jesus, shut the fuck up already. I wince at the noise.

Slowly, I pry an eye open and vaguely see Will's form in the kitchen. I grimace at the sound of the blender.

My throat struggles to work as I wilt under her scrutiny. "What the hell happened to you last night?" Her voice cuts through the air. Sharp and deadly.

I struggle to sit up straight, my head spinning and my body tremors. Shit, I'm crashing. What a fucking wreck. I grimace.

I brush my hand through my hair and assess myself. My

shirt is open at the top, and my shoes are on the floor. When did I take them off? Where the fuck is my jacket? I scan around the couch, looking for my jacket.

Will plonks a smoothie in-front of me. "Figured you'd need that," her no-nonsense voice snaps out.

My eyes slowly make their way up her body. Her smooth legs stood in-front of me, her sleep shorts low on her hips and her cami top tight around her breasts. Will's chest rises and falls rapidly as she gazes down at me. Her hazel eyes glisten with hurt. She clears her throat. "You... you, erm, have lipstick on your collar," she all but chokes out.

I flit my eyes away as my hands dart to my collar. I try to remember my night. My nose feels wet, I brush absentmindedly at the wetness.

Will's gasp causes me to tilt my head up again. The expression of horror on her face causes my stomach to roil. "You're high?"

Shit.

I jump up on my unsteady feet and push past her. She follows, hot on my tail. "What the fuck, Con. You're high?"

My legs move toward my bedroom, almost blindly.

"Jesus, Con. I fucking trusted you," she chokes on a sob. "You bastard, I trusted you."

"Leave me the fuck alone, Will!" I slam my door before she comes in. I tug on my hair in frustration. Shit.

Shit. Shit. Shit.

"Con, we need to talk." Her voice is stern and empty of the previous emotion. Her knock on the door penetrates my insides. She needs to talk about leaving me, that's what she's going to say.

My heart throbs painfully, my fingers tremble. I glance around my bedroom. I fucking hate it. She can't step foot in here. Not here.

"Don't come in my room, Will!" I all but scream back at her through the door. I don't want her in here. Not here. I go into my bathroom and struggle to turn on the shower. My hands have a mind of their own, they're shaking and uncontrollable.

I tug off my clothes in disgust. Such a fucking failure. I slump against the wall, my nose now streaming. Such a mother fucking failure.

Will

I've left Con in his pit to fester. His shower turned off hours ago, so I can only assume he's sleeping.

My mind keeps playing over and over the events of last night and this morning. His neck covered in lipstick. I squeeze my eyes shut tightly to try and banish the images. I'm hurting. I'm hurting because the man I love, the man I want to build a life with has betrayed me. Us.

If he's cheated, there's no going back. You don't ask someone you love to marry you, then spend the night with someone else.

Then what about the drugs? Does he have a problem? I can't be with someone like that. I can't have Keen around someone like that. Sickness coils in my stomach. Does he even want us here? He won't even let us step foot in his own room. Whenever Keen attempts to go in there, he tries every tactic to distract him.

I shake my head as the thoughts consume me. We need to talk. Decide where to go from here, then I can make a plan. With or without Con.

I speak to Lily, who happily agrees to keep Keen. Bren had told Cal about the night's events, who then told Lily. So, they were expecting my call in some capacity or another at least.

I hear the click of Con's door as I turn and pour myself a drink.

Followed by smooth hands on my stomach. I still at his overt movement. Is he kidding me right now?

His breath brushes against my ear. "I'm sorry."

Sorry? Rage fills my veins.

I choke on my words. "Sorry? Sorry for what, Con?" I spin around and face him head on. His jaw shifts and his blue eyes struggle to meet mine. "Sorry for fucking me in a jealous rage against a bathroom stall door? Proposing in a bathroom? For storming out and leaving me? Flirting at the bar on the same night you left your cum inside me?" He winces and his fists tighten beside him. "Sorry for coming home at four a.m.? For not coming home with me?" My voice grows louder. "Or are you sorry for coming home off your fucking face on drugs, Con?" I'm shouting now. "For the lipstick covering your neck?" I choke on the hurt.

"Is that what you're sorry for, Con?" I lick my lips in battle. "Did you sleep with her? Or were you too high to remember?"

He falls back a step, almost stunned, before his eyes meet mine again. Anger glaring back at me with such intensity my heart jumps. "You think I'd fuck someone else? Seriously, Will, you think I'd do that to you? To Keen?"

I shake my head. "I don't know, Con. Truthfully, I don't know what you'd do because everything you've just done..." I shake my head. "It's not anything I'd have thought you'd do. You need help, Con. And if you don't get it soon, it's going to be too late."

His words falter. "Wh... what's that meant to mean? You aren't leaving me." His words soften, "Please, Will."

I take a deep breath. "I can't keep doing this. You're all in one minute, then completely detached the next." I lick my lips as I consider my next words, calling him out I proceed on. "I'm not sure all the things you're saying you really mean."

He scoffs, making a face of mortification, "Like fucking what?"

"You keep saying you want me. But do you really Con? Or do you just like the thoughts of having me again. Like the thoughts of a family. We aren't allowed in your room; you don't want us there. I mean, we fuck, but we're just fucking." My voice trembles. "You won't even let me see you. We just screw." I shrug as though it means nothing. But it does, it means everything.

His hand grips my chin tightly, causing me to stare directly into his eyes. They glisten with unshed tears. "You don't think I want you here? Seriously?" His voice raises. "I can't have you in that room, Will." He points angrily at his bedroom. "I don't want you in there—you or Keen." Taking a step back, I move to back away, but he pulls me closer. "Will, I can't have you tarnished by the shit I've done in there. I don't want you near any of that." He lowers his head and shakes it back and forth.

His voice wavers as he looks into my eyes, honesty pooling around them. He brushes the hair from my face and tucks it behind my ear. "I can't. I can't see the hurt in your eyes when I have you." My body shudders against his openness. He can't meet my eyes when we have sex, because he doesn't think he's worthy?

The question must show on my face because he goes on, licking his lips and steeling himself for another breath. "I can't see the hate, the disappointment, the sadness. Everything I've caused. I can't see it, Will. I want you to want me like I want you." His lips tremble. His fingertips shake against my face.

His words seer into my heart. He doesn't think I want him? Need him? Like him? Love him? My heart suddenly aches for him. To prove to him how worthy I know he can be.

I shake my head; his hands fall away in defeat, but I clasp his wrist. I pull on his hand and we head to my bedroom. His body stumbling with me.

The door slams shut as I spin on my heel to face Con. I

stare into his blue eyes. "You didn't sleep with her?" I question again.

His face transfixed on mine; raw emotion sprayed across it. "No. Lena tried to kiss me, and I pushed her off. I called my driver and came home. I was worried I'd had too much and didn't want to regret anything."

"Besides doing coke, you mean?" My eyebrow raises in question, because if he thinks I'm letting him off with that indiscretion, he can think again.

"Yeah. Besides that." He nods solemnly. His eyes cast down at the ground and his voice is low. "I'll see someone about that. It won't be a problem again, I swear." His eyes meet mine before looking away again, vulnerably.

"Look at me, Con!"

He raises his head to stare into my eyes, his dark hair covering his eyeline.

I tug my top over my head and throw it to the ground. My chest heaves up and down. His eyes fill with lust and need.

I glare at him pointedly. "I want you, Con. *All of you.*"

His pupils dilate and he swallows thickly, his Adams apple bobbing.

I hook my fingers into my sleep shorts and push them down, leaving me naked before him. Con licks his lips. His chest heaving, his palms twitching beside him.

I walk over to the bed and lay my head on my pillow, my naked body sprayed out for him on display. I watch him as he takes short sharp intakes of breath, his eyes glued to my body.

"Come over here and make love to me, Con. Show me how you love me." His eyes flare at my words.

He throws off his t-shirt before pushing down his basketball shorts. His cock bobs free.

My eyes watch his every movement as he approaches the bed. He tugs his length in his fist, his eyes never leave mine.

His body climbs over me, settling between my legs. His soft thumb grazes my lip and gently strokes it. "This what you want, Will? Me?"

Our eyes transfixed on one another; I nod gently. "Yes," I swallow, unsure whether to tell him how I feel, knowing there's no going back once I do. I lick my lips, "I love you, Con. I want you to make love to me."

His body stills, his eyes widen in disbelief. I stroke my hand down his face, then up toward the curls hiding his eyes. I brush them away as he stays stoically still, almost in shock.

He chokes, his eyes blurry. "Say it again."

I stifle a giggle and bite my lip. "I love you, you idiot. Now make love to me and fuck me good." I raise my eyebrows in challenge.

His mouth crashes down on mine. His tongue plunders into my mouth, searching for my own. I meet his kiss; the passion engulfing us both. My hands grasp his shoulders, my nails dig into his skin as he grinds himself against me, bare.

Con's hands move around my body, grasping my hips, my breasts, my face. He can't get enough of me. He doesn't know what to touch next, his whole body desperate for me.

"Fuck. I love you so much, Will. So fucking much. I'm going to spend the rest of my life showing you. Proving myself to you. Fucking you."

Grabbing my leg, he lifts it slightly, so it's over his hip. He thrusts himself forward, his cock driving into me with such force he pushes me into the mattress, causing the bedframe to hit the wall.

I peer down to his face that is now sucking on my breast. His head rises, and he smirks at me before driving into me again.

"Fuck Con, again."

Thrust.

He grips my breast in his hands and twists my nipple, causing me to scream, wetness pooling my pussy. "Fuck yes, give it to me, Will."

His tongue sets me on fire as he laps greedily at my nipple. He pulls back from my nipple with a suckle, causing a pop. I hiss at the sensation before he dips his head and gently kisses it, followed by a lick. "Jesus, Con."

Con pushes into me hard and deep. The headboard hits the wall repeatedly. "Tell me again." He demands, as he glares into my eyes fiercely. His gaze penetrating through my body. The desire and need in them almost too much to bear. I clench at the thought. His moans echo my actions.

"I love you." I tug his head to me by his hair, our kiss hard and passionate. He grinds into me whilst moaning into my mouth.

My orgasm builds with each of his thrusts. "You'll never be free. Tell me you'll never be free from me."

"I never want to be," I admit as my pussy spasms around him. My thighs will bruise with the intensity of our love making but this is me and Con and we don't do slow and sensual. We do raw and passionate. Desperate and hungry.

"I'm going to..." My orgasm rips through me like a tidal-wave. My legs tighten around him to pull him closer.

"Oh Fuck. Fuck," Con chants out. My walls squeeze him and send him over the edge with vigor, his body crashes against mine with force. Wave after wave of euphoric bliss engulfs me as his cock pulses deep inside me.

His forehead falls against mine. "I love you, baby." His eyes meet mine and watch me closely, as if waiting for the change in me.

"I love you too." I smile softly and Con's whole body relaxes against mine.

He collapses beside me and pulls me into him, his lazy hands stroking down my spine.

Chapter Twenty

Con

Absolute. Mother. Fucking. Bliss, that's what this is.

I lay with Will, her body draped over my chest. My hand trails absently up and down her back. Her hair, damp from our lovemaking, sends chills up my spine. I tighten my hold on her. She's mine, she loves me and she's never leaving.

I kiss her head, making her sigh into my hold. I take a deep breath and decide to be honest with her she needs to know how sorry I am.

I lick my lips contemplating my thoughts. "Will." She moves her head so her eyes meet mine. I swallow the lump in my throat. "I wish I could take back what I asked of you, baby." Her body stiffens beneath me but I ignore it and plough on, needing to get it out. "I was fucked up after Keenan." She nods in understanding, her lip trembling. "The shit I said," my own eyes glaze over and I shake my head back and forth. "I regretted it, but then I heard you'd been to the clinic." I choke on emotion. "I thought I'd done it. Pushed you to do it. I fucking hated myself, Will. I knew you'd hate me too," I admit.

Will searches my face before ducking her head back onto my chest, she squeezes me gently and place a soft kiss on my heart. "I forgive you, Con." Her words are a whisper, but I hear them, my arms tighten around her in gratitude.

"I love you." I whisper.

I feel her swallow against my chest, "I love you too."

We lay in silence, both aware that the other is awake. I feel like a weight has been lifted from me. She forgives me and loves me, what more could I ever possible ask for?

"Tell me about your mom," I ask gently. It's something I've been thinking about for a while now but haven't found the right time to talk about it. I guess now might not be such a good time either, because Will's body tenses in my arms. I loosen my grip on her and begin stroking her hip, creating small circles with my fingers.

"She died when I was little. Eight, I think?"

"You don't remember?" my eyebrows knit together in confusion.

Will tilts her head up at me, resting her chin on my chest. "I remember her dying. How, why. And after, but no, I don't remember my exact age." She trails her finger up and down my arm, almost copying my own movements now onto her back. "My dad came home from work late one day. My mom commented that his dinner would be cold. He smacked her around. But this time, she taunted him." Will shakes her head at the memory. "She normally never stood up to him. I don't know why she did this time. He turned on her, hit her with a frying pan. She fell to the floor, but he didn't stop there. He climbed on top of her and kept punching her in her face. Over and over." Will's fists tighten as she speaks.

I gently unclench one of her fists and lace our fingers together. I kiss her head. "It's okay baby, I'm here."

She licks her lips and continues. "Milo and I just stood there and watched. We both just stood there, Con. While he was hitting her. So much blood. Her beautiful face was gone. And we just stood there."

"You were a kid, baby."

Will agrees with a nod. "I know. Eventually I talked to a therapist. I know I was a kid, but I felt guilty for a long time."

I squeeze her hand in understanding.

"My dad got Milo to help him. They wrapped her up in some bed sheets, like she was a bag of trash, Con." She sobs into my chest. "She's buried under our porch." My brave girl shakes at the admission.

I tighten my hold on her. He buried her under her fucking house. Under her porch. The sick mother fucker. My teeth dig into my lip in temper.

Will clears her throat. "Milo. He was a teenager. We never truly got along. He's always scared me, I guess. But after then, he was different. Colder. Meaner. I know he suffered trauma too, but... he changed. He was my father's right-hand man, and he loved it." I nod in understanding. The little fucker has been a pain in our asses for a while now, running drugs in and out of our district. Cheap shit. Nasty shit that causes kids to OD.

There was even a rumor going about that he was into human trafficking. After hearing Jack and Oscar's break-down of the little shit hanging around with the lowlife Russian gangs, nothing would surprise me. And disposing of Will when she needed him? Ordering a hit out on her?

Potentially on Keen too? Yeah, the fucker has got some sins to repent for. I grit my teeth.

"I'm not going to let anyone hurt you again, Will. I swear it on my life." I hammer the words out with force.

"I know." Her voices softens, and the trust in it makes my eyes close with smug pride. She trusts me, needs me.

"I love you, baby."

She turns her eyes to meet mine. "I love you too." A smile breaks over my lips as hers descends onto mine.

Chapter Twenty-One

Con

The buzzing noise is annoying the fuck out of me.

"Con, your phone is ringing." Will's sweet voice cuts through my dream.

My amazing fucking dream, replicating her on top of me like earlier. Grinding those luscious tits into my chest. "Ah... fuck," I scrub a hand down my face as Will continues to shake me. I grab the phone from her nightstand. "Yeah."

Bren's voice clips through my haze. "About fucking time. We got him."

I sit up straight, the sheet pooling around my cock. "Who?" I question already knowing the answer but needing him to confirm it.

"Milo, you dick. Who else?"

My heart pounds in my chest, my veins pumping the blood furiously around my body. "Where?"

"Basement of Club 11." The line goes dead.

I spring out of bed and begin tugging on my jeans. "Con, everything okay?" I stop in my tracks and stare down at Will. Her hair sprayed out on our pillow, her tits on display. The marks on her chest showing every fucker who owns her. Fuck, she's gorgeous.

Do I lie to her? I shake my head. No. We need to do this, be honest. I need to be a better man for her, for them both. I lick my lips and steel my spine; gently I bend down and brush her cheek with my hand. "They got him, baby. They got Milo."

Her eyes widen, uncertainty seeping through. "Are you... are you going to finish it?"

I kiss her forehead. "Yeah baby, I'm going to end this. Then we can start our lives together, okay?" I stare at her pointedly, waiting for her acceptance.

Will nods. "Be careful." I tighten my hold on her head and kiss her lips with bruising force, before turning and tugging on my t-shirt.

I pound on the back door of Club 11 and glare into the camera. You'd think the mother fuckers would have had someone waiting here for me. Instead, it's like getting in Fort fucking Knox.

The door opens, my eyes meet one of our security. "About fucking time." I grunt as I barge past him, making a right turn and descend to the basement.

I can already hear Bren's bitter chuckle as my chucks scramble down the stone staircase.

I take in the room; all my brothers are here. Oscar's sitting at the back with his tablet, he raises his cold eyes to meet mine and then dips his head. Cal is sitting in a chair overseeing things. Bren has his shirt pulled up to his elbows. Clearly, he's got his hands dirty tonight. He circles Milo, who's tied to a chair in the center of the room. Finn is knelt down in front of him. The knife he holds is glistening with blood.

I take in Milo's current state as I approach. His T-shirt is ripped down the center, probably courtesy of Finn. A crisscross of cuts marring the skin on his chest courtesy of Finn's finn-finishing, as we like to call it.

His hands are tied to each arm of the chair. They're disfigured and judging by the hammer beside Finn, he's shattered the bones in them both. A smile curves onto my face at the thought. Milo's head hangs forward, but his chest still rises. Good fucking job. He's mine.

"What do we know?" I ask no one in particular.

"Informant on the street rang it in. Finn and Bren went to check it out. Turns out he's been hiding out at a crack whore's house." I nod in acknowledgment to Cal's words.

I stride toward Milo. Then, bending down I grip his hair punishingly, pulling his head back to face me, I take note his face a mangled mess. "Did you know about my son?" I spit out. My veins strumming with rage.

Milo chuckles to himself, boiling my blood further. My fists clench on instinct, the one in his hair almost wrenching it from his scalp, lifting him in the chair, causing him to try and pin his toes to the floor. His defiant eyes meet my own. He spits blood out from between his lips. "I had a hit out on them both." He grins manically, his face lighting up with delight as I recoil at his words.

"Motherfucker!" I snatch the blade from Finn.

Plunging it deep into his thigh before twisting it, I take delight in his screams. The sounds echoing off the concrete walls.

Milo grinds his teeth. "Did Will tell you how bad our dad beat her? How he almost killed your kid?" He laughs to himself.

I bring the blade to his face and pull his head back to watch me, his sick grin consuming his face. "She bled like a pig, Con, her cunt bled everywhere," he taunts.

I want to cut out his tongue and feed it to him. I watch him, stunned at his words. "Our daddy tried to sell her cunt. I knew you were fucking her; an O'Connell deflowering my little sister." He laughs. "She tried to deny it. The little whore tried to deny it." I tug his head sharply at his words. "Go on, do it, slit my throat," he mocks, trying to push the knife into his throat.

A firm voice breaks my thoughts. "Con." I glance toward Finn. He shakes his head at me. I look at Bren. His head nods firmly at me in support. I straighten my spine; this fucker is goading me. But he will not die quick. No, he's going to suffer, like Will suffered. Like her mother suffered. Like my son would have suffered.

I lift the blade, dig it in and slice it down his face, cutting off his ear. It drops to the floor. Milo squirms in the chair, shaking, trying to pull away. His screams should turn my stomach. They should.

I watch in sick fascination as blood oozes down his body. I twist his head to the other side, and pull my knife toward the other ear, prepared to take him apart bit by fucking bit.

The door to the basement opens, and I glance behind

me at the footfalls descending the stairs. My uncle's large frame fills the entryway. "Don." I nod in his direction.

His broad smile fills his face. "Seems ya caught a pig." He laughs in Milo's direction as he squeals uncontrollably. Just like the pig he is.

"Let me out of this fucking chair and I'll have ya, Con. Come on. Be a fucking man."

I laugh at his antics. "You aren't going anywhere, Milo. Apart from hell, that is. After, of course, I've sliced off every limb and taken every organ from your body," I gloat, meaning every word.

He shudders and flails in his chair. "I... I... I've got information. So much information, the Russians. I can tell you everything," he desperately wails. My body relaxes at his heightened state of panic.

The thoughts of him losing his cock turning him inside out, no doubt. I chuckle at the thought and shake my head at him. "We don't want or need your information, Milo. And we'd get it anyway, don't you think? You aren't exactly in a position to argue otherwise."

He looks down at himself and probably realizes he is indeed in no position to negotiate.

Then he changes his tactic, laughs, throwing his bloody head back, licking his lips. "You dumb fuckers. Think you know it all, don't you? You don't. You know nothing. Everything you ever thought was a lie."

Bren bristles at his words. Oscar's eyes shoot up. "Do you know about the connection between the Dimitriev's and Mexicans? You know fuck all!" he shouts jovially.

I draw the blade closer to him, his hairline to be precise. I've learnt a thing or two from Finn and how to de-scalp someone is one of them.

"You betrayed your sister, Milo; you betrayed your nephew, and you betrayed your mother."

I dig in the blade, but the lunatic doesn't stop with his bleating. He laughs through the slice. "You know nothing about betrayal. Look at your own first, Con, the saddest thing about betrayal is it never comes from your enemies. There's a viper in the nest, Con and you've no idea." His devilish smile taunts. My eyebrows furrow at his nonsense words before I peel back the skin from his forehead.

A shadow looms behind me before a loud popping noise vibrates from the walls, causing Milo's body to sag into the chair. My eyes spin around and land on Uncle Don. Bren's body straightens and Cal jumps from his chair in temper. "Ya as sick as him," Don points the gun in Finn's direction. "Theres feckin blood everywhere. Ya get off on this, ya sick cunts. Shoot em in the fuckin' balls and stick a bullet in their heads, easier." He shrugs as if it's nothing. He's just stuck a bullet between Milos' eyes. Milo's dead. Fucking dead and not by my hands.

I launch at him; Finn and Bren hold me back. "You bastard. He was mine. Fucking mine!"

Don shrugs off my explosion, tucking his gun back into his jacket. "Got shit to do, boys. Not sitting round here all night while you're creating an unnecessary bloodbath."

"Nobody asked you to come, Don," Cal cuts in, his words seething. Damn fucking right nobody asked him to come.

Don's accusing eyes hold Cal's hostage. His finger points at himself. "It was my feckin men that found the bastard. Mine. Not yours, ya ungrateful fuckers."

I sag in Finn's hold. He's right, we owe him. If it wasn't for him and his men, we wouldn't have found him, potentially ever. The thought causes a shudder down my back.

He's dead.

As if hearing my thoughts, Finn clamps me on the shoulder. "He's dead, man. It's over." I nod in agreement.

He's gone.

It's over.

Chapter Twenty-Two

Con

It's been two days since we wiped that scumbag off the face of the earth. The euphoria still resonates inside me. When I got home, I held Will as she sobbed with relief, knowing that she and Keen are safe, and that part of her life is finally closed. She can finally let me in, and we can become the family we always should have been. A sudden wave of nausea washes over me as if questioning, is it really the end? I can't seem to shake Milo's words from my mind, "You know nothing about betrayal. Look at your own first, Con, the saddest thing about betrayal is it never comes from your enemies." What the fuck is that meant to mean? I scrub a hand through my hair in annoyance. What matters is the here and now. Will and Keen are safe, and they're fucking mine.

Me and my brothers sit around Bren's dining table for our poker night.

It's actually one of my favorite nights, apart from when I'm with Will and Keen. Or deep inside Will, or when Will's sitting on my face, or with my dick in her mouth. Basically, anything with Will or my kid. But yeah, tonight I'm at fuckin ease with my brothers and there's only one other place I'd rather be.

"You and Will good now, brother?" Bren asks, while dragging a hand through his shaved head. This is as emotional as Bren gets. He's a muscle headed, emotionless Neanderthal.

I throw some chips into my mouth. "Yeah, we're doing great."

"You start therapy yet?" Oscar's clipped voice asks. He's always the one to put a downer on things. Fucking prick.

I glare at him in response. "Next week, Mom," I deadpan. He ducks his head sharply as if I've passed some fucking test.

"What exactly is it for?" Cal asks, the concern in his voice clear.

I sigh. Jesus, I just wanted a game of poker, for fuck's sake. I fidget with my cap, spinning it from the backwards angle to the front, hiding my eyes, because I fucking struggle to hide the guilt when discussing my brother Keenan. I shrug, trying to act nonchalant. "Will thinks I need to discuss shit about how Keenan died. And she wants to make sure I'm not a fucking addict."

Cal's eyes sear into me. "Are you? An addict I mean?"

I scoff. "No, I'm fucking not. Jesus."

He holds his hands up in defense. "I was only asking."

I sag into my chair, take a pull of my beer. "I use it recreationally, to party and shit." My eyes flare to Finn's because we've both used together. His to help take away his sorrow of losing Angel and mine, to take away the guilt and pain of losing Keenan and Will. Finn holds my eyes, his darkening at my admittance. He knows I won't drop him in the shit, but he still holds me hostage, anyway. I shake my head and turn my head away, not about to give his secret up.

Cal clears his throat and claps his hands together. "Well, I'm proud of you, brother." The table erupts with welcomed slaps on my back, the clanging of beer bottles and the cheers in my direction. Warmth spreads through me, the acknowledgment of their support bringing a smile to my face. My family loves me.

We discuss Keen's birthday. Tomorrow me and Will are taking him to the zoo together. I can't fucking wait for our first family day out.

Then Sunday on his actual birthday, we are having a birthday party at ma and da's, complete with a bouncy castle and shit. I've never looked forward to a party so much. And I've been to some amazing fucking parties.

"So, how's things going with Marianne?" Finn asks, changing the subject from the cards we were just dealt.

Bren sighs and strokes his stubble. "Fuck. She's a grade A bunny boiler. Seriously, she wants to permanently jump on my dick." We all chuckle at Bren.

"That woman just wants power. Nothing more." Cal states.

"I'm not so sure. She's wanting a fucking ring on her finger. No doubt about it."

I watch Bren. "You going to give her one?"

His hand goes to his head again, brushing the fuzz. "Fuck no. It's just business."

"Does she know that?" Oscar deadpans.

"Pretty sure she got the message last night." Finn grins.

"Fuck, what did you do?" I ask on tender hooks because when Bren does something, he's like a bull. Charging forward with little consideration for those surrounding him, he makes sure he's heard.

Bren laughs to himself. "I got dinner reservations at the restaurant I knew she had a business meeting at. Took a couple of escorts out for a meal." He shrugs.

I choke on my drink. "Back the fuck up. You did what?"

He rolls his eyes. "She's been bitching about me joining her for this business meal she had going on. So, I thought, fuck it, I'll go, just not with her. Made sure I hired a couple of hot bitches and shoved the fucker's tits under her face." I stare from him to Cal, whose eyes are wide open in shock. Finn's laughing his head off and Oscar is glaring at him like he's a piece of shit.

"Was she pissed?" Finn asks through a stifled chuckle.

Bren shakes his head, laughing. "Man, you've no idea. That'll teach her to not get any big ideas."

"You could just tell her you aren't interested," Oscar spits out, always the advocate of common decency.

"You don't think I did? She wasn't fucking getting it. She wanted to move into my fucking apartment. Even bought herself a fucking engagement ring." His fingers go up to make air quotes, "to make sure she gets the right one."

We sit wide eyed as he gives us the rundown on Marianne. "I swear to Christ I told her, she's just another pussy. One I also do business with, not to blur the lines."

"How good of you," Oscar chimes.

Bren holds his hands up. "Hey, just explaining I haven't led her on. She comes up with this insane, possessive shit on her own."

"Yes, well, don't go upsetting her too much. We need to

keep her a little happy and her daddy very sweet." Oscar says sensibly.

Bren ducks his head and takes a swig of his beer. "Don't worry, I'll stick it in her every now and again to keep her happy. I just don't want her pussy teeth locking me in." We all nod in agreement. A shiver runs down my spine at the thought of Bren being lumbered with that nut job. Hell no.

Finn's voice cuts through the air. "So which escort agency did you use?" he grins to himself.

Bren throws his head back, laughing. "Indulgence." His eyes shoot to Oscar's, whose narrow on him.

Oscar fidgets uncomfortably in his chair before sitting up straighter, his jaw working from side to side. "And where did you hear about that company, Bren?" he asks with a controlled, sharp, annoyance in his tone, as if he owns the damn company I've never even heard of.

I watch the exchange between them. Bren raises his eyebrows in challenge. "Actually, Reece recommended them."

Cal splutters. "What! What the hell do you mean, Reece recommended them? Oscar?" He shoots his eyes toward Oscar as if asking him to explain.

Oscar breathes out slowly, aggravated at having to explain. Slowly drawing his words out. "Clearly your son has been poking around my business yet again," he deadpans. "Perhaps you could keep a better rein on him? You are his father, after all." He lifts an accusing eyebrow at Cal.

Cal jumps up from his chair. "I'm going to kill him. Fucking escorts. Escorts! He's barely fifteen. Fucking fifteen."

"He's almost sixteen dude," Finn chimes in with a smug smirk, correcting Reece's age. Fucking gaslighting the whole situation. That's what he's doing.

"He's a kid. A fucking kid." He brushes his hand through his hair, his chest rising and falling faster by the second. We watch on in amusement as my brother's sheer panic goes into overload. He's like a woman on the rag the best of times. "I need to go... I need to speak to Lily. Jesus, do you think he's having sex with them?" he asks no one in particular as his eyes dart around us all. We all make non comital sounds and shrugs. I mean, the kid is nearly sixteen.

"Try not to overexert yourself. I'm pretty sure he was poking around and passed the information on to Bren to gain favor of some sort," Oscar talks calmly.

Cal's eyes study him. Oscar's head darts up to look at Cal, an aggravated expression on his face as he goes on to explain with a roll of his hand. "I have alerts on my tablet regarding Reece's activities. The boy has vaguely looked at porn and that's as far as it's gone. I also have a good relationship with the agency discussed, and I'd be made aware of any forthcoming intentions on Reece's behalf." Oscar speaks like he's in a boardroom delivering a presentation.

Cal throws his arms up in the air, spluttering. "P... porn?"

I sit back with my arms crossed, watching the show before me. Another handful of chips in my mouth for good measure. Bren chuckles into his fist while Finn cracks up, laughing at the sheer terror on Cal's face, before asking with a raised eyebrow, goadingly. "What sort of porn, Oscar?"

Cal erupts, "I'm fucking out. I'm done. Had enough of this bullshit. Don't fucking leave escort fucking shit around my son again, Oscar," he points at Oscar angrily, "I swear to God I'm done. Fucking escorts! Porn! For fuck's sake." Cal storms to the door before slamming it shut behind him.

Oscar rolls his eyes at his dramatics.

"Seriously though, what sort of porn?" Finn grins.

"Shut the fuck up, dipshit." Bren hits him around the back of his head, causing him to grunt.

I smile at my brothers.

Fuck, life is good.

Chapter Twenty-Three

Will

We arrive at the zoo for our first day as a family to celebrate Keen's fourth birthday. Keen and Con have matching T-shirts saying, "I'm Roarsome!" on them with a huge tiger face. Both Con and Keen have matching backwards caps, jeans, and chucks. Keen looks cute as hell and a mini replica of Con, who looks hot as hell. I grin inwardly, proud of my little family.

My white sundress floats around me in the breeze. My wedge sandals put me closer to Con's height, making it easier to kiss him as we work our way around the zoo hand-in-hand.

I'm not sure who is more excitable between the two boys. I take a multitude of photos at Con's insistence. The silly faces and infectious smiles are adorable.

We lean over the alligator enclosure while eating our ice-creams, Keen absolutely covered in his. "This has been the best day ever," Keen declares through his melting chocolate ice-cream.

I glance at Con and smile. He leans in closer to me so only I can hear his reply. "Couldn't agree more, watching you lick that ice-cream has made my cock rock hard." He grasps my hand and brushes it against his hardness, making me gasp. My eyes quickly dart down to Keen, who is completely unaware of his father's predicament.

I flit my eyes back at Con and raise an eyebrow at his flirtatious smile. Leaning into him, I whisper into his ear. "Later your cock is going to drip more than ice-cream, believe me, I'll be covered in your cum." I pull back and watch Con's eyes flare with lust. His eyes dart to my lips, so I give my ice-cream a seductive flick of my tongue before covering it with my mouth, mimicking my promise.

Con's mouth parts and a low, "Fuck," is muttered. I smile internally at his reaction.

The day has been amazing, the weather beautiful, and we're now sitting at the picnic table with our lunches spread out in front of us. I sit opposite Con. The sexual tension between us is off the charts. We've spent the morning touching one another or brushing each other and passing sexual remarks to one another. Tonight, is going to be explosive. I can sense it and I cannot wait. I clench my thighs together in anticipation.

"Which animal has been your favorite so far, Keen?" Con asks him while munching on carrot sticks.

Keen removes his cap, sits up a little straighter and taps his finger against his chin, thinking hard. "Ooo, the monkeys because the tiger was too lazy to do anything."

He makes us both laugh. "He was probably tired and needed a sleep," I explain.

"Nope, he's meant to be Roarsome and run sixty miles per hour. He didn't even lift his head to say hi."

Con laughs. "How do you know how fast they run, dude?"

"Reece told me. He also said that daddy tigers can eat the cubs so they can have more babies with mommy tiger."

My eyebrows raise a little shocked. "Okay, well let's not talk about daddy tigers eating babies."

Con stifles a chuckle.

"When I get a daddy, I'm going to bring him here, to this zoo. He's going to love it," Keen states proudly, with his little shoulders pulled back.

Both me and Con stare at one another before Con quickly glances away, his jaw working hard. He sighs out a deep breath and turns his cap around to cover his eyes, his Adam's apple bobs. Shit.

"And I bet my daddy will love monkeys the best, too. And chocolate ice-cream," Keen continues, completely unaware of the change in atmosphere.

My heart races a mile a minute considering what to do. Do I risk telling Keen that Con is his father and risk breaking his heart when he doesn't step up?

Then again, today we have acted like a normal family. Is it really fair of me to keep this hidden? At some point, Keen will find out the truth. I've no doubt about that anymore and honestly, now is the time for it to be known. Con isn't going anywhere and if he does, his family sure as hell won't.

I take a deep breath and turn to Keen. "Keen, sweetheart, Mommy has something important to tell you." I glance at Con, but he's completely facing away from us, staring at nothing. Oblivious to what I'm about to say.

Keen stops eating his sandwich, giving me his attention. "You have a daddy honey and he's right here." I point at Con.

Keen's eyebrows furrow in confusion, so I go onto explain. "Con was away for a while, but he came back to us as soon as he could. Now that we know he's staying, he's going to be your daddy forever."

Keen's eyes widen and then his face lights up in a smile. "He is?"

"He is, sweetheart."

"Fuck, Will." My eyes meet Con's, his face streaked in tears, his hands visibly shaking. "Come here, little dude." He pulls Keen onto his lap, and they hug one another.

"You aren't going away ever again, right?" Keen asks him.

"Never dude, I swear it."

I swallow thickly, overcome with emotion, as I watch Con bury his head into Keen's thick, wavy hair.

We drive home in a comfortable silence, Keen fast asleep after playing tag with Con on the playground and then going into the splash area. We stayed there until the sun went down and Keen was literally dropping.

Con takes my hand and kisses it gently. "Thank you for today, Will. Fuck, I never thought you'd do it, baby." His eyes lock onto mine and then they move back to the road.

"You deserve this Con, you're a great dad to Keen. You deserve the name to go with it."

Con chokes on emotion. "Fuck baby. You're killing me here. This has been the best day of my life, you know that?" Vulnerability is shining through in his voice and words.

I pull his hand to my lips and place a kiss on his. "Mine too."

He side eyes me. "Yeah?" I nod in agreement. "Better than any outings with Jack?" His insecurities make me want to laugh and scream all in one. I settle on a smile and a nod, and he grins in return.

Con carries Keen to his room, a stuffed monkey tucked under one arm and a tiger under the other.

I head straight for the shower, dropping my clothes to the floor and stepping into the hot water, the heat soothing my skin. I close my eyes as the water cascades over my head.

The possessive touch of Con's hands grasping at my breasts, my eyes dart open, his naked hardness pushes against my back. His hands fumble roughly with my tits, playing with my nipples. Con pushes his face into my neck and sucks on my skin, causing me to moan desperately.

"Con, you're going to mark me." I panic thinking of the family party tomorrow and me showing up with a hickey like a teenager.

"Damn fucking right I'm marking you. I'm going to make sure Jack knows who you belong to." My mind slowly registers what he's saying, the fact that Jack is going to be at the family party is making him insecure, another reason why Keen deserved to know the truth about Con. He needed to realize who his blood family are.

"Fuck baby, are you wet for me?" He palms my pussy with one hand while grasping my breast with the other. "So fucking wet for my cock." I moan at his dirty words.

"Turn around so I can fuck you while you watch me, Will." His deep lust filled voice sends shivers down my spine.

I slowly turn around to face him. His pupils blown, overtaking the blue in his eyes. His cock stands straight, already dripping with arousal. Fuck, he's hot. As if hearing my thoughts, he lunges forward and picks me up. My legs tighten around his waist on instinct as he plunges into me, hitting my back against the tiled wall. He holds me under my ass and leans against the wall with his other arm.

Con kisses up and down my neck and jawline, igniting the passion between us. Wetness gathers inside me as he sucks on my neck. He hits the sweet spot inside me. "Jesus, Con, there. Right there." He swivels his hips, the motion making me moan into his mouth that's now exploring mine.

I grip his ass as he thrusts relentlessly into me. His finger trails down my ass cheeks before dipping further down. He then pushes it inside my tight hole, making me instantly see stars. I erupt from the inside out. My pussy pulsating on his cock, milking him for every drop of his thick cum. "Ahhhh Fuucckkk Will. Fuck." His body stills, but his cock continues to pulse, releasing every spurt deep inside.

His mouth finds mine again, his tongue exploring mine. I can feel him hardening once again. "Fuck baby, need to fuck you again." He laughs to himself.

I grab his chin and bring his mouth back to mine; he closes his eyes, embracing me passionately.

Con switches off the shower and carries me through the bathroom into the bedroom. Gripping my hips, he pulls me off of him and throws me onto the bed, my wet hair whipping my back at the force.

Con disappears into the bathroom again before returning with a bottle of baby oil and a sexy smirk. I smile at him and raise an eyebrow, licking my lips passionately, making his cock jump at the motion.

"On your knees, baby."

I smile and roll onto my stomach before pushing up on

to my arms, my ass in the air. Con walks behind me. He moans in appreciation. "Fuck, you're incredible." He grips my ass cheek for emphasis. I push back into his palm, encouraging him.

I hear the cap of the oil flick open, then the sensation of warmth drizzles down the lower part of my back, seeping into my ass and down as far as my pussy. Oil is dripping onto the sheets.

Con's large hands start palming my ass, rubbing the oil into my skin. I moan at the sensation.

He grips my hips and pulls me to the edge of the bed, my ass the perfect height for him. His finger trails down my spine before dipping into my puckered hole, he gently plays with it. Prodding his finger in and out while his other hand caresses my cheek. I gaze back over my shoulder, Con's eyes transfixed on my ass. His teeth nestled tightly against his lip, the tendons in his neck throbbing. Jesus, he's so damn gorgeous.

"You let him fuck your ass, Will?" he grunts, his voice darkened.

I shake my head no. "I told him I didn't want it."

His finger stops with the prodding. "You saved it for me, baby? You saved your ass for me like you did with your pussy?" His voice sounds of disbelief.

I nod again, not using my words. Followed by experiencing the sharp sting of the slap to my ass. "Did you, Will?"

"Yes. I saved it for you." I pant.

"Fuck, yes. You did, baby, you saved your ass for me. I'm going to fuck it so good, baby." His voice coos heavily with lust.

His filthy words killing me. "Jesus Con." I moan shamelessly.

He chuckles. "Yeah baby. I'm going to fuck you real good."

I can feel another finger added to my hole, stretching me. "Play with your pussy, Will. Tell me when you're close."

My hand immediately goes down to my clit, and I begin to rub frantically. His hand joins mine, rubbing my wet clit together. "Fuck, that's hot," he groans from behind, his heavy breathing heard throughout the room.

"Con, that's so good. Please."

"Please what, baby?"

"I need more."

"You want my cock in your ass, Will? Say it," he spits out.

My hand twirls around my clit, the wetness gathering. "Oh, my god, Con. Please. Please fuck my ass."

"Oh Jesus," he grunts before pushing his cock into my ass without any more preparation or sensitivity. The force of his action pushes me up the bed, but he quickly pulls his hand out from my pussy and grips my hips. The sting in my ass forces my legs to widen to try and encourage my impending orgasm.

"Fuck baby. I can't move. If I move, I'm gonna come. So, fucking tight." Con talks through gritted teeth. "Keep playing with your pussy, Will. I want you to cum with my cock in your ass."

"Oh, shit Con. Move, please move." My words are desperate.

I stare over my shoulder at him. He's shaking his head. His whole body tight with tension, trying to ease off his orgasm. "Fuck." He breathes through clenched teeth.

My pussy pulsates, and I issue my warning, "Con!"

"Fuck yeah." He moves, driving in and out of my ass.

The burning sensation almost overwhelming. I place my face onto the mattress so I can move a hand to my breast and tweak my nipple.

"Fuck baby, you look incredible with my cock in your tight ass. Fucking come!" he roars.

And just like that, I scream his name as he drives himself home one more time before I feel the pulse of his cock deep inside me. My legs shake at the force of my orgasm.

Con collapses on top of me, his cock going soft inside my ass.

"Fuck. That was incredible." He moves my wet hair to the side of my face, and I can feel him smiling into my neck. "Got all your firsts, didn't I Will?"

I can't help but smile back at his jealous, childlike behavior. "You did."

"Too fucking right, I did. I own you." He rolls me onto my back, making me wince when his dick pulls out of me. His handsome face staring back at me with pure love shining through his eyes. His forehead touches mine as he gently kisses my lips. "Love you so fucking much, baby."

Gently, I kiss him back. "I love you too, Connor." I hold his eyes with the truth of my words seeping between us. His shoulders slacken at my confession.

Both smiling at one another before he lays down and pulls me into him. My head resting on his chest, he trails his fingers over my spine as I fall into a deep sleep.

Chapter Twenty-Four

Con

This morning has been truly amazing. I got to witness my son's birthday. The little excitable bundle of joy woke us super early, making it appear like Christmas morning. His excitement and smile are completely infectious. My own cheeks fucking hurt, for Christ's sake I've smiled that much.

Me and Will spent last night trimming up the apartment. Animal balloons and banners adorn the room, declaring the birthday boy is four years old.

I made Will and Keen pancakes and even mastered how to create animal faces on them with fruit. Keen's smile lit up his whole cute face.

We watched Keen together as he tore into his gifts. A new scooter, LEGOs and Paw Patrol rescue sets were the main ones. I fucking loved every second of it. I can't wait until later at the party when I tell Will I bought us a house in the same gated community as Cal. It's got a huge fucking garden that's ideal for the scooter. I'm going to install Keen, a pirate ship, similar to Cal's but bigger, better. Probably a trampoline park or something, too. Oh, and he loves water slides, so definitely one of those. Yeah, it's going to be perfect. Best. Fucking. Birthday. Ever.

Will explained earlier that me and Keen needed to go and collect a bundle of cupcakes from Sweet Treatz, in town while she and the family organized the party, so me and my little dude were now scanning the goodies in the store.

"Daddy..." Fuck, that melts my heart. "Can I please have some of those candies?" Keen points to the self-serve pick and mix display with his little finger. He's bouncing on the balls of his feet. Kid has a sugar rush without the sugar. I smile to myself.

"Let's have a look, dude." I go over to the stand and as I pick up the paper bag, the bell above the door chimes. Peering down at Keen and he breaks out in a huge grin, knowing he's won me over; I smile back at him happily.

"Con, can I speak with you please?" a slurring voice comes from behind me, causing my spine to straighten in defense. Shit.

I spin on my heels and glare directly into the eyes of Lena. Her makeup smudged, her mascara oozing down her face and her pupils blown the fuck out. I trail my eyes down her body. Her clothes are disheveled, and she looks like shit. Jesus, I scrub a hand through my hair.

"Daddy." Keen's voice cuts through my analysis of Lena. Fuck.

"Yo... you have a li... little boy?" she slurs, causing my lip to turn up in disgust at her even breathing the same air as Keen at the minute.

I turn to Keen and bend down to his level. "Keen buddy, can you fill your bag with candies while Daddy talks to his friend?" He nods his head eagerly with a grin.

I turn back to Lena, who appears struggling to stand. I grip her forearm and drag her into the corner of the room. "What the fuck are you doing here, Lena?" I drag my hand through my hair in frustration. I don't need this right now.

"I need help." Her body is shaking, probably from a comedown.

"No fucking kidding, you look like shit, Lena." I exhale with annoyance. My words causing her to wince.

"Ple... please Con. Can you get me into a rehab or something? I can't keep doing this. I... I don't know where I woke up today. Can you? Can you please help me? Please," she begs, her voice full of vulnerability and desperation.

Jesus, I can't deal with this right now. I glance back at Keen. He's happily filling his bag with free rein. "I'm scared Con. I don't think... I'm scared another hit might kill me. My dad, he's thrown me out. You're my only hope. Please." Her eyes shine with unshed tears. The girl is a mess.

Sure, I've never had feelings for her, but I can't just walk away and leave her when I could do something to help. I glance at Keen again, knowing what I'm about to do will not go down well with Will. I stare up at the ceiling and breathe out. Shit, can I really do this? Surely once I explain she'd be proud of me, right? I might not have been able to save my brother, but I can save Lena.

My hands tremble with the uncertainty but when I look back into Lena's eyes, I know my mind is made up; I need to get her help into rehab ASAP.

"Keen, that's enough for now, buddy. Let's pay and get you to your party." Keen turns with a bag full of goodies and nods his head.

Fuck, this is going to be a disaster. Anxiety ripples through me.

Chapter Twenty-Five

Will

So far today has been amazing, a crazy, bustling day. But amazing. I cannot wait for Keen and Con to get here. The place looks so incredible. Keen's going to love it.

The gardens at Con's family home have been transformed into a child's paradise. A bouncy castle in the shape of a tiger, taking up a quarter of the grounds. A ball pit that Chloe is determined to get into, a face painter and candy floss station are situated alongside the tiger castle. Huge bright coloured animal balloons littered everywhere.

Con's mom Cyn has insisted on doing all the catering, she absolutely loves it. The attention to detail on the monkey cookies is incredible. A cake maker has created a masterpiece of a four tired jungle cake and Con has taken Keen to collect the cupcakes as a distraction while we get everything ready.

"My feckin garden looks like a feckin zoo!" A broad voice bellows across the grounds. We all spin our attention toward Brennan, who is standing with his hands on his hips in the kitchen doorway, taking in his surroundings.

"Looks great, hey, Da." Cal cheerily pats his father on his back, ignoring Brennan's remarks, causing him to grunt in disapproval.

Cal has been like a hyper child all afternoon, coming up with one elaborate idea after another. Lily has been rolling her eyes at every suggestion he mentioned. How they managed to have a low-key wedding with his enthusiasm, I'll never know.

I place the multicolored streamers on the cake table as a finishing touch when Oscar declares, "they're here," only vaguely raising his head from his tablet.

I glance over at Jack, who greets me with a warm smile. It instantly disappears when he looks at something over the top of my head. I turn to see where his eyes are fixed and instantly see Brennan glaring with sheer contempt in Jack's direction. I move over to Jack and brush my hand along his arm in support. His eyes follow the movement, and he faces me with a knowing nod at my support.

Keen leaps from the backseat of the car, causing Cyn to chuckle as we all shout, "Happy Birthday!"

We all greet him with hugs, fist pumps, high fives and kisses before he runs off to join Reece on the bouncy castle.

I wait for Con to approach, but he's holding back, shifting from foot to foot in the same spot by the car uncomfortably. I begin to walk over to him and the sound of the gravel beneath my feet causes his head to shoot up and his eyes to meet mine. They're completely panicked and vulnerable.

"Con, what's going on?"

Con brushes his hand through his hair in a clear telltale sign of nervousness. He quickly glances back at the car and directly at the passenger seat. A slumped body is resting against the window.

My heart pounds. What the hell is going on?

Con swallows thickly, his chest heaving with anxiety. "Shit. I, erm... I didn't want to do this." He waves his hand at the car.

I narrow my eyes in frustration. What is he talking about?

As if sensing my confusion, Con explains. "She needs help, Will. I can't just leave her. I need to get her to rehab. She has nobody else."

My mouth goes dry as it registers. The slumped body is that of Lena, the girl who was flirting up a storm with him at the charity event. The girl he did coke with. Lena, the girl he's currently ditching us for.

He had my son in a car with her? A junkie? His quickie? Oh Jesus! My legs tremble and my heart races.

"Baby, please don't be mad at me. I'll be gone an hour, tops. I'm dropping her at rehab, then I'm coming straight back, I swear." He steps toward me with his arms open. I step back.

"You had her in the car with Keen?" I cry out.

His body jolts, as if just realizing that mistake.

"I... I didn't have time to think. I didn't want him to be late for the party. Please Will, I didn't want to disappoint anyone. Didn't want to disappoint you, Will." He explains, his voice sounding unsure and trembly.

I nod in understanding, but my jaw tics in annoyance.

I turn my back as Jack approaches.

"Will. Will, please. I'll be an hour, I swear." I ignore him and walk toward Jack, Cal now crossing the garden with Chloe to join us.

I listen to the car door slam and the gravel churn as Con speeds away, taking part of my heart with him.

I close my eyes and pull myself together.

"Where the hell is he going?" Cal asks looking toward the SUV.

"Apparently he's taking Lena to rehab." I try to mask my voice and hope it sounds indifferent, but I'm sure I fail miserably.

Cal grips my arm to stop me from walking past. "Seriously?" I dip my head in confirmation, barely able to look into his eyes as I hold back the tears of disappointment. I wanted this to be special. Keen's first birthday with us all, yet his daddy isn't even here.

And as if on cue, Keen comes barreling toward us with a Candy floss in hand and a sweaty forehead. "Where's Daddy? I wanna show him how high I can bounce."

"I'm going to fucking kill him," Cal spits his words out, storming away.

"Come on, buddy, you can show me." Jack smiles softly in my direction as he leads Keen away.

I wrap my arms around myself, sadness and helplessness encompassing me.

A giggle breaks me from my thoughts. I glance over my shoulder and find Jack holding Keen's hands as they bounce happily on the bouncy castle. Yet another sign of Jack's continual support and another stark reminder of Con's abandonment. A shudder runs through my body, the disillusion of us being a family a blow to my heart.

He'll never put us first.

I check my watch again and sigh at the time. We've been hanging on for Keen to blow out his candles on his cake, but Con is still nowhere to be seen almost two hours later.

I turn my head and I'm greeted with a dozen sympathetic eyes, all whispering words of disapproval and annoyance at Con. My heart breaks for me, for Keen and also Con. He's disappointed us all when he promised he'd be someone better.

"When the fuck are we eating cake?" Reece grunts. His eyes transfixed on the cake.

I stare at my watch again. "Can we just give it five more minutes?" I look up at Cal with pleading eyes. His angered eyes soften, and he nods, a struggling smile gracing his lips.

Chapter Twenty-Six

Will

My phone chimes as we sing "Happy Birthday," to Keen. I fumble with it, pulling it out of my pocket with haste.

My eyes quickly scan the screen, I don't recognize the number, but I open the message with curiosity.

All the wind is instantly knocked out of me. A photo of Con in the cupcake store with Lena. He's staring down at her with his hand on her arm, protectively. I squint at the image; my little boy is in the background helping himself to the treats.

Anger boils inside me. How dare they meet at the sweet store with my son? Is he using drugs again? The girl clearly looks high, a mess. He should be watching our son, protecting our son, not this trash.

"Will, everything okay?" Bren asks, nudging me with concern on his face.

I shake my head and push the phone into his chest, unable to speak as my chest heaves in anger. Bren's eyes take in the screen. "Fucking bastard. I warned him to stay away from her. What the hell is he playing at?" he spits, his veins bulging in his forehead.

I walk away to compose myself. The hurt and anger are overflowing, and I need a drink. A strong drink. "Hey, everything all right, Will?" Lily asks as I approach the patio table.

I sit down beside her and a sleeping Chloe. I can't help but soften as I stare at her angelic face sleeping in her mommy's lap. She's normally so attached to Cal.

I shrug my shoulders at Lily. "Disappointed, I guess." She pours me a wine and pushes it in my direction.

"Yeah. I think we all are. We were expecting so much better. I don't understand it. Con's been buzzing all week about this weekend. Where do you think he collected her from?"

"I just got a text with a photo of them together in the cupcake store. I'm so angry with him, Lily. He had Keen with him. If he doesn't want this," I gesture to me and Keen, "then he needs to say. I can't deal with the childish behavior. It's draining and making me an emotional wreck. I don't want Keen getting hurt, either. He's been asking for Con all afternoon."

Lily sighs heavily. "Seriously, if Cal tried any of that shit, he'd have some serious making up to do." She looks at me pointedly.

I laugh almost sarcastically. "Cal is absolutely attached to your kids' hip, Lily. He's more mommy than you," I point out in jest, but if I'm honest, I feel a pang of jealousy at their secure family unit.

Lily throws her head back, laughing. "I know, right? I mean, if he could breastfeed, he would, and boy would I have let him do that, it was hell." She looks out at the garden with an anguished expression on her face, as if even remembering breastfeeding causes her pain. I smile at her.

"Oh, my god no!" she shrieks, jumping up and waking a startled Chloe in the process. I follow her line of sight and find Pussy sitting on the tiered cake eating at the third tier with her paw digging in for good measure. Chloe's shrieks jump Cal into action, running over to take her from Lily, her little hands grabbing for her daddy.

"Shoot the feckin thing!" Brennan shouts across the garden. "Shoot it."

Reece glares at him with hatred. "I'll shoot you in the dick if you touch my fucking cat!" he spits, while stomping over to Puss. He gently picks the cat up and nuzzles into its fur. Lifting a chocolate animal from the cake, he offers it to Puss, who licks it daintily, oblivious to the drama around him.

"Will! Will! *Fuck, come quick*!" Bren's panic ridden voice booms across the garden as I jump up from the chair at the loud desperation in his voice.

Everyone rushes toward Bren, who is on the grass. My heart pounds as I rush to him.

My heart and mind shatter as I approach and find my baby struggling to breathe. "There's something wrong with him, what's wrong with him Will?" Bren quizzes, his eyes meeting mine laced with panic.

My mind won't work, my body won't process anything, I'm numb, unable to answer as my little boy's chest heaves up and down with a wheeze.

"Nuts," Oscar states. My eyes scan the grass and sure enough, the candy bag is beside Keen. "Someone call 911. Tell them it's a nut allergy." Oscar dictates as he types on his tablet. Finn walks away with his phone to his ear, his voice loud with fear.

I'm glued to the spot, unable to move.

"Will. Will. Will, snap the fuck out of it!" Jack snaps and grabs my arm. "Where's his EpiPen?"

I can't get my words out or think straight, my eyes transfixed on my babies lips, they're turning blue. He's dying. Oh, my god he's dying. "Will!"

"Table, my bag. Table. Please..." I crumple to the floor as Jack rushes off to the table.

I can hear voices beside me as I hold my baby's hand. They feel clammy. His tiny lips are open and swollen.

"Dad, is he going to be okay?" I can hear Reece. "Dad, make him okay." He's tugging on his hair and screeching loudly.

"Fuck. Lily, for fuck's sake, move Reece." She shuffles away with her arm draped around Reece, consoling him.

Jack kneels beside me but I'm shaking all over. I can't see clearly through the tears. Jack's frantic hands work on the pen, and he inserts it into Keen's thigh. "Come on buddy." He gently strokes Keen's face. The wheeze is still audible. "Please come on," he begs, the tremble in his voice clear, showing his concern.

I numbly stare up and meet Cyn's eyes. She's crying into Brennan's arms, barely able to stand.

I vaguely hear sirens, but my body isn't registering anything other than my baby is dying in front of me.

"Someone please help him," I desperately beg. My lips quiver, and my throat is dry.

"Coming through." the paramedics push through us and begin to work on Keen as Jack gives a run-down on what has happened. A frantic barrage of medical terminology and supplies are used as I stand helplessly to the side. Begging internally for a miracle. My mind a complete mess.

Finn stands behind me and pulls me into his side,

offering me comfort and support. My teeth tremble in shock and I whimper through tears. He holds me tighter. "Shh, it's okay sweetheart, they're doing everything they can. He's going to be fine, I'm sure. He's a little fighter, right?"

"We're going to take him straight through to Emergency Care, you're all welcome to follow behind." One paramedic nods at Bren.

I follow blindly behind the paramedics as they load Keen into the ambulance. Jack guiding and supporting me helps me in beside him.

I glance around the gardens of the party. Only moments ago it was full of fun and laughter and now it's a somber sense of foreboding and heartbreak.

The ambulance doors close, locking me in an eternal nightmare.

Chapter Twenty-Seven

Con

Driving Lena to rehab has taken so much longer than I expected. The girl has some serious issues and, quite honestly; it scared the fuck out of me. The drugs have completely taken over her body and now have full control. Depending on them is too soft a word, they own her. Completely fucking own her.

Lena underwent a full-blown meltdown when I tried handing her over to her doctor. In the end, they had to sedate her. I'm completely drained at the entire experience and now as I get back into my car, I take a deep breath at the thoughts of what I'm going to have to deal with back home.

I only hope Will can see my point of view and is actually proud of me for the decision I made, no matter how shitty the timing was.

I scrub a hand through my hair and pick up my phone.

My breath catches in my throat as I notice the number of missed calls and messages, no doubt calling me out on by a crappy father, husband, and brother. I sigh as I click on the first one.

Oscar: Family emergency call me ASAP.

Finn: Where the fuck are you, dude? We need you.

Oscar: This is serious.

Bren: Gonna fucking kill ya, man. Get your ass home.

Cal: We're headed to St Thomas Hospital, meet us there.

Oscar: Please call.

Reece: Its Keen. Hurry.

I read the last text and my blood runs cold. I still. My mind is blank. "It's Keen. Hurry." The words play over and over in my mind on a loop.

Jesus. It's Keen.

My hands tremble as I try to call Finn. Straight to fucking voicemail.

I accidentally hit the wrong button as I scroll through

my phone to call Cal. No answer. I blow out a breath and a pained noise leaves my body. Desperate.

I try Bren. No answer. I drag my hand through my hair. Why is no one answering? A sickness overwhelms me, the same sickness I felt when my brother Keenan... I swing open the car door, fighting for breath. I can't breathe. I can't fucking breathe. Someone help me. Please God, someone help me.

My legs shake as I struggle to stand. Fuck, I feel dizzy. Bending my knees and swooping my head down, I bend over and take deep breaths. Anything to try and stop myself from vomiting or having a panic attack. My throat is dry, my heart pounding. My legs feel like jelly.

Deep breaths in. Out. In. Out. In. Out.

Slowly I can feel myself calming. My hands are still shaking, and I wish like fuck someone was here with me. No, not just someone. I need Will. Will and my boy. Fuck.

The thought startles me into action, and I climb back into the car.

I bite my lip in frustration with myself as I stare down at my phone, trying to make myself take action, to do something. But my mind seems slow on the uptake. Why do I get like this? What the fuck is wrong with me?

Jesus.

I need to get to St. Thomas. I start the engine.

Con

The drive to St. Thomas Hospital has taken me thirty minutes and I don't even know how I got here. I abandon my car at the entrance. Slamming the door behind me, I race around to the front of the hospital.

"Con, wait!" Oscar's no nonsense voice cuts through me, stilling me on the spot.

I spin on my heel and come face to face with Oscar. A very pale-looking Oscar. He's trembling slightly and struggling to meet my eye. What the fuck is happening? I'm not sure if his behavior is down to his aversion to being at a hospital or whatever the fuck is going on with Keen. I exhale sharply.

"It's bad, Connor, but they're stabilizing him." His voice is full of sympathy.

I jolt at his words.

"Floor six room four."

I nod and rush past him.

The elevator takes too fucking long.

But finally, I can breathe when the doors open, and I push out into the family waiting area.

Everyone is here, all our family. I lick my dry lips and push forward.

The atmosphere in the room stills, as one at a time as they lift their heads to meet my eyes.

Bren pushes past the group from the back. I think he's going to tell me what's happened, but then his face contorts into unadulterated rage and disgust. Then his fist hits my face, causing me to fall back onto my ass. I'm overwhelmed with shock; my mouth drops open. Because what the fuck?

"You lowlife, useless piece of shit. Get the fuck out of here before I kill you myself," my brother spits. The veins in his temple and throat protruding.

My eyes dart away from the tower of a man above me to the whimper of a woman, my mother. Her head is buried in my father's neck, his arms tightly bounded around her. He never holds her in public. Never comforts her. Even when she has one of her 'Teddy episodes', as he calls them. The severity of the situation engulfs me. My mind scrambles to piece together what the hell is happening.

My words come out choppy, "Wh... what the fuck is goin on?" I begin to stand on trembling feet. Finn's hand tightens on Bren's arm, keeping him from me.

Cal steps forward, away from Lily. Her face streaked with tears.

"Where the fuck is my boy?" My heart races frantically inside me. "Where's Will?" I panic as I shake myself down.

"I'll tell you where the fuck your boy is, shall I?" Cal sneers. My brother is normally the sensitive one of the bunch. Our connection normally strong. But not today, not now.

"He's got tubes attached to him. Helping him fucking breathe, Con!" his words come out hurt. His lips quiver. I lick my own lips. "You fucking let him eat nuts. Nuts!" His voice shakes as he turns his back on me to try and control himself.

His words whirl around in my mind. Did I? No. No. I never. I shake the thoughts off. I didn't.

Desperation overtakes me. "I didn't. I swear I didn't." Shaking my head desperately, "When the fuck did that happen?" Uncertainty coats every word.

He spins on his heel to face me, laughing condescendingly, then his eyes narrow and his words turn venomous. "When you were with the little junkie slut, you rescued today. When you left your fucking son to choose his own candy. He chose fucking nuts!" My heart stops. I swear it stops. My whole body shutting down.

My heart ripped from my chest.

An open cavity.

"He could die." Bren's words cut into me. I can't fucking breathe; my heart has stopped.

"Fucking die, Connor." His finger points at me. Me, I did this.

My eyes meet Finn's, and he nods solemnly in confirmation. He could die. I choke on thin air. On nothing.

I don't know what to say. What do I say to that?

I hold my body up with my hand against the wall.

"Jack was right, you know. They were better off without you." Cal sneers the words out while shaking his head in revulsion. His words cutting to the core of my heart. Severing any ties to keep it beating. Any ties of any hope. Hope for my family.

My head drops. A gut-wrenching pain overrides the sickness I previously felt.

Bren's words rage from him. "Get the fuck out of here. You're not wanted here, Con. If Will sees you here, fuck." At the mention of Will, my eyes shoot up to my brothers.

They meet mine with menacing glares. I stare at their bodies. They've created a barrier between me and the room beyond them.

A barrier between me and them.

My boy.

Will.

My family.

Cal's words are soft but firm. Deliberate. "You're not needed Con. You never were." I suck in a breath.

How am I still breathing, and my baby isn't?

Without another thought, I turn and walk away.

Away from my family.

Away from my responsibilities.

My love.

My life.

Chapter Twenty-Eight

Broken, empty, a shell of my former self

Desperate, despondent, void of emotion.

Con

I walk out the doors of St Thomas Hospital with a sense of clarity.

The cold air hits me, a chill in the wind reminds me to breathe.

I vaguely recognize a voice calling me somewhere in the distance. It somehow registers as my brother, Oscar's. But I keep walking.

My feet move, one in front of the other. They know where they're going. They don't need me to tell them they're on autopilot.

As I walk through the bustling streets, I feel nothing.

Empty, lifeless. Void of feeling. My mind and thoughts don't exist. They're blank. Non-existent. Nothing.

Bodies move by me. Going about their day-to-day business. The occasional one does a double take. What they see? I'm not sure. I don't care enough to think about it. Maybe someone without a soul. A purpose. Without a family. A life. Nothing.

I shut the door of our apartment. The click of the lock engages and reminds me to continue with my actions. The numbness needs to go away. I need to go away.

Cal's words whirl around fuzzily inside my head. "You're not needed, Con. You never were."

I gasp at the truth within them. I never was needed.

Bren. "You're not wanted here, Con. If Will sees you here, fuck." He's right, I'm not wanted. And Jesus. Will; she'll hate me. I hate myself.

My father. "She was too good for you, that girl. Too fucking good!" He's right, she is too good for me. They deserve better. They both do.

Will. "You leave! You do what you're good at, you turn your back, and you go!" Will's right, I need to do what I'm good at.

Never needed. Not wanted. Hate. Deserve better. Go. Leave.

My feet stumble to a halt. I struggle to lift my heavy head. Someone stares back at me. This guy. I don't recognize him. His eyes are empty. Black underneath them. His cheek swollen. But it's his eyes. His haunting eyes. I swallow thickly for the guy reflecting back at me. They're empty, nothing left to give.

Nothing left to love.

Useless, worthless, unwanted, filled with self-loathing.
Shattered into a thousand pieces, fractured,
Destroyed beyond repair.
Save me from myself,
I need you to show me you care.

With shaking hands, I open the mirrored bathroom cabinet and sieve through the various products until I find what I'm looking for, the valium I was prescribed when my brother died. When Will left.

When I was alone.

I welcome the darkness.

The emptiness.

I unscrew the cap and close my eyes.

Chapter Twenty-Nine

Will

My hands gently clutch Keen's. His tiny warm hand a reminder of the life within him. My thankful heart stutters.

The doctors managed to stabilize him. He reacted well to the drugs they'd given him and are confident he will make a full recovery. His breathing tubes have been removed, and he's now sleeping. His body resting.

To say it was a close call would be an understatement. I feel overwhelmingly traumatized at today's events. But above all that, I cannot believe my baby is going to recover. My heart quickens when I recall the turmoil of the day.

I push them aside. Because Keen is here. He's safe, and he's going to get better. I drop my head into my hands and say another silent prayer to the God I didn't believe in until today.

Movement at the door makes me rise my head.

My eyebrows furrow together at the sight before me. Oscar stands ramrod straight against the door, shoulders tense, terror littered over his face, sweat drips visibly from his forehead. My eyes widen at the sight, he's normally so well put together.

I know he has a phobia of hospitals. Something I've always been aware of. But this? This is something else. It's off the chart's phobia. He looks... dreadful.

"Oscar, you didn't have to come. I understand how difficult it is for you."

He holds his hands up to stop me talking, the rudeness of his motion making me jolt.

He brushes the sweat from his forehead, then sneers down at his hand, at his own bodily fluids. "It's not that." He licks his lips before breathing out and explaining. "Well, its partially that. But I wouldn't have come in here if I didn't feel it was abundantly necessary."

I glance down at Keen. Unclear with what Oscar is trying to tell me. Keen's over the worst. So why is it necessary to be here now and not before?

Oscar, being the genius he is, reads my mind. "I'm not here for you. Or Keen." Ouch. If I didn't know better, I'd have taken offense at Oscar's words. But I know better, and I know what Oscar means is, he's simply here for an entirely different reason.

I watch him fidget with his hands.

"It's Con, Will." My eyes dart to his in temper. My jaw ticking in anger. He holds up a hand. "Please hear me out."

His jaw moves angrily from side to side. Before sneering, "I've tried talking to them." He tilts his head toward the door, referring to his family. "They don't understand. Con, I mean, they don't understand him, his struggles." His eyes vulnerably meet mine and I nod in acknowledgement of his words. The fact his family appears completely oblivious to Con's struggles.

Oscar's shoulders relax slightly at my confirmation before he continues on. "He was here earlier. I'm not sure if they told you?" I shake my head. No, they didn't. But then again, I don't want him here. Do I?

I stare down at Keen. He'd want his daddy; the thought sends a pained rush to my heart. His daddy let him down. I rub at the pain.

"Please Will. I... I'm worried." His words shake from his mouth, causing my eyes to dart to his.

He swallows thickly. "He left here in a mess. I'm not sure what they said but. Fuck, Will. He didn't hear me call him. He was in a trance. A screwed-up mess. I've never seen him so bad, not even after..." After his brother's death, he means but doesn't say it. This is bad. Very bad.

"I've tried to call him." Oscar stares down at his phone as if double checking it to see if he has any calls.

"I've checked the cameras above his door. He went in, but he hasn't come out." Oscar's face is normally a mask of indifference. Emotionless. But right now, right now, this is the first time I've ever seen despair on Oscar. The thought causes a wave of sickness to flow through me. He's scared for Con.

Well, me too.

I almost choke on my emotion as I utter. "Okay." Oscar visibly relaxes. "Can you come with me?" I ask him, worry coating my words.

He nods dramatically with relief. "Yes. Yes, of course. I'll text Jack. Ask him to stay with Keen." He inclines his head toward Keen's bed. I give him a curt bow of my head in agreement.

I cast my eyes down at my little boy and kiss his forehead gently. Nuzzling into his curls and scent.

"Mommy will be back soon, buddy. I'm going to fetch Daddy." I smile tightly through my own words.

I only hope I've not just lied to my little boy. I hope I'm not too late.

I spend the car journey chewing my skin on the side of my finger. Oscar's hand tight on the steering wheel.

"Do you know what they said to him?" I quiz.

"No. I wasn't there. I don't do hospitals," Oscar's blunt voice responds, and I nod in understanding. He doesn't do hospitals. But he did. For Con.

"Nothing nice would have come from them, I'm sure." He admits. Again, I nod.

"I know you don't want to hear this..." My eyes dart to his, my jaw ticking in annoyance because he's about to give a speech about how Con's screw up wasn't his fault. Oscar looks forward and doesn't meet my eyes. "Whatever he thought he was doing. He thought he was doing right. I think he was trying to save her." He looks at me pointedly. He swallows thickly. "Because he didn't save Keenan."

My breath catches in my throat and tears fill my eyes. I bite my lip to stifle the sob, desperate to escape me. He's right, of course. I shake my head. He was trying to redeem himself.

To be a better man.

I close my eyes and wish the journey to hurry along, my legs bouncing with anxiety.

The elevator doors slide open, painfully slow.

I push past them on a mission.

I scan my finger against the security screen.

The door unlocks, and I enter the living room. I scan my eyes around the room. It's just how we left it this morning. Banners and balloons litter the empty room, Keen's stuffed animal toys sit at the dining table.

Remnants of the animal pancakes Con made for us left on the kitchen counter.

I clutch at the pain in my chest.

"Con?" Oscar pushes past me and heads to the den.

I move swiftly into the master suite. The room Con normally leaves locked.

The door is ajar. I push it further open and step foot over the threshold.

My heart pounds erratically in my chest as I take in the empty room. Its eerily silent.

"Con?" Nothing. I can hear Oscar shouting his name from the other side of the corridor. No doubt checking my room, Keen's.

I gingerly approach the bathroom, the light seeping from under the door.

I push open the door and the sight before me causes the wind inside my body to instantly be knocked from me. I grip my head in agony and shriek. "Oscar call 911!"

My heart stutters. I crumble to the floor beside Con.

He's slumped on the floor, his head barely propped up against the bathtub. Lifeless.

Tablets are strewn over the tiles. Vomit covers the floor. Con's mouth has a trail of bubbling saliva around it. My hands go to his face. "Con. Con, can you hear me?" My voice waivers as emotion overcomes me. "Pl... please say you can hear me, baby. Please." I beg hopelessly. My heart crumbles into a thousand pieces, please no. Tears fall down my face, but I ignore them, holding his head up, kissing his hair, someone please save him.

I'm aware Oscar is beside me, shouting orders into his phone. Then I distantly hear him mention Bren's name, followed by Cal. The urgency behind his voice clear.

I cradle Con's head in the palms of my hand. Tracing the stubble of his jaw with my thumbs. There's still a warmth to his cheeks. It fills me with a glimmer of hope. "Please." My tears fall to his handsome face, marking him, a reminder of my love for him. "Please." I beg desperately.

Chapter Thirty

Cal

I sit with my head in my hands waiting for news on Con. When Oscar called to say we needed to make our way from the children's unit over to Emergency care for Con, to say I was gob smacked was an understatement. A fucking overdose? He tried to kill himself? I still can't get my head around it.

I mean I knew Con had been riddled with guilt since Keenan was shot and killed but this is next level shit. Jesus how my little brother must have been suffering. We're supposed to protect one another not do this, not kill him.

I scrub a hand through my hair and scan my eyes around the waiting room.

Bren is sat on the floor no doubt feeling just as shitty as me. His knees pulled up and his head hanging low between them. Finn is leaning against the wall staring into space, the fucking toothpick firmly in place.

I lift my head again and eye my brothers. "We should have known."

"Yeah, no fucking kidding," Finn quips.

Bren lifts his head, his tear-filled eyes making contact with mine, the first time I've ever seen vulnerability shine in them. His Adam's apple bobs. "You think he meant it? To kill himself I mean?"

Finn scoffs and glares at him. "Of course, he fucking meant it." He pushes off the wall. "You told him you would kill him yourself." Finn pulls his toothpick from his mouth and spits his words out at Bren his shaking finger pointing at him accusingly.

"And you, mother fucker." Finn turns on me and strides toward me, I lift my head and gaze up at my seething brother, his temple pulsating, his face contorted in malice. "You told him we were better off without him!" he shakes his head. "Told him he wasn't fucking needed."

My stomach turns at the harshness of his words, my words. Jesus I'm a bastard.

I nod and swallow away the emotion rolling inside me, a pit of sickness forming considering my role in Cons actions. My lip trembles. My words cut him so deep he wanted to kill himself.

The door clicks open, and we all jump to our feet in Will's direction. I scan her up and down, her hair is completely disheveled, and the poor woman looks broken. Her eyes puffy and red, her body has a tremble to it. I'd go as far as to say she's in shock. Plain and simple, shock. Jesus. We stand silently waiting for her reaction, but nothing comes out of her mouth, she stares into the room emptily. Is he...? Please no. My legs almost buckle.

As if hearing my thoughts her head whips round in my direction. "No. Th... they said he's going to be okay."

Relief, utter relief encompasses the room. Our shoulders sag almost simultaneously, Finn falls into a chair and openly sobs. Bren walks over to him and in complete contrast to his usual self he places a supportive hand on his shoulder.

"Os... Oscar's with him at the moment." Will's voice trembles, her eyes seem empty, faraway. Jesus, she's been through so much.

"I'm sorry, Will. Fuck I'm so sorry." My words spill out of me.

Will's back snaps straight, her eyes punishingly glaring. "What exactly are you sorry for Cal? Hmm?"

My throat is dry, so fucking dry. "For the shit I said," I admit.

Will nods sarcastically. "For the shit you said? That he wasn't wanted, wasn't needed? Is that right?" Her eyes fill with tears, she wipes them away with her hand, but they flow down her face just as fast. Her voice rises, "Well, I fucking want him. I fucking need him!" her chest heaves, "Keen needs his daddy, Cal. He's only just fucking found him! How dare you say those things to him."

She spins around faces Bren. "And you," she points then exhales on a choked laugh, "how fucking dare you threaten him, Bren. You've no idea what it takes for him to go to that god damn warehouse for your fucking meetings every week. To see where Keenan was shot." Her voice rises. "Where he died. We tried to stop the blood pumping out of him, Bren, all the fucking while the life was leaving his body. And you fucking knew how much it hurt Con to keep going there."

Bren straightens, grazing his hand over his crew cut head. "I didn't realize how much he suffered, Will." He turns his face, guilt etched over his stern features.

She licks her lips and continues. "See I think you did, or maybe you didn't care." She shrugs sarcastically. "You all knew he'd been using drugs right? As a coping mechanism."

Her eyes scan the room, we all subtly nod.

Finn's wet eyes lift, "he went to shit when you left Will. We were just fucking happy when he started going out again."

Will wheels back slightly on her heels, and her face turns to rage. Her voice is choked. "When I left?"

Finn's voice is laced in panic as he moves toward her. "Shit I'm sorry. That's not what I meant."

Her shocked face doesn't budge. "They tried beating my baby out of me, Finn."

Finn tugs his hair. "Fuck darlin. I know I'm sorry. I'm not blaming you. I swear." He puts his hands out and takes a step toward her. She holds her hands up to stop him and I move in ready to go between them, when my eyes latch onto Bren's and he subtly shakes his head. Asking me to give them chance to work it out.

"I went through all that shit. Dealt with all that shit. Was thrown to the fucking wolves by Con. The man I loved and adored since we were kids." Her finger points at her chest, emotion and anger rolling off her in waves her voice quivering but somehow still strong. "And yet here I stand supporting him, like you should have." She points back at Finn. "And you." She points at Bren, then turns her head toward me. "And you, Cal. He supported you, he rooted for you! You should have done the same for him."

Her legs buckle and I swoop in and catch her, she rests her head against my chest and sobs wrack through her body. She feels completely fragile in my arms. This sweet girl has been through hell and back yet still always had our brothers back. She's been his lifeline until we took that away from him. Destroyed him.

I sit with her limp body, cradling her in my arms. "You're right sweetheart. We let him down and destroyed him. We're going to prove to you both we're here for you. Both of you." I stroke her hair.

Will raises her head, her face mottled with sadness. Desperation seeping through her words, "He needs help, Cal."

"We're going to fucking get it him, Will. Promise ya." Bren's firm voice is low a contrast to his normal deep and demanding tone.

"Ain't ever gonna let this shit happen again Will, promise ya that." Finn's concerned eyes meet mine and I nod in agreement. Never.

We'll never hurt him like that again. And we'll kill any fucker that dares to try.

Chapter Thirty-One

Build me, help me, love my broken self,
Hold me through this misery.
Take away the pain,
Support me to stand, to feel once again.

Con

The irritating beeping and buzzing hurts my head. What the fuck? I lick my lips; they're dry and cracked. I try to swallow, but the roughness and sharp sting in my throat makes it difficult. What the fuck happened?

My eyes are closed, and I will them to open but for some reason they don't. Are they locked? I feel locked in. Where the hell am I?

My mind tries to recall what might be happening. How I came to be like this. Small flashes of Keen munching on his pancakes flash before me. Balloons, gifts. His birthday. I smile internally at his cute face, while opening his presents. My own feelings of excitement and joy flood my veins.

Then, like an impending doom, sadness and darkness hit me. Keen. Nuts. Hospital. Failure. Losing them. Both of them. My family.

I wail, a gut wrenching, ear shrieking wail.

My eyes shoot open to the whiteness of the room. I'm alive. Fuck no. I'm alive.

"Shh. Shh. It's okay baby, I've got you," a gentle voice coos. Calming me, my body gently floats back down to the bed as Will's hands soothe me all over. Her fingers stroke my face, over my stubble, up to my eyes. "Open your eyes, Con, I need to see you, baby, please." The vulnerability and desperation in her voice leaves me no alternative because I'd give this woman anything. Any. Fucking. Thing she wants.

Her beautiful hazel eyes glisten with tears. She maneuvers herself onto the bed beside me. I shuffle back slightly, and she climbs in. Her head is resting on the same pillow as mine. We watch each other. Her hands entwine with mine. Hers encapsulating mine into a fierce grip, where mine can barely hold hers. A complete contrast to our usual stance. Her strength holding my weakness. Again, another reminder.

I close my eyes. I'm not good enough. I need to be strong for her.

"Open your eyes, Con," she coaxes.

I open them straight away, almost submissively. She licks her lips, ducking her head down and swallowing hard. I watch the motion. "You scared me." My jaw tenses and I wince. She gently touches my jaw. "I love you. So much..." her words come out smothered by emotion, tears race down her face. "Promise me you'll never do that again." Her eyes glare into me pointedly, her tone serious and sharp, "Promise me!"

I lick my lips, but don't give her the answer she wants.

Because without her, without Keen? I'd rather die. I'm nothing without them. Nothing.

"Keen?"

"He's fine."

I choke on a breath, my heart skipping. I want to keel over and bawl in relief.

The wetness flows freely down my face.

"He's okay, Con. You're okay. We're going to be okay." Her hand brushes away my tears.

My voice trembles. "I thought..."

Will squeezes her eyes closed in pain. "Shh shh. I know what you thought." Her hands stroke up and down my arm. "I know, it's okay. We're going to be okay."

"I... I... can't do this without you, Will." My voice is coming out desperate, pleading, pathetic.

Her gentle voice caresses me, like a mother would to a child. "I know. I can't do this without you, either." The impact of her words consumes me. Does she still want me? I dart my eyes up to meet hers in question.

Will leans forward and lightly kisses my lips. "I love you. We're going to get you help, Con. You're going to get better, stronger. Then I'm going to marry you. We're going to live in that big house Cal told me about and have a puppy running around the big garden. And Keens going to get the biggest play structure on the block." Her voice is teasing as she tries to smile through her pain, through her tears.

My slow mind goes over her words. She still wants me. Loves me. We're going to be a family. Stronger.

Her arms band around me, and I tighten my hold on her.

"I love you, baby. So fucking much it hurts," I admit.

"I know. I love you too."

Rebuild me, fill me with love and kindness,
Show me that you're there.
Safe in your loving arms, comfort all around me.
Save me for myself.

We hold each other and just stare into one another's eyes. The connection between us doesn't need words. Our connection is everything we need. Love.

I'm not sure how long we lay like this, feels like hours. Days even. Not long enough. It'll never be long enough.

I wet my lips with my tongue. "You really want a puppy with me?" I ask her with a coy smile.

Her pretty hazel eyes light up in amusement. "I do."

"Fuck baby. This is big. I'm going to be a daddy again."

Will chokes on a laugh and bites her lip, the action making her even more beautiful. "A doggy daddy, yes."

I shrug slightly. "Yeah. Same thing. Still a daddy."

"It is," she giggles. The noise warms me inside out. She brushes the wayward hair from my face. Her fingertips leave behind the softness she exudes. Her gentle caress and warmth.

Her love.

Chapter Thirty-Two

Will

Con's brothers have been distant all day. The realization pisses me off causing my head to pound with the tension. I can feel Con's wavering uncertainty around the situation, but I'm standing tall and beside my man. He's got my full support and I won't let anyone knock him down. I feel like a mother protecting her cub.

My arms are crossed over my chest as I sit guard at Con's bedside. He's been in and out of sleep all day, after spending the night holding one another.

As if hearing my thoughts, the door gently opens, and my eyes shoot over to it. Bren, Finn, and Cal slowly approach the bed.

"Jesus." Cal chokes and falls to the chair beside Con. His hands shake as he moves them toward him. They stop and his eyes meet mine in question. I nod my head and he relaxes slightly. Gently taking Con's hand in his. The motion makes my heart ache.

"Will." Bren's voice is soft and insecure. My eyes meet his. Tears blur my vision as I take in Bren's pained face. "I'm sorry, darlin. I didn't realize he felt this way." His voice rises, "Fuck! The things I said." He scrubs a hand through his buzz cut head.

"I deserved them." Con muffles the words out, his eyes fluttering open.

Bren shakes his head violently, silently raging at himself. At his actions. "No man. We should have been there. Seen you struggle. Jesus, who am I kidding? We knew you'd struggled since Keenan. And Will." He clears his throat. "We're here now, man. We're here for whatever you need." He nods to himself.

"Gonna, need some time off." Con moves to sit up slightly. Cal's hand still in his. His brothers watch him and wait for him to elaborate. "Gonna be a daddy." My eyes bug out.

Cal chokes and winces. Bren looks borderline aggressive, struggling to rein in his true feelings, and Finn stands at the door with a toothpick in his mouth with a megawatt troublemaking grin.

I decide to clarify as I watch them all uncomfortably, trying not to give too much emotion away. I take pity on them. "He means we're going to have a puppy." I point at Con in jest. "When we're fully moved in the house." His face is alight, and he grins from ear to ear. His eyes dart around his brother before he cracks up laughing.

They all visibly exhale, followed by a round of laughter and congratulations. The atmosphere recovered and lighthearted. I smile at the surrounding scene. How could I have ever questioned their loyalty? Their support. Their love.

Cal pulls me to the side and explains Cyn hasn't been

doing too well and has retreated to her bed. Apparently, a doctor has been over at the house to sedate her. Lily is currently there with Chloe and Reece while Jack has been looking after Keen.

The guys say their goodbyes. The love obvious as they each in turn hug their brother then me.

I'm just about to relax when the door swings open, making both me and Con jump retrospectively. I turn sharply to find a very disheveled looking Brennan Senior standing in the doorway. Instinctively, my body goes into defense and protection mode. I march in front of Con's bed with my arms crossed before me ready for battle.

There's no way in hell Con is going to be a victim to Brennan's demeaning, vicious, unsympathetic tongue. No way in hell.

Brennan eyes me cautiously. His usual broad shoulders slackened. The darkness under his eyes clear of a man that has been through hell. Sympathy oozes into my heart. His normally vibrant, deep blue eyes now completely drained and remorseful.

He sighs and then shuffles on the spot, clearly out of his comfort zone. "Ya gonna let me in, lass? Ain't gonna hurt him." His sharp eyes meet mine.

"Will, let Da through the door," Con gently speaks from behind.

I lower my shoulders and move to the side. Giving way for Brennan to barge past me obnoxiously. My nostrils flare in annoyance. I breathe deep to rein in my temper before spinning on my heels to give him a piece of my mind.

The scene before me is truly heartbreaking and all my aggression instantly dismissed. Brennan is holding a sobbing Con in his arms in an enormous bear hug.

I stifle my own sob with a hand to my mouth, desperate to not interrupt the rare show of love and support.

Brennan whispers words to Con and Con holds Brennan tighter, his fists clutching at Brennan's suit jacket. A loving moment between father and son. I feel privileged to have witnessed a glimmer.

Once again, this is a reminder of the relationship that Con has with Keen. It's unlike anything he's ever received himself. He gives himself whole-heartedly to Keen, a stark contrast from his own relationship with his father. He's determined to be a better man.

Brennan pulls away and Con nods at him. Then he straightens his shoulders back, tugs his jacket at the bottom to pull it into place, raises his chin in the air and reverts back to his normal arrogant ass self, almost in an instant. The change in air a witness to the transformation.

His deep voice bounces off the walls. "Now, pull a stunt like that again, ya little shite, and I'll kill you myself, ya hear me?" My eyes bug out at his crude words.

Con's lips curl up at the corner, almost in a laugh. His playful eyes meet mine, and I know he hasn't taken his father's words to heart. Thank God.

Brennan stands towering above Cons bed waiting for a response. "Yeah Da. I hear ya." Brennan nods in approval, spins, and walks out the door. My mouth hangs open in shock at the turn of events.

We both sigh a breath of relief as the door closes.

Con's eyes dance knowingly at my reaction.

"I'm going to go and check on Keen. Will you be okay for a little while?"

"As long as you come back." Con's eyes suddenly become vulnerable.

I go over to his bed and climb in. Gently I tuck his head into my chest, I kiss the top of his wavy hair, cradling him. Con's body sags into mine at the ease of my affection. "I'll always come back for you."

"Me too. I love you always."

Chapter Thirty-Three

Con

It's been just over eight weeks since Keen's birthday and a lot has fucking changed in that time.

With the help of Oscar, he managed to get me an awesome doctor who diagnosed me with PTSD, anxiety, and depression. I'm on a few different drugs that have helped stabilize my mood. I also see a therapist twice a week. A little extreme if you ask me, but I do what Will wants. For us.

Not going to lie, it's fucking hard work going over how I feel each session. But this last week it definitely seems to be getting easier, lighter.

Me and Will couldn't be any stronger. She's my everything and I'm finally certain I'm hers, too. Keen made a full recovery. Of course, being the little warrior that he is, he bounced back like a fucking superstar.

We moved into our new home last month and it's

quickly becoming my sanctuary. I can't wait to get back to my family every day. And even when our puppy shits everywhere I wouldn't want to be anywhere else. It's home.

I pull the car to a stop in the driveway of our parents' house, I recognize I don't feel the same anxiety I used to. I couldn't pinpoint when it started, but I know when it ended. When my da hugged me for the first time in my life. He loves me and wants me, Connor O'Connell, to be with him. His family.

"You, okay?" Will asks me for the hundredth fucking time. I turn to her, and she bites her bottom lip, realizing she's asked again. Her beautiful hazel eyes meet mine in apology. I stroke my hand down her face and lean in and gently kiss those perfect lips. The lips that woke me this morning wrapped around my cock; the memory makes my cock twitch. She sighs easily into the kiss.

I pull back and lock eyes with hers. "I'm fine, baby." Brushing my mouth against her ear and softly whisper, with grit in my tone, "You ask me one more time, Will and I'm gonna spank that ass raw." She visibly shudders and breaks out into a series of goosebumps. My girl loves my filthy mouth.

"Daddy, can we get out now?" Keen whines, breaking the tension. I draw away from Will and adjust myself through my jeans, pulling my t-shirt out over the top of my raging cock. The little minx grins at me.

The family is gathered around the table as Ma proudly lays out the food. We've brought along Peppa, our family puppy, Keen insisted. He's sitting daintily on the table next to Puss. Both of them eating from Reece's hands. Cute as fuck.

"So, the dog is a male, but you called it fucking Peppa?" Finn quizzes, his eyes oozing disgust while pointing his toothpick at our puppy. My lazy, relaxed vibe I was rocking a second ago obliterated at his snide comment.

I straighten my shoulders and shrug. "It was either that or Cock. But we persuaded Keen to call him Peppa." I was quite proud I turned that one around.

Bren chokes on his meal. "You dodged a fucking bullet there."

I sit prouder. "Yeah. I suggested Peppa." My proud smile grows wider when Will beams up at me.

"Well, I like Cock!" Keen announces, making me sit forward in my seat.

"Keen, buddy. We agreed on Peppa. He makes little snorty noises just like the Peppa on television." I nod at Keen encouragingly.

"Well, I think Cock suits him better. And Cock loves Pussy." Finn's voice is laced in glee, his eyes locked onto the scene on the table. "I mean see... Pussy is licking Cock." He points at my dog.

Puss is showing him some love. Cute as fuck, but I turn my eyes on Finn and make sure he know I'm pissed at him. My voice low and deadly. "It's Peppa," I seethe the words through clenched teeth.

Finn scoffs in jest. "You sappy shit. You've completely lost your balls to a kid and a dog. Hell, the dog has bigger balls than you."

I glare venomously at him. "Shut the fuck up. Peppa's cute as shit; it suits him."

My da chokes. His voice bellows through the room. "Fucking cute? Finn's right, you've lost your feckin balls. Bet the feckin thing ate em."

Cal turns his head from side to side, scrutinizing Peppa. I wish like fuck they'd all leave him alone. He's the bomb. "The dog looks like he's had a severe case of mange."

Finn chimes in. "I mean, what the fuck is it meant to be?"

My words come out pissed, with a threatening bite to them. Because let's face it, they're being dicks. "He's a Chinese Crested."

"He's a feckin abomination. Looks like a fuckin rat. Get it off my table," Da shouts, while pointing his finger at Peppa.

Reece's eyes shoot up, blazing with poison.

He pushes his chair back and leaves the table.

We all watch him walk away. Our mouths open and eyes wide. That's not like Reece. Not at all.

Lily clears her throat to explain. "We've been working on him walking away from conflict, encouraging him to rein in his words." Her smile is proud and graceful.

The table begins congratulating them, and words of appraisal are shared. They do amazing with Reece, and the transformation in him is undeniable.

"What stage is Chloe at now?" Oscar asks. He's been monitoring Chloe's progress from a distance. Never getting too close. But his concern is touching. He hasn't said it, but it doesn't take a mastermind to figure out he's looking out for Chloe's development. To see if we have another genius in the family, no doubt.

Cal seems to miss the point completely. "She's at the teething stage. She's obsessed with Puss too." We all smile at little Chloe as she mushes up her food in the palms of her chubby hands.

Reece slumps back in his chair, drawing attention away from Chloe. His face is sulky and petulant.

We all laugh and chat around the table. The atmosphere soothing, the warmth and love of the family encircling my heart.

Cyn hands out the desserts. She's made a yummy apple pie and Brennan has his usual bread and butter pudding. The man is religious in his meals.

All too soon, the mood changes. Brennan coughs, thumping his fist against his chest. Gasping for breath.

"Da, are you okay?" Cal panics, getting up from the table. Da waves him away, hating appearing weak in some way. Heaven forbid.

"Pass him the water," Ma suggests. Cal does as Cyn instructs and Brennan swallows a full glass worth.

His cough settles down but occasionally reappearing, making him bristle with annoyance. Silently irritating him as he tries to ignore it and continues on eating his dessert. We all eye each other with uncertainty if he's okay, but not wanting to make a show of the situation.

He gasps a deep breath and chokes heavily.

Yeah. Clearly, he's not okay. What the hell?

"Da. What's wrong?" Bren snaps, impatient as ever. Like father, like son and all that.

Finn sits back lazily in his chair, watching the drama unfold.

"Can you speak?" Cal stupidly asks. The man's, face is red, and he's clutching his throat.

"I'll call 911." Oscar sighs, drawing his words out nonchalantly, as if he couldn't care less to ring 911.

Lily shoots out of her chair. "Oh, my gosh. Is he having a heart attack?" Panic floods the room as everyone rises slowly from their seats to assist in one way or another.

Reece jumps up, his chair hitting the floor with an echoing clatter. All eyes on him. "Jesus. He's fine. Calm the fuck down. It's just a bit of pepper." He shrugs, takes his seat again and continues eating his dessert.

Lily's eyes flare.

Cal can't get his words out. "P... pepper?"

Reece slowly tilts his head to face Cal. "Yeah. Pepper. Not a fucking heart attack." He rolls his eyes with boredom.

"Pepper?" Cal questions again.

I look at Finn, his grin encompassing his mouth.

"Fucking pepper?" Cal rages, his voice high. Lily strokes his arm, trying to soothe him.

"Ya son feckin poisoned me! The little bastard nearly killed me!" Da spits out. Literally spits out.

"Well, perhaps you shouldn't be so mean to Peppa. Besides, if I wanted to kill you, I'd use Botulinum." Reece shrugs.

Lily's mouth drops open, gaping like a fish. Open, shut. Open, shut. Her feet slightly stumble at Reece's admission.

Both Cal and Lily spend the rest of the meal trying to chastise Reece, who in turn scowls at their every word. Obviously, in complete disagreement with them.

I think Lily and Cal need to teach Reece to not use actions when he walks away from conflict as well as words, but I decide to keep that suggestion to myself.

Brennan retreated to his room, sulking. Cyn sits at the table proudly, smiling and shaking her head at all the drama.

I lean back in my chair, Con's arm draped over my back. I turn my head to him, my voice delicate. "You okay?" Con's nostrils flare, he raises an eyebrow and I bite my lip in response to the deep black of his pupils expanding. My blood pumps around me, my panties becoming uncomfortable.

Con pulls my lip from between my teeth with his thumb, "You won't be able to sit down for a week." His dark voice makes me shudder.

Jesus, he's hot.

"Keen, come on, buddy. Time to go home." My eyes dance playfully at Con, a smug grin spreading across his face.

Bring it on.

Bring it fucking on.

Epilogue

Con

"Face down, ass up, baby," I demand.

"Is that really necessary?" Will snarks back.

I nod my head at the bed. "Absolutely. You know, it pisses me off when you keep asking me if I'm okay. Now be a good girl and take your punishment." I smirk at my words.

Will drops her head slightly. "I just care."

I lift her chin with my fingers. "I know, baby, and I appreciate it. Now, stop with the excuses and get on the fucking bed. Ass high."

She does as I tell her. And Jesus fucking Christ, she's hot. So hot I could blow my fucking load just looking at her pert ass in the air.

We're both completely naked, locked in our bedroom. Keen and Peppa safely tucked up. Now it's time for Will to receive her punishment.

I stroke her ass cheek, tingles breaking out over my body

at the touch. Will shudders clearly, just as affected. I raise my right hand. SMACK! Straight on that perky ass. Her body jolts into the mattress. Fuck yeah. I lick my lips.

I stroke it, soothing it gently before raising my palm and repeating the action. "Fuck Con."

"Smack! You sorry, baby?"

SMACK! I soothe her once again.

"Fuck yes. I'm sorry," she pants out. Her little moans are igniting my need to fill her. To drown her in my cum.

"Are you going to do it again?" Smack.

Will struggles to catch her breath. I watch her as she bites into her lip before answering, "Honestly? Probably."

Her answer makes me chuckle. Yeah, she'll definitely do it again. I lean over her body, all the way up to her ear. Gently, I stroke her hair, pushing it behind her ear. "Guess I'm going to have to come up with a better punishment then, hey?!" She sucks in a breath, arousal filling my veins. I straighten up and move a hand to my cock, pumping it a few times before finding her dripping pussy. I surge forward, knocking the wind out of her.

I still my actions, willing myself not to come. I always have the urge to come too soon with Will. I can never get enough. Never. The desperation to own her consumes me.

I gaze down at her body bent into the perfect curve; I stroke over her spine. Up and down, all the way to her ass. As I surge forward again, I push my thumb into her ass. Will's mouth gapes open, "Oh, Jesus." I pound into her. "Oh God. Con." Her fists tighten in the sheets.

Fuck yeah. Her tight, wet pussy clenches around me. I pound and pound my hips against her tight little ass, the slapping noises of our skin filling the room. Fuck, she's hot.

I smack her ass again and her firm walls hold my cock

tighter and tighter, then they begin pulsating around me, the feeling rippling through me. Will tremors before screaming my name. "Co... nnn." The sensation spiraling my own orgasm, her walls are pulling it from me. I close my eyes and throw back my head at the ecstasy of my orgasm, the pulse of my cock flooding her pussy with my cum. I drop my mouth open in awe. Fuck, that's incredible.

I collapse beside Will and pull her into my arms. My chest still panting. She raises her head, sweaty and sticky from our lovemaking. I rest on an elbow and stare down at my girl. Absolutely fucking beautiful.

"Marry me?" Her words come out so quickly, I'm not sure I heard her, right?

The confusion on my face makes her giggle. "Marry me, Con." Her eyes implore me, "Please?"

Jesus, I can't speak. I'm utterly fucking speechless. I stare into her beautiful hazel eyes, my lips parted to talk but unable to commit to the action. My eyes flare with hope. Did I hear her right?

"Can you speak?" she asks playfully. I shake my head. No, I can't fucking speak.

I can't fucking function right now.

"Nod your head for yes. Shake it for no," Will says, while chewing her lip.

I nod my head frenziedly.

Will chuckles and leans forward for a kiss. I flip us over and pounce on her mouth, my tongue finding hers with vigor. Sliding home into her pussy, my body comes alive once again. Will wraps her arms around my neck as I make love to her.

"I love you so damn much, baby," I tell her.

"I know. And I love you too, always." She smiles into

our kiss. And I know right here and now, in one another's arms, we finally have our forever.

THE END

Afterword

Want a little more?

Would you like more of Con and Will?

Come and sign up to BJ Alpha's newsletter for an exclusive extra scene and be the first to hear about the up and coming events and book news.

Use the link to get your copy of Con & Will's extended epilogue now: Extended Epilogue

Acknowledgments

I must start with where it all began, TL Swan. When I started reading your books, I never realized I was in a place I needed pulling out of. Your stories brought me back to myself.
With your constant support and the network created as 'Cygnet Inkers' I was able to create something I never realized was possible, I genuinely thought I'd had my day. You made me realize tomorrow is just the beginning.
For that I am eternally grateful!

Tee, you have no idea the love and gratitude I feel toward you.
Thank you for giving me purpose!

To my fellow Cygnets, thank you!
My soul sister, Jaclyn for always encouraging me and believing in me. You're one in a million Jaclyn.
Nikila and Kerry for your constant support and messages.
Vicki and Sadie for all your advice and quick responses. Thank you for showing me the way when I needed it. I cannot wait to meet you in person!
Thank you to my Beta Readers, Libby, Rhi, Jaclyn, J and Em. I'm so thankful for your help and constant support.
An extra special thank you to Libby for absolutely everything, I'm in awe of your kindness. The fact that you go above and beyond for me is incredible.

A special mention to the Swan Squad.
This group of ladies lift me up and make me smile when I need it the most.
I've formed friendships through this amazing group of ladies that mean the world to me.
Emma H, Patricia B, Claire B, Caroline W and the amazing Bren with her swan cnuts. Thank you for your friendship and support.

My beautiful friends.
The crazy Kate. Your journey is only just beginning, and I cannot wait to see where it takes you! Preferably with me attached to you. Or the other way round, whatever.
Marie N thank you for EVERY. THING! Thank you for being you.
To my friends Julie and Hayden, thank you for being my biggest supporters. A reminder that family aren't always blood.
Sarah and Meg, your words and photos lift me up. Keep

going girl, super proud of you. Thank you for always being a message away. x

To my ARC readers and bloggers. Thank you for all your hard work, messages and support!

To my mum, thank you for your support. Also, thank you for not disowning me! Ha ha.
Love you more.

To my boys, thank you for everything. I'm so incredibly proud of you both, keep being you.

To my hubby, the J in my BJ. Thank you for pushing me, listening to me and supporting me through this whole process, yet again. Without you I wouldn't be BJ Alpha.
Love you trillions!

Thank you to https://www.mind.org.uk for the information available.
I'd also like to thank https://autism.org.uk for the wealth of information available to me and many others.

And last but by no means least thank you to all my readers. I really hope you enjoyed Con as much as I did!

About the Author

BJ Alpha lives in the UK with her hubby, two teenage sons and three fur babies.
I love to both read and write hot alpha men and feisty females.

Join me on my social media pages...
My website and newsletter sign up:
www.authorbjalpha.com

For all news on upcoming books, visit my Facebook pages:
BJ Alpha Facebook Page

My readers group:
BJ's Reckless Readers

Instagram: BJ Alpha Instagram

Also by B J Alpha

CAL Secrets and Lies Book 1

A Second-chance romance, secret baby, jealous/possessive hero with steamy sex scenes.

Be prepared to be taken on a journey of Secrets and Lies.

Cal

I knew her only as Carmen, the little hottie from a night of passion in Vegas, the love of my life!

Fifteen years later after tracking down a cyber thief who has stolen millions from me and my family, I'm holding a gun to her head thanks to her dumb-ass son! Only he's not just her son... secrets are exposed and just when I think things can't get any worse? The Cartel are after them.

Lily

My teenage son leaves a trail of destruction in his wake, the latest, stealing millions from a Mafia family. Cal the sexy man from my past comes barreling back into my life, as if it isn't chaotic enough, he's holding a gun to my head.

My ex-lover is now my savior, only I'm not sure he can handle the number of secrets and chaotic baggage we bring.

WARNING: This book has triggers. It contains sensitive and explicit storylines, graphic sex scenes and strong language recommended for readers aged eighteen and over.

CAL

BORN RECKLESS

A Dark High School Romance.

A bad-ass FMC makes a huge mistake causing her world to collide with a stuck-up rich boy who hates her for it.

Frankie

One night is all it took to change my life for the worse.

I grew up with no real home or blood family around.

That is until my uncle decided to be an unwelcome hero. He offered me a new life, a home in his mansion, and a fresh start at an exclusive private school. He thinks he's better than me... They all do. Especially his hot as hell adopted son, Cameron. The reason I'm on lockdown.

Uncle Jimmy thinks he's doing me a favor, but I know his secrets, just like he knows mine.

But the difference between us all, is I'd rather live my previous life than one like this.

Cameron

In one night, she destroyed something that meant the world to me.

After filing charges, I inflict what I think is hell by having her sent to a detention center, a place with no future. Lock-up. Where she belongs. I want my revenge, what was lost to me forever, but I'll take what I can get.

That is until my adoptive father introduces me to his niece, and I see before me the very bane of my existence. I refuse to look into her eyes, to give in to the intrigue she stirs within me.

I refuse to want her. Until the choice isn't even mine.

Born Reckless

MORE BY BJ ALPHA!

Secrets and Lies Series

CAL Book 1

CON Book 2

FINN Book 3

BREN Book 4

OSCAR Book 5

CAL Short Story

CON'S WEDDING NOVELLA

Born Series

Born Reckless

The Brutal Duet

Hidden In Brutal Devotion

Love In Brutal Devotion